The Laws of Seduction

By Gwen Jones

The Laws of Seduction
Kiss Me, Captain
Wanted: Wife

The Laws of Seduction

A FRENCH KISS NOVEL

GWEN JONES

AVON IMPULSE
An Imprint of HarperCollinsPublishers

Excerpt from *Various States of Undress: Virginia* copyright © 2014 by Laura Simcox.

Excerpt from *The Governess Club: Louisa* copyright © 2014 by Heather Johnson.

Excerpt from *Good Guys Wear Black* copyright © 2014 by Lizbeth Selvig.

Excerpt from *Sinful Rewards 1* copyright © 2014 by Cynthia Sax.

Excerpt from *Covering Kendall* copyright © 2014 by Julie Revell Benjamin.

EPub Edition NOVEMBER 2014 ISBN: 9780062356505
Print Edition ISBN: 9780062356512

10 9 8 7 6 5 4 3 2

In memory of my mother,
Claire Mary Sofchak Weerheim.
Au revoir, ma chérie.

Acknowledgments

Thanks to all who assisted me in shoving this book to fruition. As always, beta reader and receiver of all things angsty, fellow writer Linda J. Parisi, technical advisor and sister extraordinaire, Gretchen Weerheim and her husband, Andrew Chattaway, whose magic camera can even make me look good, fellow Papa's Pizza denizens and cheerleaders Susan Crawford and Kate O'Brien (Susan, what would I have done without those LOL pix on my waning days of this project!), the family cheering section who brought me so many shoulders to lean on during my darkest days, Lorna Maguire, Marlene Stewart, Pattie Noakes, and my feisty Aunt Helen, champion retweeter and one-woman street team Chris Clemetson and her sidekick, library goddess and Book Café hostess Rachael Dohn, the girls of the First Wednesday of the Month Book Discussion Group, Jane, Pat, and Carol, Avon editor Nicole Fischer, whose patience should be smelted and sold as gold, my fabulously glamorous agent Marisa Corvisiero and her Team Corvisiero, and above all else, my own romance hero, my husband, Frank, who will finally get to eat a meal not warmed by the microwave, but from the loving cockles of my heart. Thank you all.

Chapter One

Alpha Nailed

Center City District Police Headquarters
Philadelphia
Monday, September 29
11:35 p.m.

IN HER FIFTEEN years as an attorney Charlotte had never let anyone throw her off her game, and she wasn't about to let it happen now.

So why was she shaking in her Louboutins?

"Put your briefcase and purse on the belt, keys in the tray, and step through," the officer said, waving her into the metal detector.

She complied, cold washing through her as the gate

behind her clanged shut. She glanced over her shoulder, thinking how much better she liked it when her interpretation of *bar* remained singular.

"Name . . . ?" asked the other cop at the desk.

"Charlotte Andreko."

He ran down the list, checking her off, then held out his hand, waggling it. "Photo ID and attorney card."

She grabbed her purse from the other side of the metal detector and dug into it, producing both. After the officer examined them he sat back with a smirk. "So you're here for that Frenchie dude, huh? What's he—some kinda big deal?"

She eyed him coolly, hefting her briefcase from the belt. "They're all just clients to me."

"That so." He dropped his gaze, fingering her IDs. "How come he don't have to sit in a cell? Why'd he get a private room?"

Why are you scoping my legs, you big douche? "It's *your* jail. Why'd you give him one?"

He cocked a brow. "You're pretty sassy, ain't you?"

"And you're wasting my time," she said, swiping back her IDs. *God, times like these I really hate men.* "Are you going to let me through or what?"

He didn't answer. He just leered at her with that simpering grin as he handed her a visitor's badge, reaching back to open the next gate. "Thank you." She clipped it on, following the other cop to one more door at the other side of a vestibule.

"It's late," the officer said, pressing a code into a keypad, "so we can't give you much time."

"I won't need much." After all, how long would it take to say, *No fucking way.*

"Then just ring the buzzer by the door when you're ready to leave." When he opened it and she stepped in, her breath immediately caught at the sight of the man behind it. She clutched her briefcase, so tightly she could feel the blood rushing from her fingers.

"*Bonsoir,* Mademoiselle Andreko," Rex Renaud said.

Even with his large body cramped behind a metal table, the Mercier Shipping COO never looked more imposing, and in spite of his circumstances, never more elegant. The last time they met it'd been in Boston, negotiating the separation terms of his company's lone female captain, Dani Lloyd, who had recently become Marcel Mercier's wife. But with his cashmere Kiton bespoke now replaced by Gucci black tie, he struck an odd contrast in that concrete room, yet still exuding a coiled and barely contained strength. He folded his arms across his chest as his black eyes fixed on hers, Charlotte getting the distinct impression he more or less regarded her as cornered prey.

All at once the door behind her slammed shut and her heart beat so violently she nearly called the officer back. Instead she planted her heels and forced herself to focus, staring the Frenchman down. "All right, I'm here," she said *en français.* "Not that I know why."

"*J'ai oublié que tu avez parlé ma langue,*" he said. "But we'll keep to English so there's no mistaking my meaning." His immaculate patent-leather shoe nudged the chair opposite. "Have a seat, *s'il vous plaît.*" He tsked. "I mean—*please,*" he added, smiling brilliantly.

If there was anything she remembered about Rex Renaud—which was nearly everything because he wasn't easy to forget—it was how lethally he wielded his physicality. How he worked those inky eyes, jet-black hair, and Greek-statue handsomeness into a kind of immobilizing presence, leaving her weak in the knees every time his gaze locked on hers. Which meant she needed to work twice as hard to keep her wits sharp enough to match his, as no way would she allow him the upper hand. Yet even though he was in jail, even with him jammed behind that metal table, and herself looming over him, it was still a battle. Because with every advantage on her side he still dominated the room, the situation, the very airspace between them, so much so that Charlotte had to curl her hand around the back of the chair to steady herself.

Too much coffee today, she reasoned. *That's all it is.* Even though she knew that didn't even figure.

He nudged the chair again, his collar opened where his bow tie had been, his only concession to the situation. "Please sit. You heard the *flic.* We haven't much time."

"We haven't any time at all." She steeled herself. "It's not like we have anything to discuss."

"*Non?*" His gaze offered her a challenge. "Then why did you come?"

She smiled, with delicious, malicious intent. She waited a long time to wound him—and *all* men like him who dismissed women so easily—and as swiftly and as deeply as she could. "Maybe for the pleasure of seeing you behind bars."

"Really," he said, his eyes darkening as he drew closer.

"Though the idea of pleasuring you does hold a certain appeal."

Heat streaked through her as she slammed her briefcase atop the table. "Then take a good look, because my watching you rot in here is about as close as you'll ever be to getting me off."

He sat back, amused. "The lady finds her bliss in the strangest places. Though if watching people in pain is your thing, I am acquainted with a few gentlemen who'd pay you a nice piece of change to put all that aggression to use." He cast her a glance that near stripped the clothes from her body. "I believe all you'll need is a good deal of leather and some rather kinky boots."

Her jaw dropped. "Are you—you—" She waved her hand in front of her.

"Me? Why *non*. I do like a bit of spark in my women, but I always prefer it on top." His eyes hooded. "Metaphorically speaking, that is."

"You bastard piece of shit," she uttered, pressing her knuckles to the worn steel. "I had to be out of my mind to come here when it's clear you're guilty of everything you're accused of."

"And what's that?" he said, rising. "I'd love to hear it out of your mouth."

"Of sexual assault," she spit out. "Of everything vile and sick and violent that men and their disgusting appetites are capable."

"Oh, how right you are, *mon amie*. How truly loathsome we are. Repulsive animals." He leaned in, so closely she could feel his breath on her cheek, his eyes malevolent and cold. "Men are indeed beasts, always stooping to the lowest common denominator. Using brutality to get what they want, pugnacious and vicious to the end. Unlike women, who've crawled out of the swamp and up the evolutionary ladder to become so much more ruthlessly efficient. Who needs fists when you have feminine wiles?" He leaned in even closer. "Why shed blood when you can suck out a man's soul."

"What do you want from me?" she said, backing away. "Why would you ask me to defend you, knowing what I think of men like you?"

"Because I believe you'll want to," he said, his eyes bleeding candor and reason and some indefinable quality she found, God help her, unable to resist. "After you hear what I have to say."

"I doubt it. But even if I were to agree—which I won't— I'm no criminal attorney. Lawsuits, breach of contracts, employment law, women's rights in the workplace . . . oh Christ." It hit her like a ton of bricks. "Of *course*. That's it. You want to use me because I'm a *woman*."

He arched a brow. "Seems like you have it all figured out."

"Only because I've seen your kind before." She was often approached by men fighting sexual discrimination disputes, thinking a female attorney was their ace in the hole. She always turned them down. "You want to use my reputation as a women's activist to your advantage. You want them to see if I'd defend you, then you must be innocent." Was it possible even Rex Renaud, this womanizer, this catalog misogynist, could stoop so low? Not that she'd let him. "I won't do it. How could you even think to ask me?"

"How couldn't I?" he said, falling back to his seat, all the weariness in the world falling with him. "You're the best at what you do."

"Even if I am, what makes you think I'd agree to take your case?"

He looked to her with conviction. "Because you will, *avocate*. You've been waiting a long time for a case like this."

"I sure have—from the other side of the courtroom. But to think I'd defend you?" She laughed, incredulous. "Are you insane?"

"Arguably. But that isn't the point." His eyes narrowed. "You'll want my money. You need it. And I have a lot to buy you with."

All at once she panicked. He knew something, something about how desperately broke she was, and how he found out she could only imagine. Still, she had to play him off. She still had principles. And those principles could never allow even an inch of compromise.

"I'm a partner in a very successful law firm," she said, her chin lifting. "How could you possibly make that assumption?"

"Because it's no assumption. It's a fact. And so is this—you're broke. Although your practice is very successful, it's the other partners who are bringing in the coin with cases like . . . what was that last one? That arthritis drug that paralyzed a couple of people? How many mega-millions was that worth? While there's you, running around defending secretaries trying to squeeze another dollar an hour out of their tight-fisted bosses."

Her jaw clenched. "So secretaries aren't worth defending?"

"Depends how you define *worth*." His gaze captured the irony. "Those pro bono cases are starting to add up, aren't they? And your partners are tired of carrying you."

"No one carries me. Just last week I took on a vice-president of a very successful Internet start-up who's suing the company for copyright infringement."

"Settled before it even got out of discovery."

"Only because it wasn't necessary," she countered. "The facts were as plain as—"

"Face it, Charlotte," he cut her off. "What you lack in billables you more than aptly make up in passion. But the fact is your passions are bleeding revenue. That group you head, that band of half-naked feminists—what's it called? Occupy Vagina—is an open festering wound, even with its membership growing every day. And though a week doesn't go by without a couple of mentions in the press, all you're attracting is more desperate cases. The truth is your partners only keep you around for the high profile you bring, but even that's wearing thin. And now they're ready to cut you loose."

"Where the hell did you hear that?" she said. "They need my publicity to detract from all the slimy work they do. Who could've possibly told—"

"How about Joshua Lido?"

Another slam to the chest. A partner in the firm? "What about him?"

He swiveled toward her, leveling his gaze. "We did a little research on you before we started negotiations on Dani Lloyd up in Boston. Seems your firm was very grateful for my company's settlement, as you'd actually be bringing in some cash. Or how did he put it?" He looked away for a moment, his hand to his chin. " 'I guess we'll *have* to let her stay until the check clears.' "

"That's a lie," Charlotte said. "Why would he purposely disparage me, especially to you?"

"That's a question you have to answer yourself, *ma chérie*. As why would you want to stay on in a firm that does?"

"Why are you doing this?" she finally asked. "You could get anyone to defend you—the best criminal defense attorney in the world. Why ask me?"

"I already told you," he said evenly. "Because you're the best."

"Oh come on," she scoffed. "You'll have to do much better than that."

"Then there's this." He rose, and was on her in a second. "I watched how you operated in Boston against Mercier. How you worked a wrongful termination suit to transform that little female captain into a veritable cult icon." He looked at her with more than a bit of awe. "My God—when you believe in something you're like a terrier with a bone. You were brilliant."

Charlotte sincerely hoped she wasn't blushing. Because incredibly enough, she felt herself basking in his praise. "Wow, you sure know how to dish it, don't you? Why don't you just go ahead and tell me how nice my ass is." *Oh Christ—did I just say that?* She must have, as he was laughing with the kind of intimacy that usually accompanied a slide of naked thigh up her own.

"It is, isn't it?" he said, leaning so closely his intoxicating scent dizzied her, his dark eyes gleaming with mirth. "But I think I'll save that for another campaign. One I also plan on winning."

If she was reddening it was only because she was seething. "You know, they have a word for men like you."

"You mean the one that pays tribute to the greatest part of my anatomy?"

"That wasn't quite the one I was thinking of."

His mouth crooked. "Neither was I of its feminine correlation."

"That's it, I'm done. Finished! *Va te faire voir*," she spat, grabbing her briefcase, ready to bolt out the door.

"Charlotte—*c'est bon*—I'm just playing with you," he said, latching hold of her arm. "*Mon Dieu*, I'm fucking incarcerated. The joke's already on me. What can be funnier than that?"

She shrugged him off. "I don't know—waterboarding?"

"Not when I've already made your day. Now please, have a seat." He returned to sit at the other side of the table and folded his hands atop it, looking as serious as she'd ever seen him. Charlotte remained standing, needing the advantage of height to keep her balance. After a few moments he continued.

"Someone is out to ruin me—for whatever reason, I'm not sure yet. But when I find out ...." His eyes narrowed, face turning hard and steely. "Look, if you defend me I'll make it more than worth your while. I'll make it so god-damned worth it you'll never have to depend on anyone again, let alone those two-faced sycophants at your firm. And we can win this, I know we can, because anyone who puts as much passion into their work as you do will always succeed. And Charlotte . . ." The look he gave her was as close to pleading as a man of his kind was capable of. "I need you to work that passion for me."

She didn't answer, turning to the window instead. Which was pointless, the outside as dark and muddied as her thinking, her mind racing so fast she was unable to process a sensible thought. Maybe because nothing made sense anyway. Because if it did, why would she even contemplate representing someone like Rex Renaud, a man who could've been CEO of any of a dozen multinational corporations, but chose to stay on as chief operating officer for a company as misogynistic as Mercier Shipping? True, perhaps now it was a bit more friendly to women since its president, Marcel Mercier, married the independent-minded Dani Lloyd, the company's only female captain. But Rex Renaud, second in command or not, was his own man in every sense of the word. And that made her trust him even less, no matter how physically aware of him she felt every time she was around him. As she was now, catching his reflection in the window, watching her. Waiting for her answer.

"Charlotte," he said, his rich baritone enveloping her from halfway across the room, "You need my money and I need your expertise. Now I want to hear you say you'll do it."

WANTED HER TO? Rex *needed* her to. And for one more reason than the obvious. From the moment he met her in Boston he couldn't get her out of his mind. A frustration almost as bad as being in this hellhole of an American jail.

Quite frankly, he wanted to get *out* of it so he could get *into* her as soon as possible.

Crude, but he also knew there was only one way to get over an obsession and that was to confront it directly. And Charlotte Andreko was quite simply a confrontation waiting to happen.

And why was that? Because she certainly wouldn't be the most beautiful woman he'd ever been with, the amount of which he stopped counting by the time he'd turned twenty. The same number of years later his choices in women had only become richer and more varied. Yet the moment he made Charlotte's acquaintance all the others seemed lacking. There was just something about her, whether it was her overconfidence or sense of self-importance or an intelligence that always kept him on his guard—he couldn't be sure.

Because it couldn't just be her juicy breasts, her slim waist, that delicious double handful of *cul* he ached to squeeze, those slim, endless legs he longed to part. Could he really be that base? He smiled to himself—*oh, he most certainly could*. Ever since Boston he dreamed of burying himself inside her, taking her fast and hard and in someplace not quite respectable. Against a car. In some dark corner of a barroom. He glanced over. Right atop this table. Fist those blonde twists of hair between his fingers as her neck arched back, those lusciously plump lips open in a silent scream of release as he pummeled her senseless.

But there was something else he needed to accomplish before he'd let his lust take over, and that was to destroy whoever was doing this to him. And as with any business challenge it'd be a complete annihilation, no prisoners, no looking back. Except, he knew, for Charlotte. *Charlotte.* Because as much as he wanted out of this jail, this ridiculous charge, this whole infuriating mess, he wanted her more. Infinitely so.

"Get me out of here," he said.

She snapped her fingers. "Just like that. Do you really think it'll be that easy?"

"Why wouldn't it? Are you thinking I can't make the bail?"

"Oh, I'm sure you could. But what was it they called you?" Those blue eyes swiveled upward. "Ah yes—an extreme flight risk. And your own jet to do it with."

"I'd have to be an idiot to jump bail."

"You would think." She bent toward him, her creamy décolletage in plain view. "And then you thought to call me. That alone has me questioning your sanity."

"You're here, aren't you?" As he knew she would be. "What does that tell me?" Hopefully, that she found him as irresistible as he found her.

"That maybe you should be questioning my sanity as well."

"At this point I really don't care," he said, strangely apprehensive. He wasn't used to feeling this on edge. But then again, he'd never been arrested for sexual assault before. "Will you do it or not?"

"Don't you think you'd better tell me your side of the story?"

He shrugged. "It's actually pretty simple. There's a funding bill Mercier wants Congress to pass. It has to do with dredging harbors to deepen them for the new larger ships and tankers we'd like to purchase. In this region there're two ports vying for consideration. Here in Philadelphia, and Elizabeth in North Jersey where Mercier has a terminal. Naturally, Mercier wants the funding for Elizabeth, but the bill has been stuck in committee so long, it's becoming more and more apparent it'll never get to the floor for a vote. Especially since Congress is due to adjourn this week until after the elections. After that the bill may as well be dead."

"You seem to know a lot about American politics," Charlotte said.

"When you're working with international trade deals, learning what you're up against becomes second nature." *Just as when you're working with women, you learn their vanity comes first.* "Just as I'm sure you've come to know every labor law on the books to be as good as you are."

She tilted her head slightly, a subtle nod to his praise. "I suppose. But what does that have to do with you being in Philadelphia? You'd think you'd be haunting Elizabeth."

"Not when one of the committee members is in town for a fund-raiser."

"You mean Congresswoman Lilith Millwater?"

"Well, this is her district."

She eyed him over. "Hence the tux. So you were here for a bit of a schmooze."

"Only because nothing gets done in Washington anymore," he said, shaking his head. "Used to be ninety percent of business was accomplished during cocktail hour. Now the righteous lot of you are afraid to be seen with a drink in your hand. You seemed to have forgotten the immense value of a tumbler of scotch. Why is that?" He looked at her, truly curious. "Why is it that Americans have created every type of pleasure for themselves but are vilified if they indulge?"

"Perhaps because some forget there's a time and place for everything."

"Perhaps they should realize it doesn't have to hurt or taste bad to be good for you."

"Is that what happened, Monsieur Renaud?" she asked. "Were you looking for lightning in your glass of champagne?" She crossed her arms in front of her, throwing up the gate. "Perhaps you were showing someone the value of pleasure only to have it explode in your face? Is that what happened when you took that lobbyist in the next room and tried to rip her clothes from her?"

He clenched his fists. "Bravo. You've well-proved you can read a police report."

"And a good thing I did as you're telling me nothing." She huffed, tossing her hand in futility. "You know, out of everything you've said so far the one item you've omitted is that you're innocent." She eyed him speculatively. "Are you?"

He rose, coming around the desk, remaining at a respectful enough distance so he could read her reaction. "They say a good defense attorney doesn't need to know that. That all they need are facts and evidence."

"But I'm not a defense attorney, am I?"

Now she was just irritating him. "Don't be flip with me, Charlotte."

"And don't play me for an idiot. The one thing I need more than facts and evidence is to absolutely believe in what I'm doing, and I can't defend you if you lie to me. So I'm only going to ask you this once, and I expect absolute truthfulness." She met his gaze squarely. "Are you guilty of what they're accusing you of? Did you sexually assault that woman?"

A knock came at the door. "Ten minutes," they heard the guard say.

He looked down on her. "Well, let me tell you . . ."

Chapter Two

By Any Other Name

Earlier at the Ritz-Carlton Hotel
Philadelphia

REX NEEDED A drink like a car crash needed an ambulance.

The day had not started well in Marseille, not with the dockworkers threatening to strike again, and rumors of the board entertaining the idea of going public. Prospects weren't looking much better on this side of the Atlantic either. Credit that to U.S. Representative Lilith Millwater, staring daggers at him from across the ballroom. What a couple, she and her horndog of a husband, the Honorable Stanley Millwater, a circuit court judge. They'd make a fine pair of blackmailers if they ever decided to leave politics, but then why give up when they'd honed their skill to a polish? For now the judge was busy keeping his mojo in form with a pair of female law clerks he was energetically chatting up. Rex caught Lilith's glare and held it for a moment before he aimed toward the bar, knowing she'd soon follow.

He ordered scotch, narrowing it to Glenfiddich when asked for a preference. He told himself even before he left France that if he didn't get what he came for on this trip, there'd be no point in pursuing it any further. And if that happened, he was going to need a good deal of Glenfiddich for the anger-fueled binge he intended in the aftermath. But he wasn't about to give up yet. He had one last try in him. Too many jobs, too many billions of dollars depended on his success getting this harbor dredging bill passed, and this time he'd do whatever it'd take, even throw her own words back at her. So he took out his phone and turned on the voice recorder, setting it on the bar. By the time Lilith joined him, he was already sipping his scotch.

"Malbec—any kind," she said to the bartender. When he left she turned to Rex. "You were supposed to be here last night. What happened?"

He took another sip, staring straight ahead, like he was listening to the jazz quartet or watching for a friend to arrive. "Sorry, *ma chérie*, but some people actually work more than two days a week. A strange concept, but true."

"That's not what I meant and you know it." Her gown

rustled as she reached for the wine, a strand of silver-blonde hair slipping from her otherwise impeccable updo. She lifted the glass to her lips. "I've missed you," she said, sotto voce.

He glanced to her husband, his stomach jiggling as he laughed. *And my contributions to your campaign.* "So nice to be wanted, Lilith."

"Two months," she said. She snatched a napkin from the bar, blotting her lips. "That's a long time to make me wait," she said, looking down at the ruby-red oval her impression had left.

"*Oui*, it is. Even in the congressional time-space continuum. Two months more the goddamned bill's been in that vacuum you call a committee."

"That's right. Go ahead and blame me," she said, crushing the napkin and tossing it. "I've tried to get it through, but no one wants to budge. No one wants to admit to spending a dime these days, not with the midterm elections a month away."

He swore under his breath. "Not with any election ten *years* away. It's going to die in committee and you're not going to lift a finger to save it, are you?"

"Who says I've given up?" She reached to her hair, setting the single strand back into place. "In fact we may get it out on the floor for a vote this week. We're just waiting on one member."

Rex knew exactly who. "It's still Brendan Hitchell, isn't it? Jesus, why haven't you closed it with him by now?"

"I will. He's assures me—"

"That it's going to die." Suddenly a girl across the ballroom caught his eye. She looked vaguely familiar. And she was staring at him hard, unwaveringly. He drained his scotch, signaling for another, the bartender filling it before he continued. "Madame Congresswoman, you need to tell me something new, or your campaign funding will dry up before it gets another dime out of me."

"Rex. Please." She gripped his arm, but one withering glance and she snapped it away. "I'm meeting Hitchell for lunch on Wednesday. He assures me we can work it out." Her mouth crooked. "At the Hay-Adams. You do recall the hotel, don't you?"

The last thing he wanted to do with her was take a trip down memory lane. "Get to the point, Lilith. Why is he taking so long?"

She took a sip of wine, waving dismissively. "Oh, he wants to tack some waivers onto the bill. But I'm certain we can work it out."

"And you will. Because I'll be there alongside you to make sure you do." *I've seen that girl before. She most definitely looks familiar.*

Panic flared in Lilith's eyes, but she quickly suppressed it. "That's not necessary. If you know anything about how D.C. works, you'd know it always goes down to the wire."

"Perhaps. But unfortunately, time is a luxury I don't have." *The Hay-Adams Hotel . . .* "I'm going to your meeting with Hitchell. Twelve-thirty, the usual time?"

"Rex, please, it's not necessary." She laughed lightly, but he could tell it was forced. "I can handle him. If you show up, he may get suspicious."

"About what, Lilith? He'd have to be an idiot to not know I want this dredging bill passed. Why should he care if I'm there?" He leaned in, gifting her with his most seductive smile. "Are you afraid he might read more into it?"

"What's to read?" she said, eyes flashing. "Tell me the truth. You wouldn't even have bothered to come here if it wasn't for the bill. You didn't come to see me."

"Who says I didn't?" His finger brushed her arm. "Didn't I just cross an ocean for you?"

"Oh, don't tease me, Rex." She turned to the bar, looking into her wine. "I really did miss you. Why, I was as excited as a teenager getting ready tonight, knowing I'd see you. Rex . . ." Her face softened. "I'm not leaving for Washington until tomorrow. How about I come to your room later and we could . . ." She squeezed his hand. "We can talk about the bill. Then we can both take the train down in the morning."

"Talk? Seriously?" He swirled the amber liquid in his glass. "That'd be a first."

Her jaw tightened, her anger returning. "All right— fuck, then. You remember fucking me, don't you?"

He could see the rage building inside of her, which was precisely why he couldn't ever let his guard down. Lilith Millwater was as useful as she was unpredictable. Which was also why he'd have to take every precaution. He gripped the bar rail and bent into her. "Oh yes, Madame Congresswoman. I remember fucking you and fucking you often. It's what you required. That, and regular contributions to your favorite political charity—

yourself. But I'm here tonight to tell you I'm turning off the tap unless you get that bill out for a vote." He picked up his phone. "And this is to make sure you do."

Her jaw dropped. "Rex," she whispered, her hand flying to his wrist, "you *didn't*."

"Didn't what, Lilith? Besides insure the price of doing business?"

"Who do you think you are?" she said, her voice seething. "If that ever gets out, I'm ruined."

"This is just between the two of us, of course. You get that bill out for a vote, and whatever's on here goes away." Rex removed her hand, slipping the phone into his inner pocket.

"You son of a bitch," she uttered, her throat emitting that tiny, desperate sound women often made before they broke into tears. "You're a cold, hard man, Rex. Is this how you treat your friends?"

"Friends bleed the bottom line, *chérie*. I buy acquaintances when I need them." He took one last pull on his scotch. "*Bonsoir*, Lilith. Until lunch on Wednesday." He set the glass to the bar and walked off, leaving her white with rage.

Not that she had a right to be angrier than he. He had spent nearly a year cultivating Lilith in order to get that bill through, only to have her end up whining and simpering like a thirteen-year-old. *Goddamned ridiculous*, he thought, weaving through the crowded ballroom. This was what happened when women tried to play the same game as men. When they'd get their emotions all mixed up with what they wanted and what they needed to do, when they should know the two were totally separate things.

He stopped, staring straight ahead. *I have seen that girl before.*

The Hay-Adams—of course. All at once the memory tumbled back.

Along with the realization he could always feel miserable later.

The girl pushed away from the piano. Their gazes met and she smiled It *had been* the Hay-Adams where he first met her. She was the little lobbyist he'd met in the bar.

This was exactly what he needed. Nothing like the balm of a warm body. He aimed for her, grabbing a champagne from a butlered tray of flutes. She kept her gaze locked on his, conveniently moving to a velvet settee near a darkened corner.

Perfect.

He didn't waste any time. "Haven't we met before?" he said.

She looked up, her expression noncommittal, her long, straight hair curling under the bodice of her low-cut gown. "My goodness," she said dryly. "*Très originale.*"

He stared her down. "Apparently not," he said and so lethally, even he was surprised at the speed her jaw dropped. "*Pardon moi, mademoiselle,*" he said. "*Je suis vraiment désolé.*"

"Oh no—I *do* remember, Monsieur Renaud," she said, jumping to her feet, her hand on his sleeve. "You bought me a Gibson and you had—a scotch, wasn't it? A single malt?"

That impressed him. Her memory was certainly better than his. "I believe it was."

"It was. I haven't forgotten . . . You see . . ." She tilted her head, blushing as she smiled coyly. "I've been hoping we'd run into each other again."

Mon Dieu, she was delicious little thing. Still on the juicy side of twenty-two. He recalled very little of their conversation, only that he wanted to take her back to his room. Just as he wanted to now.

"Well, it looks like you got your wish . . ." Rex racked his brain. " . . . Amanda, isn't it?"

She beamed. "You remembered, Mr. Renaud. I'm flattered."

"Please, call me Rex." He was probably old enough to be her father. "So . . ." They began to stroll. "What brings you to Philadelphia?"

"I'm *from* Philadelphia," she said, grabbing her own champagne from a passing tray. Her hip brushed against him before they squeezed through another bar line for drinks. "I suppose I didn't mention it."

"Visiting your parents, then?" he said, rejoining her on the other side.

She laughed. "That's as good a reason as any, I suppose. But actually I'm here with my boss." She turned, her bare shoulder pressing against his arm. "There he is, over there. See?" She held up her flute, one manicured fingernail indicating the direction.

"Oh. Really," he said, not seeing and certainly not caring. The only thing he did see was how pert and perfect her body was encased in that burgundy gown, and how much he'd like to hike it over her hips. "So you're working then?"

She gritted her teeth. "Seems like I always am—ooh! I think I just made the mistake of making eye contact with my boss." She whirled around. "Don't look now, but standing next to him there's this flabby old man with really bad breath he wants me to keep schmoozing. But I've already spent an hour with him and the only thing I got out of it was an ass grab and his cell number." Her nose wrinkled. "Ew. Look at that gut. Talk about gross."

Rex silently gave thanks for his personal trainer. "You poor thing."

"I know! And he wasn't the only one who grabbed me tonight." She ran her hand down the slope of her *derrière*. "This crowd's like wading through an octopus tank. I bet I won't be able to sit down for a week." She frowned. "I'd duck out of here, but I'm getting paid for tonight, and with all the student loans I have, I really can't turn down the money."

He was all about seizing opportunity. Rex leaned into her. "We could go hide."

Her eyes lit. "Could we? Where?"

"I'm not sure, but there's the exit." Which led to the elevator right up to his suite.

She thought a moment. "Oh! I know. There's some conference rooms right outside that door. But first, why don't we—"

She gulped back her champagne, Rex doing likewise before they stopped a butler. They replaced their empty flutes with two fresh ones.

"Perhaps if we stood here long enough the tray of canapés would also pass by?" he said, his stomach rumbling at the thought. He really didn't remember the last time he ate.

"Who has time!" Amanda chirped. She grabbed his hand, pulling him toward the exit. "Let's go!"

They scuttled from the ballroom and into a conference room right out the exit, closing the door behind them. Inside was a long table surrounded by chairs and on one side, a credenza with a towering bouquet of fresh flowers, on the other, the city skyline shining through the casement windows. Amanda whirled around, sitting on the edge of the table.

Rex went to the flowers and plucking out a rose, brought it back to her.

"Mademoiselle," he said, handing it to her. "*Pour vous.*"

"*Merci*," she said, bringing it to her nose. She laughed. "And with that, I think I've exhausted my French."

"Then it's a good thing I've enough English for the both of us." Actually, he preferred if they didn't talk at all.

She slid the rose against her jaw, regarding him. "Then what do you suppose we should do? Now that we're properly hidden." She leaned back on her arm, the thin strap of her dress, sliding off. She glanced toward it. "Oops."

"Lose something?" Rex said, moving closer, slowly sipping the champagne.

She glanced to the strap. "This is what happens when a fat man sits on your dress. Got all stretched out when I tried to get up." She set down her flute, slipping the strap back into place. "There," she said. "All fixed. Or if you'd rather . . ." She flipped it back down, then, looking to the other shoulder, flipped that one down, too. "Or better yet . . ." She gathered the two straps together in front and tugged, both easily breaking loose from the back. Then she let go, the bodice falling to her waist.

Rex's gaze dropped to her bare breasts, small yet exquisitely shaped and pale in the moonlight. "Well." He took one last sip from his flute before setting it next to hers. "What does this mean?"

Her smile was lazy and lust-filled as she latched hold of his lapels and pulled him toward her. "It means I'm not going back out there. It means that fat old man can kiss my ass."

"What a lovely idea," Rex said, raking his fingers through her hair. "But why should he have all the fun?"

"He won't have any fun at all." She tugged at his bow tie, unraveling it. "But maybe you will."

He held her face between his hands and whispered, "*Coquette* . . ." before brushing his lips against hers.

She seized his greedily, plunging her tongue into his mouth as she threw her arms around his neck, taking him with her as she fell back against the mahogany table. What she lacked in grace she made up for in enthusiasm, Rex conceded. She slipped her hands inside his jacket and under his cummerbund and around to the small of his back.

"I want you to fuck me," she said, biting, nipping his ear. "I've been waiting for you to fuck me ever since you bought me that drink in D.C."

"Really," he said, kissing her neck, his hand sliding down to her breast. She felt more petite than he originally figured, though every part of her seemed fit and firm, almost unnaturally so. "So what have you been doing since then?"

"Thinking about your cock," she said, her hands wasting no time in finding it, snaking around to the front of his trousers, where she quickly went to work undoing them. "How much I wanted it inside me." She made speedy work of his zipper. "How much I want it in me now."

Apparently his body had the same idea, while his mind wasn't yet fully vested. He kissed a trail up her neck. "I have a suite just an elevator ride away."

"I can't wait that long," she said, her fingers grasping his rod. "I want you to fuck me *now*." She wriggled beneath him, her gown hiking up as she spread her legs. "Rip my underwear off."

He stopped, mid-kiss. "What?"

"I *said* . . ." She grunted with impatience, grabbing his hand. "Rip my panties off!"

He whipped his hand back and straightened. *Oui*, he was hard and *oui*, she was one hot little package. But he was still old school enough to want to drive the bus. "*Excusez-moi?*"

"My panties." She palmed her breast, nudging him with the heel of her stiletto. "Rip. Them. Off. *Comprendre?*"

Merde. For one split-second he entertained going back to his suite and just turning on the Playboy Channel. Instead he spread her legs and stepped between them, tossing up her gown until it puddled atop her chest. Then placing his palms atop her knees, he said, "*Chérie*, I'm much older than you as you're probably aware."

"I know that," she said, looking confused. "But that doesn't make any difference—"

"Eh!" He raised a finger, stopping her. She silenced immediately. "What that means is you get the benefit of my experience, as I have much, much more than you." He leaned in, looming over her. "Trust me, I know what to do and can do it so well, you'll scream with so much pleasure the back of your head will cave in."

Her legs twitched. "Oh."

"*Mais oui.* Now." He bent over her. "What is it you wanted me to do . . . ?" he asked, trailing his finger down her belly.

She shivered under his trace. "Rip my panties off," she whispered.

"*Qu'est-ce que tu as dit?*" he said, his fingertip rimming the top of her pale pink boy shorts.

"My panties . . ." She groaned, swallowing hard. "*Rip them.*"

"*Avec plaisir.*" He gripped the top of her panties and yanked down, the fabric shredding in his hand.

Amanda lifted her head and fixing her gaze on him, screamed.

And screamed and screamed and screamed.

Rex turned, hearing the door open. "Oh Christ," he said, her underwear dangling from his fingers, "it's not what you think."

Chapter Three

A Marriage of Convenience

Center City District Police Headquarters
Philadelphia
11:58 p.m.

"AND THEN?" CHARLOTTE said.

Rex sighed. "I was caught *in flagrante delicto*, or was it *corpus delicti*?" He flipped his hand dismissively. "You pick the poison, it's all the same to me."

"But you say it was consensual," Charlotte said, again citing the police report.

"Isn't that what I told you?" he said, getting annoyed.

"You can tell me what you want, but I operate on facts and evidence."

"Then why'd you ask?" he said, his expression darkening.

The last thing Charlotte expected was to enjoy herself, but watching Rex getting perturbed was more fun than she had thought. "To see how you'd answer."

"*Fils de pute*," he said, "what would you expect me to say?"

"I really don't know. From your side of the story, it almost sounds like she was out to attack *you*. Or is the very idea a challenge to your manhood?"

Being well acquainted with Gallic views on male virility, she expected an eruption. But what she got was a most malevolent smile. "*Non*. In fact, it's what I'm counting on to clear me."

"But why—" She stared at him. "You didn't turn your voice recorder off after your chat with the congresswoman, did you?"

"*Non*." He sat back, relaxing again, as if recalling his phone was the only tranquilizer he needed. "I didn't turn it off until the police came. And once they listen to it, everything will be perfectly clear."

"Don't be so sure of that," Charlotte said. "Her sexual aggression is one thing, but her prolonged screaming won't be so easy to explain."

"What's to explain?" he said, perturbed again. "It was all part of setting me up."

"You really believe you were set up? Why?"

"I don't know," he said angrily. "*Yet*. But my position makes me an easy target. Rest assured though. I'm going to find out."

His attitude had to come from frustration, Charlotte surmised. Not knowing the *why* of something was probably a situation he didn't often find him in. "I suppose that's something we'll get out of the investigation. I imagine they took your phone when you were arrested?"

"*Oui*. It should be with the rest of my things."

Charlotte glanced at the tan line on his wrist, his open French cuffs. She could only imagine what the rest of those *things* were. "Well, aren't you in luck. The cops can't search your cell phone when you're first arrested anymore, not without a warrant. But if they find out what's on it, you'll never get it back. So don't say anything, at least for now."

"Why Charlotte, are you advising me to suppress evidence?" He smiled again, and quite brilliantly. "You must have decided to be my *avocate*."

A moment later they heard shuffling outside the door. Then it swung open. "It's time, Ms. Andreko," said the officer.

Rex looked to Charlotte. "So, are you going to get me out of here?"

"At least," she said, picking up her briefcase. She met the cop at the door, then turned. "After that, if everything works out the way you say it will, you'll hardly need me anyway."

"That, *mon amie*," he said, rising, "has yet to be determined."

"What isn't?" she said, the door choosing behind her.

"*Bonjour, avocate,*" Rex said as Charlotte entered the small office aside the courtroom the next morning. "Guess what I just found out from this lovely young lady here? You could've gotten me released last night. Did you know that preliminary arraignments are held twenty-four-seven?"

She shivered with a small jolt of awareness. Even after spending the night in jail, dressed in the same tuxedo he had more than likely slept in, he still exuded a sharpness and a command of the milieu that never failed to throw her. For all he'd been through in the last twelve hours, he still looked as dead-sexy as if he'd just walked out of a photo shoot. With his hair tousled, his eyes hooded, his jaw alluringly bristled, the Rex she kept in her head was now ablaze in all his womanizer glory, smiling blindingly as he half perched on the edge of a desk, a cup of coffee in his hand. No doubt it was bribed out of the way-too-attentive sheriff's deputy looking just as comfortable on a chair before him. Apparently Charlotte had just interrupted a rather animated tête-à-tête.

She looked to the deputy. "I'm sorry, but my client and I need a few minutes before we have to go in."

Did the deputy actually just look to Rex for permission? She must have because he nodded, saying something *en français* Charlotte couldn't translate, but sure sounded awfully suggestive. The deputy answered in kind, albeit with a girlish grin and a Caribbean lilt, taking way too long to rise from her seat.

"*Plus, chérie,*" he said as the deputy beamed at her charge like an ingénue, slowly closing the door behind her.

Charlotte couldn't help rolling her eyes. "My God, what is this strange power you hold over unsuspecting women?" She crossed to him, taking the deputy's seat. "You ought to come with a warning label."

"And what would you suggest?" he said drolly. "Slippery when wet?"

"How about just plain slippery," she answered, digging into her briefcase for an iPad. "I'll draw up a formal document when I get back to the office, but before we begin, I need you to sign for my retainer."

His mouth crooked. "So you've decided to represent me after all."

"Let's just say we're taking it one step at a time." She brought up the form, handing him a stylus. "Sign right here," she said, tapping the spot.

"Not so fast," he said, sliding off the desk. In one swift movement, he was towering over her, staring her down with well-honed, authoritarian hauteur. "You didn't answer my question. Normally, I make it my practice to know exactly what I'm involved in, but last night you had me at a disadvantage." His eyes darkened. "Though I'm right back on it this morning. Why didn't you get me out last night?"

She rose to meet him, more than a little peeved. "Because it took me all night to figure out what the hell I was going to do with you. Which, by the way, included four hours of research, two hours with the French consulate, an hour in transit, and roughly forty-five minutes to shower, change, and ingest a stale bran muffin and some astoundingly bad coffee."

After a moment he said, "You didn't sleep at all last night? No wonder you look so wretched."

Damn, if he didn't have passive-aggressive down to a science. "Thank you, I'm sure," she said, blowing a strand of hair from her eyes. She twisted it around her finger and tucked it back into her upsweep. "I'll be sure to repay the compliment real soon."

"I didn't mean it that way," he said. "I only meant you're usually so put together and today you look . . ." He peered at her. "A little worn around your edges."

Praise, however faint, from Rex? She scowled inwardly, trying to ignore the flip deep down in her belly. "Well, no thanks to you."

"Yes, I know." He gave her hand a squeeze. "Thank you."

She looked to where his fingers grasped hers. She always thought she could tell a man's personality by the look of their hands, but in Rex's case, she was utterly confounded. By all accounts they should have been soft, unabraded, and well manicured, the pampered paws of the unapologetically privileged. Instead his carried a few nicks and scratches, the underside toughened by calluses, his grip firm and amazingly warm. Part of her was pleasantly surprised, but a larger part fought the contradiction. Because in no way did she want him to be playing against type, let alone offering his gratitude. She needed to remember he was only using her because as a female lawyer, she could save his ass. But that was all right. Because she'd be using him, too. The only thing she wanted from him was his cold, impersonal cash, and if she had to be a bitch to siphon off as much of it as she could, she would. She slipped her hand from his.

"I'll take your thanks in the form of a cash transfer," she said. "But first . . ." Again she tapped for his signature. "You need to pony up for my retainer."

He half sat on the desk. "A few preliminaries first. How fast can you get me out of here?"

"How fast can you sign your name?"

"At the speed when-my-shoes-hit-the-sidewalk."

"My shoes ought to walk out of here right now."

He tilted his head, his gaze trailing down her legs. "Go ahead. You sure don't want to keep the next pro bono waiting."

"Very funny." She clenched her eyes against the burn racing down her spine as *sucker!* rolled through her head. The work she'd done so far, any rookie would've already dragged a fat fee out of him before going any further. "Look, you're aware you've been charged with a felony, right? That alone carries big bail. But you're also a foreign national and a flight risk, not to mention you're a person of considerable means."

"Oh?" His mouth quirked. "Look into my bank account, did you?"

"Didn't have to. They did at the consulate. I just peeked." She grinned. "And what a pretty thing it is."

"And now I know two things that get you off—seeing me suffer and my big fat wallet." He leaned in. "Want to try for a third?"

He just loved to knock her off her heels, didn't he? "I'd rather talk countries without extradition treaties."

"That, I would've never have figured." His eyes darkened. "Now why is that?"

"Because your Cayman reserves sure are sexy. Oh, the bribes they could buy."

"But as we determined before, I'm innocent."

"Then tell me what happened after the screaming or better yet, just before?"

The look he gave her shot straight down her spine. "First things first. What's your price, *avocate*?"

She swallowed hard, leveling her gaze. "Five hundred thousand."

If she was waiting for his jaw to drop he didn't even blink. "All right."

So neither would she. "Then sign right here." She tapped the spot one more time. "And we'll get this ball rolling."

"To where?" he said, still unmoved.

"Come on, they'll be calling us in any second." *Tap, tap.*

"I'm not doing anything until I find out what's going to happen."

"Seeing as I'm not the judge," she said evenly, "I can't predict how he or she will react, but you have two strikes against you already—privilege and being a French citizen. And if the judge is a woman?" She shrugged, and not without smug satisfaction. "You could be screwed from the start."

He laughed. "So much for blind justice."

"Yeah, well, if we were in Paris, how much would my being American help *me*?"

"If we were in Paris, this farce wouldn't be happening."

"Anyway, the consulate has agreed to be responsible for you. So more than likely the judge will order you to stay there until the preliminary hearing, which could be anywhere from three to ten business days from now."

"And what's the purpose of that?"

"To show if a crime has been committed and whether or not you're the likely offender. The evidence against you will be presented either by the detective on the case or the assistant district attorney. If there's enough, the case moves forward."

"They'll get a statement from the girl, then."

"They already have."

"Did you see it?"

"Yes." How much should she tell him? He berated her for taking pro bono cases, and here he was, demanding the same. "Take what you told me and reverse it. Basically that you lured her into the next room and then assaulted her."

She could see his jaw clench. "Have you spoken with her?" he said quietly.

"That's not the way it works. I have access to whatever statements she gives to the police, but outside of that, I'll have to wait until I could cross-examine her in court. I hear she's gone into hiding anyway. At least she's not at her parents' home in the city."

He obviously wasn't pleased with that information, but there was nothing she could do about it. "So what happens if they can't find enough evidence to substantiate her statement?"

"Then you'll be free to go."

"Hm." He fell silent, looking askance, crossing his arms over his chest.

Charlotte leaned against the wall, exhausted. She last slept in days not hours ago, and the only thing she really wanted was to get this morning over with so she could drop atop her pillow. So unlike Rex, who looked miraculously revived, always seeming precision-cut out of marble. Her gaze drifted to the slope of his jaw, his wholly sensuous mouth. She idly wondered how many women that mouth had kissed, how many times it'd scorched down fevered . . . *Jesus.* She stopped herself, pinching her eyes shut. *Where the hell did that come from?* From wherever it did it had to stop. He was a client, at least he was probably going to be, and that was it. No matter how attracted to him she was—and there was no denying she was—she'd learned long ago men like Rex were bastards to the core and good for only one thing—turning a good woman bad.

" . . . other options, don't you think?"

She looked up. "What?"

His mouth crooked, even more sensuously. "You weren't listening, were you?"

"Sure I was." *Focus.*

"I *said*"—he enunciated the word—"what are my options?"

"Options?" She was mystified. "There aren't any. Either there'll be enough evidence to move the case forward or not. This part really isn't all that complicated."

"No, I mean about my release. I don't want to stay at the consulate."

She laughed. "I don't think they'll care what you want. Unless you have family here, or another party who has established ties to the community and is willing to take responsibility for you, I don't see where you'll have a choice."

Rex eyed her dubiously. "There's always a choice."

"Like the one you've given me?" She laughed again. "You've practically held a gun to my head."

"You could walk away."

"I could. I *should*. Especially since I suspect there's a lot you're not telling me. You can't hold out on me if you expect me to form a rational defense."

"I never said I was and besides, I won't need a defense when they see there's no crime. I didn't assault that girl, and that'll become evident enough very soon. The only thing you have to concentrate on is getting me out of here."

All at once the reality of what she was doing descended on her. "And then what? After I've compromised my reputation by working with you, how do I redeem myself?"

"By proving those fuckers wrong," he said. All at once he grasped her by the shoulders. "And you start by trusting me. Can you do that?"

"How could I? I hardly know you at all." Then right there and that suddenly, she found she wanted to, to really know him, to really understand him. And why was that? It was those eyes. *Damn* him! She couldn't think with those inky eyes so focused on hers. She could drown in them, in fact it seemed she was, all reason swirling down the drain.

"Why should I?" she finally said. "All you probably want me to do is manipulate the facts anyway, truth be damned. Isn't that what a good defense attorney does? Twist the truth until it suits the purpose?" She shoved him away, all professionalism going out the window. "Then you'd better cough some up, monsieur. Why did she start screaming?"

"I told you—to set me up."

"For *what*? Why would she be out to get you?" She shoved him again. "Tell me!"

"*I don't know!*" he hissed, reeling on her until her back was against the wall. "Get me out of here so I can find out. If you do I'll make it worth your while."

"Yeah?" She stared at him. "How much?" She honestly wanted to know. Didn't she already push him over the edge with her retainer?

"Two million," he said. "One for your firm, and another as an endowment for Occupy Vagina."

"Two *million*?" She stared at him, speechless. There was only one reason he'd offer her something so outrageous. "Jesus, you really must be guilty."

His gaze dropped, fixing on her mouth. "That's the last thing I'd like you to think of me. For now I only need you to trust me."

The deputy opened the door. "Time to go in," she said, smiling at Rex.

He nodded. "*Merci. Nous arrivons.*" He looked to Charlotte, adjusting his open collar. "Shall we?"

"Oh no." She tapped the iPad. "Not before I get this is writing."

"And I will. After." Then he took her arm, leading her into the courtroom.

"ALL RISE."

A female judge. Rex rose as she took her place behind the bench. *Good.*

Charlotte leaned in, whispering, "You're fucked."

He whispered back, "Then at least let me enjoy it."

She stared at him, blushing furiously.

Rex smiled to himself. He was starting to enjoy doing that.

" . . . the Honorable Sophia K. Jennings, in and for the County of Philadelphia and the Commonwealth of Pennsylvania. Please be seated."

As he did he looked over his shoulder. For so early in the morning the courtroom was packed, and if he wasn't mistaken, there were a few spectators who looked way too comfortable.

"Yes, you're right," Charlotte whispered.

He peered at her. "About what?"

"Those *are* members of the press back there."

"Surely not for me."

"Eventually, yeah, they will be. They're looking for a story, and when they find out who you are and what you're here for, they'll get one."

He sighed. "Just what I need."

"And just what I don't," she said, scribbling something on a legal pad. "Their story won't only be about you, you know."

The judge looked up from her blotter. "Rex Renaud?"

Rex and Charlotte stood. "We're here, your honor," Charlotte said.

"Approach the bench."

"Don't answer unless you absolutely have to," Charlotte whispered as they made their way to the front.

"That's what I'm paying you for," he said.

"Or not," she answered. They took their place at the bar.

After a few moments the judge said, "Mr. Renaud?"

"Yes, your honor?" As he gifted her with a deferential curve of his mouth, he could almost feel Charlotte groaning beside him.

"You're a foreign national, correct?"

"Yes, your honor," he answered. "Of France."

"In this country for business or pleasure?"

"Business."

"And what is the nature of that business?"

Charlotte answered instead. "My client is the chief operating officer of the international corporation Mercier Shipping, and is often in the U.S. for business. Mercier and its subsidiaries have a shipping presence at several major ports and on both coasts throughout the United States, including Philadelphia."

A small rumble went through the courtroom until the judge glanced up, immediately silencing it. "I'm aware of Mercier," the judge said, looking askance. "Something about one of its captains chaining herself to the mast of her ship here last summer . . . ?"

A few titters from the crowd. "Yes, your honor," Charlotte said.

Then just as quickly, the judge turned somber. "But there's nothing quite as amusing about this incident, now is there, counselor?"

Charlotte glanced to Rex with a you're-so-screwed expression before answering. "No, your honor. Not at all."

She raised a brow. "And you of all people should know that, Ms. Andreko."

More rumbling as Rex watched Charlotte blanch. He almost reached for her hand.

The judge ruffled a piece of paper, looking to Rex. "Mr. Renaud, complaints of sexual assault and indecent assault have been filed against you, sections 3124.1 and 3126 of the Pennsylvania Criminal Code. Are you aware of their seriousness?"

So much he was ready to crush the party responsible. "Yes I am, your honor."

"As well as I am aware you're a very wealthy man," the judge said, shuffling a few more papers. "One that could afford, say . . ." She thought a moment. "Five million dollars' bail."

More rumblings went through the court as Charlotte said, "If I may, your honor, isn't that bail a bit . . . overcautious?"

"No, counselor," the judge said. "No for someone who has a plane at their disposal to flee the country with."

"Not that I would, your honor," Rex said, to Charlotte's immediate jab of a spike heel into his toe.

"*Ow*," he whispered, scowling at her.

"Excuse me?" the judge said, looking up.

Charlotte coughed. "Nothing, your honor. Sorry."

The judge squinted at her before returning to the sheaf of papers. "So, as a man of considerable means being accused of a felony, who's a foreign national, and who has an extraordinary means of transportation that could whisk him out of the country at a moment's notice, please tell me Mr. Renaud, why the court should grant you bail?"

"If I may, your honor," Charlotte said.

"Yes, Ms. Andreko?" the judge said a bit impatiently.

She cleared her throat. "Mr. Renaud, in all his forty years, has an impeccable record in his private life, and a long history of service to the international community. And since he's the COO of a major corporation, and with the nature of his charge no doubt soon to be picked up by the media, it would be very hard for him to slip out of the country. Even so, the French consulate here in the city is willing to take responsibility for him until the hearing if he's released into their custody in lieu of bail."

"Which won't be necessary," Rex interjected.

"Oh?" The judge looked over. "Why is that?"

"Because I'd rather make bail than become a burden and distraction to the consulate," Rex said.

Charlotte shot him a look of horror. "Jesus—will you keep quiet?" she muttered.

"Admirable, Mr. Renaud," the judge said, "but let me ask you a question. Do you have any family in this country?"

"No, your honor."

"Do you own a residence?"

"No," he answered.

"I see." The judge thought a moment. "So, Mr. Renaud, and this is no reflection on your character, but with such a serious charge leveled against you and no ties to this country except through business, it wouldn't seem quite reasonable to just let you out to wander the streets."

"And I wouldn't be," he said. He glanced at Charlotte. "I have an alternate place to stay while I'm in America."

"Oh?" the judge said. "Where might that be?"

"With my attorney. She's agreed to take full responsibility." He turned to Charlotte with the full force of his personality. "Isn't that true, *avocate*?"

Chapter Four

There's No Place Like Home, There's No Place Like Home

HE HAD TO be joking. Charlotte gaped at Rex, following the line of that self-assured jaw to an expression too god-damned determined.

"Seriously, Ms. Andreko? You're willing to take responsibility for this client?" The judge hardly sounded convinced.

"She had agreed, your honor," Rex answered, "if I were unable to stay with the consulate."

"You don't have a choice," she mumbled under her breath.

"No—*you* don't," he said, grinning again.

Charlotte hissed through her teeth, "Why you son of a—"

"Ms. Andreko," the judge snapped. "Please address

the court. Will you take responsibility for Mr. Renaud or not?"

If she said no she'd look like an idiot. But saying yes was almost worse. It was bad enough the head of in-your-face Occupy Vagina was defending the COO of a company who'd been labeled misogynistic, branding her an opportunist for risking every feminist principle she ever stood for. But if he was *convicted*? The idea nearly gave her the shakes. Her reputation would be blown clear back to the Victorians.

Son of a bitch had her over a barrel and he knew it. And there was only one way to fight back. By proving the *connard* was as innocent as he said he was. She slanted him a scowl. *And he goddamned better be.*

"Yes, your honor," Charlotte finally said, formulating a reasoning on the fly. "I believe that since Mr. Renaud has never been convicted of as much as a traffic citation, his public stature and financial capabilities would make him less of a flight risk, not more."

"Perhaps, but I'm not quite so sure. Which brings us to the question of bail." She looked to Rex, and not altogether kindly. "Your unique circumstances as well as the severity of this charge demand a bond." Then she paused, as if for effect. "Five million, to be posted before your release. As well as your absolute assurance you will not fly yourself down to South America. Is that clear, Mr. Renaud?"

"Perfectly, your honor," Rex said, unflinchingly, the courtroom rumbling in response. "I haven't the slightest inclination to go anywhere until all charges against me have been dropped."

"I should hope not," the judge said, "but your five million bond will give you all the more incentive. And Ms. Andreko?"

"Yes, your honor?"

"I need *your* assurances you won't let him out of your sight until the preliminary hearing."

Out of her sight? She must be joking. "Do you really think that's necessary?"

"Are you questioning the judge?" Rex said sotto voce, feigning astonishment.

"Are you questioning me?" the judge asked.

Jesus—who's been charged here? Charlotte thought. She looked to the judge, cornered. "No, your honor. You have my assurance."

"That's all I want," she answered. She shuffled a few papers on her desk before looking back to Rex. "Mr. Renaud, you're to report back on Friday, October 3, ten a.m., for your preliminary hearing. That proceeding will determine if sufficient evidence exists to hold the case over for trial. At that time the court may also discuss a reduction in charges or dismissal of the case. Do you understand?"

"We do, your honor," Charlotte said.

The judge peered at her. "Well, that's excellent." Then to Rex. "Mr. Renaud, please follow the deputy out so you may post your bond. Ms. Andreko—my chambers, please."

"I'll meet you out front," Charlotte said to Rex.

"Oh, you most certainly will," he said, squeezing her arm as he left.

Charlotte hoped that shiver came from rage, or what a week it was going to be. A minute later she was standing before the judge's desk inside her chambers, the judge plopping into a chair behind it. And most pointedly not asking Charlotte to take a seat.

"Just what do you think you're doing?" the judge said.

"I beg your pardon?" Charlotte answered, taken aback.

"I'm pretty familiar with your Occupy Vagina," the judge said, tapping her nail against the armrest. "My daughter even has even started wearing that—that—" She hastily shook her hand in front of her. "That ovary-appliqued bikini top of yours to the pool."

"Oh." Charlotte laughed slightly. "Sells even better than our 'See Dick Run' T-shirt."

"I'm definitely *not* laughing," the judge said.

"No, of course not." *Jesus.*

"The point being," the judge continued, "you have a solid reputation in this city, probably in this state. Maybe even wider than that when you think about the shenanigans Renaud's company pulled last summer. But back then you and your organization stood tall empowering women, not railing against them."

The judge repositioned herself and gave her a quick once-over, both actions designed to telegraph Charlotte's insignificance. But she wasn't buying it. She'd met her kind before. Women were always infinitely crueler than men as their standards were always higher. She thought back to Rex's earlier observation. *Why shed blood when you can suck out a man's soul.* He'd nailed it without even trying.

He did know women. At least that was one thing to admire him for. Had she the inclination.

"Ms. Andreko," the judge went on, "I'm not trying to tell anyone what to do, and you're certainly free to conduct your business anyway you want. But personally I'm a bit confused how you can risk the backing of your many female supporters by representing a man who's obviously just out to use you. Don't be surprised if they're angry and see it as a betrayal, wondering why you're not directing your efforts toward the woman in question. I mean—my goodness." She squinched her face in horror. "What would Gloria Allred say?"

If Charlotte had been taken aback by the judge's reaction she knew she shouldn't have been. Her motives had been questioned before. Even so, the judge had picked the wrong morning to give her a schooling. It was bad enough she was flying on no sleep and bad coffee, not to mention a week with Rex waiting on the other side. She hardly needed this woman maligning her judgment, as that always got her hair in a kink.

Even more than it usually was.

Charlotte planted her Louboutins, pressing her fingers to the desk. "All due respect, your honor, but I think Gloria Allred or Gloria Steinem or even Gloria Vanderbilt would do the same as me—correct an injustice when they see one and the sex be damned. You of all people should know that."

The judge's eyes widened in outrage. "Are you questioning me again?"

"You're questioning *me*, and I haven't gotten as far as

I have by letting you or anyone roll over me. Believe me, I know what I'm up against."

The judge stood, slowly and with a glare Charlotte was sure could have melted steel. "Then you better hope to God that man is innocent or I'll make it my personal mission to drag your name so low you'll be looking down to look up."

Charlotte met her gaze. "If he's guilty you won't have to. My obituary will already have been written."

"Especially since there's this. You and that man better be making like Siamese twins until the hearing because if either of you try to flout my order, and I find out he's even crossed the street without you, I'll issue a bench warrant so fast his *derrière* will back in jail at the speed of light." Her eyes narrowed. "Not that that should be a problem. I saw the way he leered at you."

Charlotte turned to leave. "Then you've nothing to worry about because I'll be only one getting screwed, won't I? You have a wonderful morning." She opened the door and walked out.

She wondered if she went too far. But hadn't she done that the moment she said yes to Rex? As she left for the elevator bank she shuddered, thinking of how many more times in the next few days she would again.

CHARLOTTE ROSE FROM the bench in the lobby as Rex entered from the street. "Where in holy hell have you been?" she said.

It took him a moment to register what she'd said

before he could speak. "I got a ride back to the station to get my things," he said. "But when I got there . . ."

She tossed her hand, hoisting her briefcase atop her shoulder. "Yes . . . ?"

"My phone was missing," he said, still not believing it.

"What?" She looked incredulous. "How is that possible? Didn't you sign for it?"

"Oh course I did," he said, irritated she'd even ask. But it wasn't there, and they could offer me no credible explanation why it wasn't. They said they'd look and call me if they found it."

"This was at the property room?"

"*Oui*. They took my phone from me at the scene, but after I was brought to the station they gave me a receipt for it there. Look."

She scanned it. "And here's the phone. Was anything else missing?"

He looked over his shoulder and back. "Can we continue this discussion someplace else? I'd really like to get out of here." He flicked the lapel of his tuxedo. "And out of this."

"Not before I have a chat with the nice folks in the property room." She grabbed her briefcase. "We're going back."

"Don't bother," he said. "You won't get any cooperation from them. I left them with a string of French curses that are probably still hanging in the air. Besides, they don't have it."

"How do you know?"

"Because if they were out to just steal anything of

mine," he said, pulling up a sleeve, "it sure as hell wouldn't be my four-hundred-dollar iPhone."

She stared at his diamond and platinum cuff links. "Jesus," she whispered. "What's something like that worth?"

"Maybe five grand." He shrugged, pulling the sleeve down. "Give or take a grand."

"*God*. How good does it feel to be that rich?"

He pointed to a tear in her leather briefcase. "How bad does it feel to be that poor?"

"You're such a smartass."

"And you ask too many rhetorical questions." He pointed to the door. "Can we go now?"

"Sure, but I have to warn you that after your arraignment, you can fully expect some of the media to approach you. See what I mean?" She jutted her chin toward the door. "There's news vans out there now. And I'm not entirely sure they're just out to get you. I'm sure there's one or two of them ready to make an example out of me." Then she stopped. "I know a back way out to the street. C'mon."

As he did, Rex almost felt sick. What the fuck would he do now? Who the hell would want to steal his phone? Who would gain by it? Could it possibly have been . . . Lilith? With her husband a judge, the idea fell within the realm of possibility. But it was also true they hated each other. At least that's what Lilith led Rex to believe. But then you never could tell what went on between two people. Maybe they had struck a bargain a long time ago to cover for each other, both living so visibly in the public eye.

Charlotte pulled open a door, entering into a stairway, Rex watching her as they descended. She truly didn't know how goddamned hot she was, did she? How effortlessly seductive she was with her blonde hair piled high, allowing a few strands to frame her long neck, her silk shirt straining across her breasts, a pencil skirt hugging up and around that gorgeous *cul*. And those legs. Even though they went on forever, he had a good idea how to make them stop. By wrapping them around his hips and burying himself inside her.

Not that he needed to be thinking any more about his libido. Had he paid it a little less attention, he wouldn't be walking out of a courthouse now.

"So where are we going?" she said, opening another door to a service corridor.

"How about my hotel?"

Her eyes narrowed. "Oh, that's so not happening."

One more door and they were out on the street. "Quench your dreams of glory, mademoiselle. I need to wash and change. Though you'd better decide where we're going after that, as it's either your place or mine."

Which she looked none too happy about. "All right, mine then."

"*Très bien.*" He looked up and down the street. "Where'd you park your car?"

"I didn't bring it," she said. "I don't use it much in the city. It's easier to take the subway."

He gaped at her with mild horror. "You honestly don't expect I'd get on—"

"Calm down, your majesty. The Ritz is just down the street. See?" She pointed to it. "We can walk."

"Oh, stellar," he said, taking off his jacket to sling it over his shoulder. He thumbed his collar. "Nothing says Eurotrash like evening clothes in daylight."

Charlotte laughed. "But you wear them *so* well." She slipped the briefcase strap to her shoulder with a wince. "This way."

"Give me that," he said, taking the heavy leather satchel from her.

She pulled back. "I can handle it. I don't need your help."

"I'm sure you don't," he said, yanking it back. "But the cad in me is just gentlemen enough not to ignore a lady struggling in the street. So indulge me, please?"

She let go, crossing her arms. "Fine—it's all yours."

He hoisted the handle, wincing. "What do you have in here, hammers?"

"No, just the evidence of your guilt."

"Which means we'll have to hire a truck to carry the evidence for my side."

"Hm . . ." was all she said.

They walked for half a block more before he finally broke the silence. "You didn't think I'd get out today, did you?"

She slanted him a glance. "I didn't think it'd be easy. There was that jet to consider."

"You still think me capable of all kinds of mischief, don't you?"

"I wasn't the one you had to convince."

He took her arm, steering her around a pile of broken glass. "You do have a point."

One more block and they were at the Ritz-Carlton, entering into the cavernous marble lobby. She aimed for a sofa. "I'll wait here."

"Not on your life," he said, taking her arm again. "Remember the judge's order. We're to remain as thick as thieves."

"Doesn't mean I have to visit your den of iniquity," she said.

He turned, regarding her. "*Ma cher avocate*, if you so fear my turning into a sex fiend the moment you and I occupy the same enclosed space, then by all means, wait near an opened window. I'm sure your screaming is pure poetry." He pressed the up button for the elevator. "For Christ's sake, what are you going to do when we get to your house and we're really alone?"

She didn't reply, watching the floor indicator instead. "Where was that fund-raiser last night?"

"The ballroom. On the second floor."

She looked at him. "Take me there."

He had no idea what she was about. "All right."

The fund-raiser had run late into the night, and the staff was still shuffling tables and setting up for the next reception. As they stood in the doorway Charlotte said, "How crowded was it last night?"

"Packed to the jowls," Rex said. "Took us quite a while to squeeze through the crowd to get out."

"When you left to go . . . ?" She let the obvious simply hang there.

"Yes," he said.

"Take me to it."

As they walked across the ballroom he became inordinately aware of her beside him, the way her hips shifted beneath her skirt, the clip-clop of her heels across the parquet flooring. It stuck him how different she seemed alongside him than that girl did from the night before, so much more natural, unlike how he had felt chasing down the scent of rut. *How foolish I'd been,* he thought.

"It's through here to the right," he said, holding open the exit door for her.

She slipped past him, then halted almost immediately. "Oh," she said.

Bright yellow and black tape X'ed the door with "CRIME SCENE—DO NOT ENTER," the knob and moldings still white from the fingerprint dusting.

Rex shook out his handkerchief and tried the doorknob. "It's locked."

"As I figured it would be. Yet our coming was inevitable, wasn't it?" She laughed, a short harsh burst of irony. "They say the perp always returns to the scene of the crime."

He hadn't seen the point in coming, and he sure didn't want to pursue it any further. He knew he had enemies, but he didn't understand why they had followed him here. "Are you through?" he said, turning to the elevator bank. "Or would you like to see me squirm some more?"

She regarded him a moment. "No, I've had enough. Let's go."

A few silent minutes later they were at his suite, Rex surprised when his key card actually opened it. But then again, suspected felon or not, wealth did have its perks. She followed him inside to a sitting room.

"Can you give me a few minutes?" he said, setting down her briefcase. "I need to decontaminate myself after a night in that cell."

"Go ahead," she said, positioning herself on the sofa and crossing those long, creamy legs. Suddenly he found it almost unfathomable how he could have thought someone so much younger could look better than what he saw right in front of him. "But can I ask you a question first?"

"Sure," he said, further loosening his collar, something he would have done long ago if he didn't look so ridiculous already. "What is it?"

"It's something I've been thinking about for a while now." She seemed to ponder it a bit more. "Why is it that when older women go after younger men they're called cougars, but older men are almost expected to trade up for younger women?"

"I don't know," he said, removing his cuff links. "I've always appreciated experience."

"Yet you left the congresswoman for the little lobbyist." She looked askance. "Huh."

"Let's get one thing straight," he said, going to her. "There was never any love lost between me and Lilith."

"Yes, I know. It was strictly business." She spread her arms across the back of the sofa. "Or so you said."

He huffed, yanking off his jacket. "I'll be in the shower," he said, closing the French doors to the bedroom.

"Damnable woman," he muttered *en français*. He ripped off his clothes, leaving a trail of them to the bathroom, knowing there'd be no housemaids to pick up after him like at home. Maybe he'd gotten used to too many things he shouldn't have these past thirty years. Maybe he should try to remember what it was like before. Didn't matter, he knew, as he stepped in the shower. He broke his back to get where he was. He soaped his face, grabbing his razor. Just like he'd break his back to stay there as well.

After he shrugged into his jacket he returned to the sitting room, still tying his tie when suddenly he stopped short. There was Charlotte lying on her side atop the sofa, her clasped hands tucked under her chin, dead asleep. It was a sight that shot straight to his core, and he would have drawn the curtains and left her there had her eyes not popped open. She sat up, her hair tumbling down around her.

"Oh," she said, red-faced and yawning, "I think I fell asleep."

"I think you did, too," he said, finishing his Windsor knot. "Would you like to go lie down on the bed for a little while?"

She stared at him as if he'd just proposed a leap out the window. "No," she said pointedly, standing. "If I'm going to do any sleeping I'll do it in my own bed, thank you." She eyed him up and down. "Are you ready?"

"Just let me grab my bags," he said, leaving a hundred-dollar bill for the maid.

As they rode the elevator down, as he settled his bill, increasingly Rex became aware of her, so much that even the smallest things, like signing his name and retrieving his wallet, became distractions. How would he ever spend the week with her? Perhaps it wasn't so much Charlotte who was disorienting, as how the little things she had said made him inordinately mindful of himself and his position. She had no idea what he had lost and how hard he had fought to get where he was, though he thought that maybe one day he would tell her. But at the moment he hardly found her perspective endearing. So when they finally hit the sidewalk it was with some relief he found a bit of secondhand familiarity parked at the curb. Julie Knott's Channel 8 News van.

"And where do you think you're going?" said her cameraman, Denny O'Brien, as he rolled down the driver's side window.

"That would be my house," Charlotte said. "Hey, is Julie in there?"

"Yes," Julie said, her monstrously pregnant belly hardly allowing her to swivel toward them from the passenger seat. "Oh hello, Rex. Sorry about what happened last night, but I do love how the family keeps feeding me copy."

"As well as how it keeps you in maternity clothes," Charlotte said, gaping at her enormous belly. "Jesus, Julie, ovulate much?"

She laughed. "Not lately. But I'll tell you, when they start coming in pairs, it's time to stop." The TV reporter winced as she adjusted herself in the seat. "So Charlotte, what the hell are you doing here? I came for Rex's story, but yours is a hell of a lot better. Jump in and let me give you a ride while you tell me all about it."

"I don't want to inconvenience you," Charlotte said. "We can take a cab."

"Not on your life," Julie pressed. "Or would you rather someone outside the family gets ahold of both your stories, and who'll be sorry then?"

Rex tapped Charlotte's arm. "Better get in," he said, and reluctantly, she did. The inside of the news van was so crammed with production equipment there was hardly room enough for her and Rex to squish themselves into the jump seats.

"So Rex," Julie said, struggling to turn to face him, "ça va, mon ami. Andy assures me you may be a conniver and an opportunist, but a ravisher of women, you're not."

"How gracious of him," Rex opined, his knees nearly hitting his chin.

"Then what's the story?" Julie asked. "Come on, I'm having a drought here."

Rex knew in order to control this story he had to own it, and the only way to do that was to feed his version directly to Marcel Mercier's sister-in-law. Even though she usually did the lighter side of the news, he was well aware that was hardly why she was here.

"I didn't have sex with that woman," he said.

"Gee, where have I heard that before?" Julie said. "But we're not exactly talking a tryst. We're talking assault."

"Exactly," he said. "Which I'm sure you hardly think me capable."

"So naturally, she's lying," Julie said. "Now why would she do that?"

"I don't know." He wished he did. "But I'll be sure to let you know when I find out."

"Of course," Julie said, "but for now, we need to do better than that."

"Where're we going?" Denny asked. "I'm guessing not the Four Seasons."

"We're going to my house," Charlotte said. "Turn up Fourth Street."

"On the other hand . . ." Julie's face lit. "Now *there's* a story more like I'm used to. Why would the biggest feminist in town be playing for the other team? And for an alleged felon, no less?"

"I resent that," Rex said.

"No offense intended," Julie said. "But I only think in tabloid headlines. So Charlotte, give me an exclusive. Why did you decide to lawyer for this man? Especially if it means risking the wrath of your supporters who will obviously see it as a betrayal?"

"Then it'll be they who're the real opponents of equality," Charlotte said. "I fight for justice on both sides of the gender line. It's as simple as that."

"What a headline. I love it!" Julie said, her eyes lighting. "Why this is even better than the twelve-year-old who chews nails. Imagine the two of you, double-teaming it. Like Susan B. Anthony and Dominique Strauss-Kahn."

"It's hardly like that," Charlotte said, her eyes narrowing.

Julie looked to Rex. "You must be paying her a boat-load of money. Get it?" She prodded his knee. "A boat-load!"

He regarded her blandly. "*Très amusant.*"

"The next block," Charlotte said to Denny. "That one with the blue door."

Denny pulled to the curb, Charlotte practically leaping out. Julie looked to her from the window. "So no joke—you're really and honestly his *lawyer*?"

It's a good thing she's a woman and Marcel's sister-in-law, Rex couldn't help thinking. Because if Julie were a man, he wouldn't be responsible for what he'd do next. "Didn't she just say that?"

The reporter slowly shook her head. "It's just too bizarre. *Too* bizarre." She shrugged. "Well then, *au revoir*! And don't forget to keep me posted."

Charlotte sighed, looking to Rex as the van pulled away. "We are so fucked."

Chapter Five

Potent Potables

REX LOOKED TOWARD the house. "You have anything to drink inside?"

Charlotte turned from the stoop, key at the lock. "Coffee or tea?"

Was she joking? "I said a *drink*."

"What do you expect, absinthe?" She glanced at her phone. "It's ten a.m."

"Which makes it four in Paris and already too late for a champagne lunch."

"Champagne? As if we've anything to celebrate."

"Which is why we'll make it scotch. Do you have any?"

That pert little nose lifted. "What would you say to a Balvenie forty-year-old single malt?"

"I'd say what are we still doing on the sidewalk?" *Mon Dieu*, she was a surprising woman. "Take me to it."

The inside of Charlotte's closeted row house was a marked difference from Rex's airy little waterfront home on Vallon des Auffes in Marseille. Instead of pastel shades and sun-washed tile, there were velvet curtains and a worn-looking sofa against dark paneling, the living room's faded green carpeting bleeding into a dining room that didn't appear to ever host a meal, its table cluttered with books, papers, mail, and a laptop. Charlotte shifted around equally overflowing chairs to a sideboard housing a rather interesting rye and malt collection, gleaming glassware beside it. Apparently, she took her liquor seriously, which pleased Rex to no end.

"I know it's messy, but believe it or not, someone comes and spruces up all the essential parts every Tuesday." Then she winced. "At least they used to." She poured two fingers into each glass.

"So you're joining me, I see," he said.

"With as much sleep as I got last night? I suppose it's barely the shank of the evening after all. Ice?" she asked, retreating into the kitchen. When he declined she added, "Oh you Europeans. You like everything at room temperature."

"While you Americans"—he heard the clink of two cubes hit her glass—"like everything frozen."

"Not everything," she said, handing him a glass. "*Santé.*"

"*Santé,*" he said, clinking hers. He took a sip as well, savoring the smoke as it warmed his throat. "Ah, very nice."

She smiled over the rim of her tumbler. "Yes, isn't it."

He came around the side, regarding her. "You surprise me. It's the rare woman who appreciates a good scotch."

"I'll take that as a compliment," she said, her mouth crooking ever so slightly.

A shaft of sunlight through the window caught a streak of red in her hair. "As it was intended."

She flipped her hand toward the living room. "Shall we?"

Rex waited until she sat on the sofa before joining her on a chair opposite. She leaned against the arm, crossing those impossible legs. "So . . ." he said, savoring another swallow.

"So . . ." She took a demure sip as a few moments of silence yawned between them. "Perhaps this would be a good time to discuss the elephant in the room."

"Oh, right." He looked around. "A rather big fucker it is, too."

"Freaking huge. Sucks all the air out of the place, doesn't it?"

"I think it needs a name. Why don't we call it . . ." He thought a moment. "Rex."

"T-Rex," she said, her eyes widening. "It's that ginormous."

"It is." He swirled his scotch, glanced into his glass. "Charlotte, I do appreciate what you're doing." Maybe he even felt a bit sorry for forcing her into it. "I don't think I would've enjoyed being jailed at the consulate any more than I enjoyed my stay with the city police. Thank you."

"Oh don't worry," she readily assured him. "*I'm* going to enjoy being a millionaire."

That's what he got for going soft. "Don't order the

Bentley yet, *ma chérie*. You still have to get me out of this."

"And I will. At least I'll do my best. But you have to be straight with me. Because the minute you start taking me for granted I'm out the door."

"I'd have to be insane to do that," he said.

Her eyes flashed to his. "Yeah, well." She sniffed. "Just so you know."

"I won't forget."

"Good." She took another sip, smiling cordially, but then the elephant returned, the air nearly vibrating around it. After a moment she said, "Perhaps you should continue where you left off. What happened after the police burst in."

"And ruin our scotch? *Non*. Perhaps we should first get to know each other a little better."

Again her eyes flashed to his. This time with heat. Not that it was an invitation. Not yet anyway. "And we will. After you tell me what happened."

He always operated on the principle to only divulge information on a need-to-know basis, and with Charlotte, he needed to know her a bit more. But since she was his attorney, she certainly had a point. "Well, the first thing I did was shut off my phone."

"Why?"

"I was still recording, remember? And aside from the fact I didn't want them to know that, I didn't want to get myself on tape saying anything they could hold against me."

"Sound reasoning," she said. "But who were you really

protecting yourself from? The police, or . . ." She met his gaze. "Who was behind the door?"

He took a sip of scotch. "Good catch, *avocate*."

"Who was it?" She leaned closer. "Tell me."

Her eyes told him she had already guessed. "It was Lilith."

"She followed you."

"*Oui*."

"Well, it doesn't take a detective to figure out why," Charlotte said. "*Ou un génie non plus*."

"You know, I've been wondering—*où avez-tu appris à parler si bien le français?*"

She laughed, swirling her drink. "*Qu'est-il arrivé à l'anglais seulement?*"

Although nearly perfect, her American-accented *français* heated him as thoroughly as the scotch. "All right . . . where did you learn to speak French so well?"

"I ought to ask you the same thing about your English."

"I asked you first," he said, watching her throat as she swallowed. *A very nice throat.*

"But if you want any more of that scotch you'll be a good little detainee and do as I say."

"You have me there." He loosened the top button of his collar. "I took my first English lessons in primary school, but I polished it on both sides of the Atlantic. At Cambridge, where I got my undergraduate degree, then for my MBA at Harvard—"

"*In* Cambridge," Charlotte finished. "My, my, Mr. Renaud. That's rather redundant of you, isn't it?"

"Doing something well once is worth doing again,

don't you think?" he said. "And the name's Rex, by the way."

"Rex . . . yes . . ." she said, sliding a leg under her, her face flushing slightly. She brushed a few loose curls from her eyes. "Rex it is."

"Now you," he said. "Where did you learn to *parlez vous*?"

"Ah-ah!" She waggled her finger. "*Pas de français*, Monsieur—er, Rex." Apparently the scotch was going to her head. "Phew . . ." She laughed slightly, holding the glass against her cheek. "Apparently the scotch is going to my head."

"I was thinking the same thing."

She fanned herself. "Oh? It's going to your head as well?"

"The scotch?" He shook his head slowly. "Oh *non*."

She took another sip, her fanning speeding up.

"Perhaps we should have some breakfast," Rex offered. *Perhaps I could eat it off your belly.* "But first, answer my question."

Charlotte set the glass on an end table. "Well, if you must know, I've been speaking it since birth. Honed at my grandmother's knee."

"Oh? Was she French?"

"*Oui*—the Frenchiest. *Ma grand-mère était une Parisienne.*"

"Really? From Paris?" Which explained Charlotte's snobbery. Parisians were like New Yorkers. Everyone and everything outside their immediate orbit were *les beaufs*—trash—not so much a matter of money as style, of which the denizens of Paris thought themselves the official arbiters. As far as Rex was concerned, he was definitely one of *les costume-cravate*—the suits and ties, corporate entities who only cared about making money. Which, he had to admit, wasn't too far from the truth.

Until now. Since the night before, making money seemed to have lost a bit of its imperative. He looked to the *avocate* across from him. Since . . .

"She was a war bride," Charlotte continued. "My grandfather was one of the first American soldiers who marched into Paris after liberation. She ran out in the street and threw herself into his arms. He didn't let go."

"How romantic," Rex opined. "So she came back with him after the war?"

"Yes. They were married in Paris, and they lived there for two years after, as my grandfather wound down the war and, I guess, set up the peace. My mother was born there, and she lives there now. Went back for good when I was still in high school."

"So you have dual citizenship," Rex deduced.

"I do," she said. "I go to visit my mother and the rest of the family at least a couple times a year. As a matter of fact, my aunt wants to leave me her apartment in Saint Germain des Pres."

"The Left Bank?" He *was* impressed. "*Très chic.*"

"I suppose, though she's had it forever. But don't get me wrong." She used her glass for emphasis. "For all my French roots, I'm American to the core. The only left bank that means anything to me is here in Philly, as it's only on the left when you're looking from Jersey."

"New Jersey?" He laughed. "Are you seriously trying to compare that industrial wasteland to *Paris*?"

"You really ought to get away from those container terminals a bit more," she said, taking umbrage. "Off the flyover, it's really quite a beautiful state."

"I'll take your word for it," he said dryly.

"You should because it's true. That's where I was born and where my grandparents came back to live." She took another sip, looking away. "And where my grandfather was killed."

"*Je suis tellement désolé.*"

"*Merci*, but I never knew him. It happened before I was born. He was an executive at a steel mill up the river in Roebling. Just as my mother was entering college, he was killed in an industrial accident."

All at once Rex felt his jaw tighten and spasm, the fingernails of his right hand digging into the chair's frayed fabric. He bolted upright. "Would you mind if I poured myself a bit more?" he asked, taking one last gulp.

"No," she said, peering at him. "Go right ahead. Though you're the one who said we should have something to eat."

"Just a bit more," he said, already at the sideboard, his hand shaking as he tilted the bottle over the glass. "It's just that good."

"Well . . . thanks," she said, a bit warily. "I'm glad you're enjoying it."

He sucked three-quarters of it back before he even set the bottle down, relishing the heat as it sank into his stomach. He took a deep breath, exhaling slowly, relieved he was out of her sightline. After a moment he felt better, setting the bottle back. He rejoined her.

"So it seems your mother left you for Paris when you were still a schoolgirl," he said as he found his seat again. "Mind if I ask why?" When she seemed taken aback, he shook his head. "I'm sorry. You don't have to answer that."

"No, it's okay," she said. "I'm just a little surprised you'd ask. I guess you can say she left because of a broken heart." She looked into her glass, swirling the ice a bit. "My father left her for another woman."

"I see," Rex said quietly.

"I know what you're thinking," she said, looking up with accusation. "You're thinking—oh, those Americans. So prickly when it comes to relationships. But it wasn't like that. My mother was oh-so-very French in her sensibilities. She would've overlooked his having a mistress. But it went beyond that. When he chose this other woman over her, he threw back in my mother's face everything she was about." She drained her glass, then, staring at it, jiggled the ice. "I think I'm going to need more of this myself."

"Do you think you should?" Rex asked.

The look she gave him brooked no discussion.

"Well, all right," he conceded.

Charlotte went to the sideboard and poured herself a bit more, topping off the little that was left in her glass. In all actuality, Rex thought she needed the trip to the sideboard more to ponder whether to continue, and it struck him how much that little gesture showed what they had in common. She returned to the sofa, facing him directly.

law department, as this was the glory days of arbitrage, and Mom was as ruthless as they got. So while she raked it in representing companies eating each other alive, the firm got richer and richer and the 'rents couldn't live life large enough. Until I threw a wrench in the picture."

"Your mother got pregnant."

"Exactly." She laughed harshly. "I guess that's when Mom had to put down the coke spoon."

Rex cocked a brow. "I get the impression you're not your mother's biggest fan."

"Let me put it this way. My mother never let me forget she had to start working part-time after I was born, while Dad went full-bore into more and more lucrative cases—rich men killing their wives, international embezzlement. All headline stuff, all Main Line, and boy, did his cock get big then." She scowled into her drink. "After that he was home even less, and I think she resented me even more."

"So I'm going to take the leap and assume this is when he started taking on mistresses."

"*Oh no*," she said with lethal emphasis. "This is when he started fucking anything with a pulse. Like the new clerk fresh out of law school."

Charlotte rose and went to the window, bracing her hand against the molding as she crossed her legs at her ankles, showing Rex the bloody-colored sole of her shoe. "I don't know what it is, maybe it dates back to something primal. Like when two tribes would go to war and after one side would win, they'd kill the other tribe's men and their babies, then impregnate their women with their issue. Maybe it was the same thing with my father. Maybe he needed to slough off the old for the new."

She held the tumbler of scotch to her cheek. "But that would've been too ordinary, and my father was more original than that. This was back in the day when an ass grab at the office was fully sanctioned, and although women were expected to produce, expecting to advance because of it was almost laughable."

She reeled on him, her anger almost palpable. "So yeah, he took up with the law clerk and yeah, he started fucking her and eventually he stopped coming home at all. By this time he was bringing in so much dough he was made a full partner, even though my mother had earned twice as much when she was working full-time, and in far less time than it had taken him. Didn't matter. And apparently, neither did she. Not anymore. Because after that he dropped the coup de grâce. He got the partners together and had her fired, putting the law clerk and her brand-new degree in my mother's place."

After a few beats, Rex said, "I don't know what to say."

She turned back to the window. "How about"— her fore- and middle fingers curved in faux quotation marks—"*and your point is*? Standard operating procedure in your line of work, isn't it?"

He got out of the chair and went to her, grasping her arm as he turned her around. "You don't know that. You don't know anything about me. You don't know how I run my company or how I work."

She pushed him away. "I know enough that I had to put up with your CEO a couple months back. Had to watch him worm his way into Dani's shorts until he wore her down."

"Oh come on," Rex scoffed, "they were *in love*."

She stared at him. "Do you have any idea how absurd you sound saying that?"

"Oh, *oui*. So much I took a sock in the mouth just for doubting he meant it."

"Then you know what a ridiculous notion it is. How people use it to manipulate each other."

She didn't know how close to the Meaning of Life she just came by saying that. He could almost kiss her for her perspicacity. "I know."

"Of course you do," she said. "It's your modus operandi. I'm sure you have seduction down to a sixth sense. I wouldn't doubt you have forms of it tailor-made for each of your victims. Though this time it didn't quite work out, did it?" She came closer. "*Did* it?"

He took a step back, though it made him feel larger in context. "You're drunk."

"You bet I am. And it only brings me clarity." She poked his chest. "You're a snake. A creepy-crawly-gut-to-the-ground bottom feeder."

"My, aren't we colorful."

"You brought that girl into that room for one reason only—to seduce her and throw her away."

He laughed, as if it was obvious. "Now that's a news flash. Did you think perhaps we were out to debate Thomas Piketty and his economic theory?"

"How can you do that—" She waved her hand in front of her. "How can you be like that?" she said, swaying so much Rex once again grabbed her arm, this time to steady her. "How can you use women in that way?"

"Use women?" He shook her slightly. "*Her?*" He pulled Charlotte up to him. "I'll remind you *she* was using me. That now, for whatever reason, she's lying. Why do you suppose she's doing that?"

She pushed him away. "You tell me. Or are you saving that for the big reveal?"

He almost laughed. Drunk or not, there really was no getting over on her. "I don't know, but someone behind her does, and for one reason or the other they're out to make me look bad."

"Now why is that? Who did you piss off? Besides Lilith, that is." She let out a short "Ha!" her gaze woozily shifting to his. "Or wasn't she the first?"

"Look, I came to Washington for one reason and one reason only," he said. "So Mercier could bring super-sized container ships into our East Coast terminal, and for that we need a harbor deep enough to accommodate them. Hence the dredging bill. And that's it. No hidden agenda."

Her fingers latched around his arm. "So you figured you had to dredge *Lilith's* harbor to accommodate her, hm?" She laughed again, downing more scotch. "*Très original*, indeed."

"*Tu es complètement givrée,*" he said, shaking her loose.

"*Oh oui? Et je peux pas te supporter,*" she countered, poking him again.

"Enough of this shit." He grabbed her hand, mid-poke, snatching the tumbler of scotch. "I think it's time to get something to eat." He looked past her. "How about I make us an omelette?"

She laughed. "You? *Cook?*"

"I've been known to break an egg now and then."

"Unless you can make them out of ice and condiments," she said, her hair falling in her eyes. All of a sudden she slumped against his chest. "That's about all I have in my . . ."

He looked down on her, grateful the change in subject at least calmed her down. He wondered how she'd feel about that when she sobered up. "Don't like to cook, I suppose?"

"It's not so much that I mind cooking," she said after a moment, fascinated with the knot of his tie. "It's that I like making reservations so much better."

"Then how about we go out?" Rex said. "Didn't we pass a deli down the street?"

She straightened. "That's not just a *deli*," she spun the word. "That's the Famous. *Now* you're talking omelettes. They have a smoked salmon and—"

Suddenly the window exploded over her head, Rex throwing them both to the floor.

Chapter Six

Or Are You Just Happy to See Me?

"WHAT THE HELL just happened!" Charlotte cried, squirming beneath him.

"Keep still!" Rex hissed. All around them was shattered glass.

Charlotte grabbed his jaw, forcing him to look at her. "Oh, don't worry about me, I'm all right. Thanks for asking."

"Quiet," he said, sliding her hand to his shoulder. He looked to the window above them. The top pane had a hole in, as just past them lay a brick wrapped in lined paper. *Subtle*, he thought. He looked to Charlotte, her hair loosened and fanning across the carpet, her eyes a bit boozy. "*Are* you all right?" he asked.

She huffed. "Didn't I just say so?"

"Maybe I didn't hear you." He liked the way she felt

under him, like a live wire ready to spark. Though getting her there wasn't exactly the way he had pictured it.

"Maybe because you never listen to me."

He felt the rapid rise and fall of her breasts. "Maybe because you're always busting my *couilles*."

"I have no idea why you just said that although . . ." Charlotte grinned, her knee shifting past his groin. "Isn't it strange how life suddenly tosses opportunity in your lap?"

"Just make sure it's your lap, not mine." Rex raised up and stretched past her, peering over the window's edge. Obviously, the brick thrower had been a drive-by. "Come on," he said, pulling Charlotte up with him. "And watch where you step."

She scrunched across the broken glass to the brick, peeling off the lined paper. "Christ," she said, handing it to Rex.

"TRAITOR" was scrawled in pencil across it.

She looked up, anger in her eyes. "Those bitches," she said. "After all I've done for them."

"Fuck them," he said, just as angrily. "You don't believe it, do you?"

"No, but damnit—I should've been ready for this. The judge warned me this would happen. That there were people out there who wouldn't take my defending you lightly. I told her I knew what I was doing." She looked to Rex, her face filling with consternation. "You may not believe me but I really do think injustice is gender-neutral."

"I believe you," Rex said softly. "Though in this

case"—he hefted the brick—"I'm hardly your target audience."

She laughed. "That's because *I'm* the target."

Someone knocked at the door. Charlotte looked to Rex with a silent *who the hell is that?* "Stay there," he said, going to it.

"Where else would you like me to go?" she said, steadying herself against a chair.

He opened it, saying, "Yes?" to the suit on the other side of the screen door.

A squat, portly man peered back at him. "Detective Spencer, Philadelphia Police," he said, flashing a badge. He jutted his chin toward Rex. "You Rex Renaud?"

Christ, he thought. *Word sure gets around.* "Yeah. Why?"

"Where's that hot little attorney of yours?" He scraped a nail down his jaw, grinning. "This *is* her house, isn't it?"

Rex hated him on sight. He looked to his left. "If you mean the one with the brick hole in the window."

The detective leaned back to look. "Oh look at that." He turned back to Rex. "Yeah, that's the one."

"She's right here," Charlotte said, peering over Rex's shoulder. "What do you want?"

"I think you need to ask me in," Spencer said. "Before something with a bit more bang lands in your living room."

She glanced to Rex. He kind of liked that she did. "Okay," she said. Rex moved aside, letting the man in. The detective sauntered over to the shards of glass, glinting in the sunlight.

"This came courtesy of the brick," Charlotte said, passing Spencer the note.

"Uh-huh," he said, glancing at it. "Can't help admiring the old-school delivery system. Who needs high-tech?"

"Is there a reason you're here?" Rex said.

Spencer glanced to the empty tumblers on the floor. "Uh, sorry to interrupt your cocktail hour, but you need to pack your things."

"What?" Charlotte said. "What for?"

"Because we just got a bomb threat for your home-sweet-home down at the station. And after this here?" He pointed toward the brick. "Your house is going to be a pile of them if you don't take it seriously."

"Are *you* taking it seriously?" asked Charlotte.

"We can't afford not to," he said. "Especially this one." He poked his elbow into Rex's side. "Oh those women scorned, eh buddy?"

"I'm not your *buddy*," Rex growled, spinning the word. "*Enculés de flics.*"

The cop peered at him. "Watch it, Frenchie. We still got a cell with your name on it." He turned to Charlotte. "Anyway, you got someplace you can go for the next few days?"

She glanced to Rex again, this time with caution. "I might."

"Well, make it a definite, because I'm not leaving until I lock you and this door behind us. Go get your things."

"But I can't," Charlotte said, her hand flinging toward the broken window. "I just can't leave my house opened."

"Don't worry, we'll throw a board over it." The radio

at his hip squawked. He yanked it to his mouth. "Spencer here."

Charlotte pulled Rex aside, her back to the upstairs railing. "Might not be a bad idea to get out of town. I have to agree with him. Things will probably get worse."

"And just when Philly was starting to feel like home."

She crossed her arms, throwing up the gate again. "Oh please, I'm not in the mood."

He leaned in, latching on to a post. "And what will it take to get you into it?"

He savored her little burn of chagrin—which quickly dissipated when it turned to anger. "Stop it, Rex. I'm scared."

And when the crease between her eyes deepened, he started to believe she was. "Well don't be. I'm right here and I won't let anything happen to you."

"My, aren't you chivalrous. I thought it was my job to protect you."

"Kind of works both ways, doesn't it?" Though the idea of anyone even thinking of hurting her made him want to smash things. "And here I thought you were fearless."

"Yeah, well." Her gaze flicked to his, a little bleary-eyed. "Allow me a little humanity. It's not every day you get a bomb threat and a brick through the window. Plus a strange man camping out in your living room."

"Living room?" He glanced over his shoulder. "What else have you got?"

"If you think there's crap on my table you should see my extra bed."

"I'm sure we can make alternate arrangements."

She slinked out from under him. "Talk about your American Dream."

"Okay folks," Spencer said, holstering his radio. "Tick-tock. In case you haven't noticed, there's someone with a mic out your window and your neighbors are starting to get a little irritated."

"Damn," Charlotte cursed, peering out the front door. A reporter was checking out the broken window from the sidewalk, while a news van idled in the street. "Can they do that?"

"City owns the street and sidewalk, so yeah. Anyway." He huffed. "You got a place to go to or what, because I really don't have all day."

"Do you?" Rex asked. Because if she didn't, there were certainly more hotels than the Ritz-Carlton, and he rather liked the idea of taking her to one.

"Yes," she finally said. "But I'll need to get my car. I'll have to get past those people out there."

"After which, they'll just end up following you," Rex added.

"Not necessarily," Spencer said. "Where's your car?"

"About ten doors down . . ." She turned, pointing to the street. "It's blue. A Fiesta."

Rex looked to her, amazed. "*Merde*, you need to start chasing more ambulances."

She tossed him a scowl. "And you need to keep your comments to yourself like a good little detainee."

"Children—please." Spencer waggled the fingers of his outstretched palm. "The keys, counselor."

"Why?" Charlotte said.

He tilted his head to the back of the house. "Because I'll move the car to the next street over while you slip out the back door." He waggled his fingers again. "Now hand them over."

Charlotte retrieved the keys from the sideboard, tossing them to the cop. "Is this really necessary?"

The detective glanced outside to where a man in an undershirt and suspenders was yelling at a reporter. "I think your neighbors will insist." He pocketed the keys. "Meet you in five. Now get going." He left out the front door.

"Damn," Charlotte muttered. "This is not how I planned on spending my week."

Rex smiled. She was angry yet she seemed to take things in stride. "Though isn't it strange how life suddenly tosses opportunity in your lap?"

"Go ahead. Make jokes," she said. "*You're* not the one getting thrown out of your house."

"You're so right," he said. "So much better to be thrown into a goddamned American jail for some trumped-up charge you didn't see coming."

"Think about that the next time you take a teenager into a darkened room."

"You have more than ably made your point on that, Charlotte. Any more remarks on it, and I going to start thinking it actually bothers you."

"Stupidity always does."

"Point taken." She had the tiniest mole near the corner of her mouth. "Now tell me where we're going?"

She bent to retrieve the fallen tumblers, her skirt straining against the pull of fabric as she set them on an end table. "It's at the ocean. Or as we say around here—down the shore. It was my grandmother's retirement house. She left it to me a couple years ago when she died."

"So do you like the sea?" If she did, that would please him immensely.

"Of course I do," she said, almost looking insulted. "And I've always looked at the house as my refuge."

He crossed to the window. "We don't have to leave town, you know. I could get us a suite somewhere—a penthouse, even. You choose the hotel, and I'll happily pay for it." Spencer was right. He didn't like the look of those people standing across the street. When he turned she was right beside him watching the street. He caught the scent of her hair, both fresh and exotic. "How's that sound to you?"

"I'm sure you'd like that," she said, peering past him, "but I'd rather get out of town. I have a feeling wherever we'd go around here someone will recognize either one of us, and then it'll only get worse. At least down there, with the town thinned out from the summer crowd, our *admirers* will be easier to spot."

He glanced to the brick. "Then let's hope this is the last of their love letters."

"Yet somehow I don't think it will be. Oh God, why did you call me?" She huffed, her hand to her forehead. "I may as well have a target on my back. I mean there's a lot of crazies out there, and you have to be a little nuts to join an organization called Occupy Vagina to begin with, don't you think?"

His mouth crooked. "Or to found it?"

She looked up sharply. "Is that what you think of me?"

"Charlotte, listen to me." He braced his hand against the wall, caging her. "I called you because you're the best at what you do. Don't ever forget that. And when I get out of this—which I will—it'll prove to all those idiots how wrong they were and you'll be vindicated. You believe me, don't you?"

She smiled weakly. "Maybe, but what'll I do until then if another brick smashes through my window?"

He slid her hand from her forehead to hold it over his heart. She was scared because of him, and all for what? A tryst with a silly young girl. He wanted to pull her into his arms and kiss her fears away. "Until then I'll be there to deflect it and keep you safe. And I will, Charlotte," he said, wanting her to believe it. "I'll stake my life on it, I swear."

Her eyes widened at that. "All right."

"Then the sea it is," he said, squeezing her hand lightly before he let it go. "Now go up and pack. And don't forget your bikini."

She swallowed hard. "I don't think I'll need one."

"You're probably right," he said, stepping back.

EITHER SHE WAS really drunk, or she could've sworn Rex was just about to kiss her. She reached to the top shelf of her closet and dragging down an overnighter, tossed it to her bed. "Oh God . . ." she groaned, she *must* have been drunk. For all his gallantry and double entendre, she needed to remember the man was a cad to the core.

Which meant he probably only wanted to sleep with her.

Huh, she thought, opening the bag, *big surprise there.* It's what most men wanted, and why should he be any different?

But the difference was she almost wished he had kissed her—*no*. There was nothing *almost* about it. She wanted him to. So badly if he hadn't stepped away she would've done it herself. Maybe even a whole lot more. *Way* more. Just to see how it felt.

Yep, she told herself. *Drunk.*

She yanked the zipper back, spreading the bag wide. The thoughts she was entertaining were so unethical. And even though there was a definite bond between her and her clients, Charlotte sincerely doubted sleeping with Rex was the attorney-client *privilege* American jurisprudence referred to. And wasn't that a goddamned shame.

Oh, most definitely hammered.

She made a quick sweep of her bathroom, stuffing a cosmetic bag with all the essentials—mascara, face cream, lipstick, anything that wasn't already down there. One thing that never was loomed in her medicine cabinet—glaring at her like shrapnel from her latest exploded relationship. She slid the packets between her fingers, counting. Twelve. *Twelve!* The number nearly made her blush. Twelve times with Rex? She felt a twinge deep down. Would it be enough to get him out of her system?

She pictured him out of that million-dollar suit, his broad shoulders, the hard planes of his chest, thighs like iron and oh, what lay between. She imagined even one time, her hips twisting with the thought. She had to be crazy for even picturing it. Still . . . She dropped the twelve into her cosmetic bag. Better to be safe than sorry.

Shit-faced, oh yeah.

She went back to her bedroom yanking open her dresser drawers. A sweater, T-shirts, jeans, a skirt, underwear, bras. A teddy. She fingered its lace, its button-up back, the oh-very-slippable straps. Charlotte glanced to the overnighter.

She was lit. *Défoncée.* Totally.

She tossed the teddy in and zipping it, left for downstairs.

DETECTIVE SPENCER WAS just getting out of Charlotte's Ford when she and Rex slipped from the alley to the street. "Did anyone see you?" he asked.

"I don't think so," she said. At least she hoped. "I didn't see anyone, at least."

"We didn't," Rex affirmed. "I would have noticed."

"Now tell me where are you going," Spencer said, passing the keys to Charlotte.

"Do you absolutely need to know?" Charlotte said.

"Yes," he said. "Have you forgotten about your little friend here? I believe the judge said you need to tuck him in at night."

"Oh don't worry about me," Rex said, plucking the

keys from Charlotte's hand. "I can brush my teeth and everything."

"Hey," Charlotte said, watching as Rex slipped into the driver's seat. "I can drive."

"Oh *oui*? So now you're up for the jail experience?" he said, sliding the key into the ignition.

"Hey—jurisprudence." Spencer looked to Charlotte. "Just call me OnStar. What's the destination?"

Her head was starting to ache. "Margate. Down the shore," she said. "I have a house there."

"Jersey?" He stared at her. "You're taking him out of state?"

"You're kicking me out of my house, remember? You asked me if I have anyplace I could go, and that's the place. Unless, of course, the Philly PD wants to foot the bill."

"Go," the cop said. "Just don't forget to check in with the police when you get there. Because if you don't, say, by three this afternoon . . . ." He glanced at the back of her car. "We'll just have to go looking for that license plate."

"Fine." Charlotte tossed her bag in the back before she climbed in. She glared at Rex. "Do you always have to be in the driver's seat?"

"Another rhetorical question," he said, looking over his shoulder as he pulled into the street. "Do you actually think I'm just going to sit there while you drive me around, half-cocked?"

"It's my car, for Christ's sake. And it's not like you know where you're going."

"Who says I don't." He glanced to the rearview. "But first we have to lose the cops tailing us."

Charlotte looked to the side view mirror. "You mean that white van about a block back?"

"That's the one, with the municipal plates," Rex said, making a quick left down a side street. "We passed it while we were walking to your car, parked a few spaces down." He mashed the gas, making another quick left before he speeded up and whipped the car into the opened garage door of A–1 Auto Repair.

"Yeah?" a man said, wiping his hands on a rag as he sauntered over.

"I think I have a slow leak in my right back tire. Can you take a look?"

The man tossed the rag. "Let me pull it up on the lift."

While he did, Rex peered out from the edge of the doorway, Charlotte close behind. After a minute or so the white van rumbled past, the Ford already on the lift and out of view.

"Smooth," Charlotte said, honestly impressed. "Credit the criminal mind inside every successful businessman."

"Strictly nonviolent," he said blithely, though the intent was clear. "But yes, you're right."

"So where'd you learn to do that? Rum running?"

"Father running. I just couldn't get them home before midnight." He looked over his shoulder. "What's your curfew?"

"What's a curfew?" she said, pivoting toward the lift and inside.

"WHAT THE HELL is that?" Rex said, neck craned into the windshield. "Damned thing must be fifteen meters tall."

Charlotte jolted awake, eyes blinking into the late-morning sun as she tried to focus. As soon as she'd set the GPS the combination of scotch and a lost night's sleep had claimed her, and she collapsed against the door. She followed Rex's sightline to the wood-and-metal pachyderm complete with howdah.

Too funny, she thought. *I'd forgotten about her.* "You mean Lucy?"

He was still staring at Margate's own elephant even after they'd passed it. "What the hell is it for?"

Charlotte yawned, straightening. "Lucy was built in the late eighteen-hundreds for a real estate scheme. Now she's on the National Register as an historic site . . ." She yawned once more. "She's quite famous."

"Really," Rex said. "For a moment I thought it was our little metaphor come to life."

She may well have been, Charlotte mused. Because Lucy's compatriot had certainly been in that car with them, crowding out all that lay unsaid between them and surely what was coming. Up until a moment ago it'd been easy enough to ignore, which made her falling dead asleep so convenient.

"Sorry I passed out," she said, flipping open the mirror on the visor to the dark circles under her eyes. After too much coffee, court, and the cops, not to mention a healthy dose of scotch, she looked like shit and felt even worse. "I just couldn't keep my eyes opened anymore, and long car rides always seem to put me to sleep." She smiled briefly. "Must be a holdover from my childhood."

He glanced at her. "Oh? I've heard of parents riding their squalling kids around until they'd fall asleep. Was that how it was with you?"

She flipped the visor closed and sat back, looking out the window. "I have no idea. Though I'm pretty sure my father never did."

"You never said what happened to your father," Rex said.

"Didn't I?" She laughed. "Tells you how much I give a shit. He moved out to California a few years after he and my mother divorced. Got even richer defending Hollywood scumbags. I'm surprised O.J. didn't show up on his doorstep. He never sent me as much as a birthday card. My mother hung around a few more years after that, waiting for my grandmother to retire so she could dump me on her and go back to Paris. She hasn't been back since."

"Which is why your *grand-mère* raised you," Rex said, stopping for a light.

"That's it." She rolled down her window, looking out. "Someone had to."

"*Ma pauvre petite fille perdue.*" His arm stretched across the back of the seat to her headrest. "I don't remember much of my parents either. My *tante* mostly raised me, when anyone actually did. I had my aunt and you, your grandmother. Looks like we have that in common, at least."

"Yeah, similarly hellish childhoods. We ought to write a book." She flicked her hand out the window. "Make a right at that next block."

He shifted his arm away, murmuring something in French. The closer they came to her neighborhood, the more edgy she felt. She couldn't dismiss the feeling something was simmering between them, almost since the moment they met up in Boston, and whatever it was, it was quickly coming to a head. And once it did Charlotte knew there'd be no turning back.

Couldn't blame it on the scotch now. She was stone-cold sober.

"Turn left." They passed a mix of small, squat cottages and older two- and three-story houses on either side of a block to the end of the beach. Many of the homes had flowerboxes under their windows, and above, striped canvas awnings, giving the block a comfy, old-school feel. "That's it, the next to the last house. The one with the geraniums out front." She pointed to a smallish two-story with a green canvas awning over the second-floor porch and a separate garage off to the side.

Rex pulled the car to the curb before the driveway. "Is there room in the garage for the car?"

"Yes. Good idea," Charlotte said, reaching into the glove box for the remote. She aimed and pressed and the garage door opened, Rex pulling it in. He shut off the car as it closed behind them, leaving them in near-darkness.

"You know," Charlotte said, "it's such a lovely day, we should go to this great little outside café just up the street. We could have lunch and talk about what we're going to do next." She unbuckled and twisted toward the back seat. "Just let me get my—"

"*Non*, not yet," he said, his hand on her shoulder. "Not with Lucy still breathing down our necks. There's something we really need to get out of the way first." He unsnapped his seat belt and turned to Charlotte, his hand suddenly cradling her cheek. "*Ma belle . . .*" he whispered, drawing her in.

"My father was a lawyer, as was my mother. As was her grandfather, as I am." She laughed a bit. "I guess you can say law's the family business. My grandmother's family had quite a successful corporate law firm in Paris, where she was a legal secretary. But then the war came, and they lost everything. And after she married my grandfather and came back here, she took on the traditional role for American women at the time, which was being a house-wife and raising a family, even though she had all this experience behind her. Then my grandfather was killed, just as my mother was about to enter college, so she went back to work as a legal secretary. And then she received a large sum in compensation from the steel company."

"A settlement," Rex said, taking a swallow of scotch.

"That allowed my mother to return to college and go on to law school," Charlotte said. "By this time my *grand-mère* was working for the district attorney's office, where she became acquainted with a pretty cocky up-and-coming defense attorney by the name of Jake Andreko."

"Your father," Rex said.

Charlotte's brow knit in anger. "Yes." She took an-other sip, belting it back. "Look, I'll cut to the chase as we should be talking about your case, not about my family skeletons. Eventually my mother graduated and passed the bar, and all during that time my father was pursuing her, so the day the letter arrived saying she passed the bar was the same day they got engaged. They had a huge church wedding and a honeymoon in Venice, after which Mom went to work for Jake's firm which was, by that time, pretty successful. See, she was killing it in the corp

Chapter Seven

Shooting an Elephant

DAMN IT TO HELL, he couldn't help himself.

Rex kissed her, savoring the warm, soft feel of Charlotte's lips until he deftly parted them, his tongue lacing around hers. Then something so incredible happened he damned nearly lost his breath.

This beautifully gorgeous woman kissed him back.

"Rex . . ." Charlotte murmured, her hand falling against his chest not to push him away but to pull him in, her fingers twisting the fabric of his shirt until he could feel her nails beneath, her hitching breath matching the eagerness in his own.

"Charlotte . . ." he whispered, leaning her back against the seat, Charlotte sighing as he cupped her chin and explored every corner of her mouth. She tasted of sleep and cinnamon—no idea where the last came from and he didn't care. All he knew was he wanted more of her, as much as he could get.

"*Très belle, très belle* . . ." he whispered, kissing her neck. She had to know—how couldn't she? He wanted her from the second they met back in Boston.

"Oh Rex, please . . ." She squeezed his thigh—as if he needed that. He was already hard. Had been, from the moment his mouth met hers, and he knew he'd stay that way until she offered him sweet release. "We really shouldn't," she whispered. "We can't. We—oh *damn*." She kissed him hard, her hand sliding straight to his cock, caressing it.

"*Jesus*," he whispered, groaning, his hand falling to her breast.

"No," she suddenly said, pushing him off. She scrambled back against the door. "*No*, goddamnit."

"Okay," Rex said, moving away. "I do understand the meaning of the word."

"Thank you," she said, straightening her blouse. She tousled her hair in a nervous gesture, all at once looking very beautiful, and very grave. "I'm very sorry for that"—she blushed profusely, tossing her hand—"grossly improper gesture."

"Don't apologize to me," Rex said. "Obviously I was all for it."

"Obviously." She blushed even deeper, glancing down. "But that needs to stay right where it is. For both our sakes." She dug her fingers into her hair again and sighed. "I'm not going to lie, Rex. I am attracted to you."

"The feeling is mutual," he said, relieved he could finally say it.

"Even so, outside of the ethical issues, I still have problems with your reputation and what you represent."

He couldn't believe they were having this conversation. Not with his cock still hard and her lips lusciously swollen. "I'm not the enemy here."

"And I'm not one of your employees," she snapped. "You may be buying my services, but you're not buying me. Know that everything I'm doing, everything that happens between us, I'm doing because I want to and for my own reasons."

That stung, even though he could sense her true intent. Because what she said earlier was right. He did like being in the driver's seat. And because of that maybe he also needed to put *her* in her place, if only momentarily. "And we know exactly how much those reasons are worth, don't we?"

Her eyes flared. "Keep your two million. Do you think that's buying me?"

"It certainly got your attention."

"You bastard," she spat, snatching her purse. She threw open the car door. "And just so there's no mistaking my meaning—" She slammed it, leaning into the opened window. "*Va te faire voir!*"

"Son of a bitch," he muttered, hurrying after her. "Damnit Charlotte, you know I—"

He found her at the opened side door of the garage, her hand still gripping the knob. Two uniformed men stood on the other side of it.

"Hi ya, folks," the police officer said, touching his hat. "How are you doing today?"

Did he just catch a snicker coming from the man behind him?

"We're fine," Charlotte said with perfect courtesy. "And you're here because . . . ?"

"Oh." He grabbed a notepad from his top pocket. "You're Charlotte Andreko, right?"

"I am," she said, her thumb jutting over her shoulder. "And this is Rex Renaud, to answer your next question."

"*Bonjour,*" Rex said, sliding past her to stand outside.

"Yeah, they told us you were French," the other patrolman said. "We get a lot of French tourists down here from Quebec." He smiled. "I'll bet you're from Montreal."

"No," Rex said. *Jesus.*

"*Anyway,*" Charlotte continued, "who did you speak with?"

The first patrolman glanced to the notepad. "We got a call from a Detective Spencer from the Philly PD. Said you were going to check in with the department when you got down here. He said Mr. Renaud is out on bail." He eyed him directly. "For a felony."

"We just arrived," Rex said. "We've hardly had the chance."

"Right." The first patrolman cleared his throat. "But that's not mainly why we're here." He looked to Charlotte. "He told us about the bomb threat you received."

"And the brick," said the other cop.

"Anyway," continued the first officer, "we were patrolling the area and just happened to catch your car pulling in the garage, so we figured we'd save you the trip down the station." He slid the notepad back into his pocket.

"But when you didn't come out right away . . ." He smiled briefly. "We decided to give you a few minutes."

"Oh," Charlotte said after a moment.

Funny how Rex could already interpret her subtle reactions, how her seemingly calm exterior belied a range of emotions inside. More than likely she was mortified, but anyone looking would only have noticed a slight hesitation. Anyone but him, that was. Which gave him an idea exactly how to play this.

"Thank you for saving us the trip," Rex said, moving back beside Charlotte. He slipped his arm around her waist, feeling her flinch, but to her credit, that was the extent of it. "Charlotte's been a bit worried, but knowing you're keeping an eye out will make her feel a lot better."

"Yes," she said, tensing a bit as his hand fell to her hip. "Thanks."

"You're welcome," the patrolman said. "We'll do a drive-by a few times a day, but do give us a call if you see anything suspicious."

"Of course," Charlotte said. "We should only be here a couple of days."

Rex slid his hand up her back to the back of her neck. "And it's not like we're planning on going out much, right, *chérie*?"

She turned to him, her glare lethal enough to melt glass, Rex instantly grateful the officers couldn't see it from this angle. "Oh, you're so right, hon," she said, eyes narrowing.

"Stay as long as you like—or don't leave at all. As you can see . . ." He looked around him. "We're having some great weather and almost everything's still open. So go on, have a good time." He touched his cap again. "Take care now."

"Good-bye," Charlotte said, watching as the patrolmen returned to their cruiser and pulled away.

"He acts as if we're here on holiday," Rex said, massaging her neck.

Charlotte shook him loose. "Okay, they've left, game over," she said, brushing past him and in through the side door of the house.

Rex went after her, catching the door before it closed. "So now you're going to make me sleep on the porch?"

"No need for that when the beach is just two doors down." She tossed her purse to the table, turning toward him. "Look, I don't know what you were trying to do back there—"

"I was throwing them off the scent, Charlotte," he said, coming toward her. "So if I decide to give them the slip, which I think I'm going to have to, they won't bother us if they think we're inside . . ." He came even closer, backing her up against the sink. "Well, do I have to spell it out for you?"

"No," she said, crossing her arms in front of her. "My imagination works just fine. And that's exactly where it's going to stay."

"Why?" he said, those blue, blue eyes watching as his gaze traced the curve of her jaw to her lips, still rouged from their kissing. "You want me and I want you. And we started something back there I'm very eager to continue. Aren't you?"

"Doesn't matter." Her chest rose, fell. "I don't think that's a good idea."

He leaned in, whispering, "Then give me a reason why, *chérie*." He brushed his nose against the shell of her ear, making her shiver. "When it's something we both want." He brought his hand to her chin, angling his lips over hers. "When I'd very much like to kiss you again."

"Yet you won't," she said, her hand against his chest.

"I don't think so, *ma petit*," he said, his mouth falling to hers.

After a moment, she tore her mouth away. "You have an ongoing problem with the word *no*, don't you?"

Rex froze, his hands dropping to his sides.

THE MOMENT THE words left her mouth she wanted to take them back. "Rex—oh my God, I didn't mean that."

He backed away, his face blank. "It's all right. I'm sorry. It won't happen again." Then he turned and walked out the door.

Charlotte watched him leave, unable to move. What she'd said had been cruel. So why did she say it? How could she? But then how could she be so undeniably attracted to him yet repelled by all that he was? What was the female equivalent of misogyny? She recalled reading about it once. *Misandry*. Was that what she was—a misandrist? Did she really hate men? She never thought so. It was always more the things they did. Yet one thing she knew for certain. She didn't hate Rex, no matter how hard she tried. Then why had she said it? Did she *want* to hurt him?

It didn't matter because she had. She pushed away from the counter and ran out the door.

Where had he gone? She trotted to the end of the driveway, looking down the street, the rows of houses on either side of the mostly summer homes now unoccupied. She looked up the street, only one more house on her side and then the beach, the bright white sand gleaming in the autumn sun. It was there she spotted a pair of sock-stuffed men's shoes atop the short seawall at the head of the beach, and halfway down it, Rex with his trousers rolled to his knees, his hands in his pockets as he strolled toward the water.

She laughed to herself. How did he know everyone did this at the shore? During the summer, there'd be rows and rows of sandals at the entrance to the beach, no one ever bothering them. Could they do the same now, with their thousand dollars' worth of shoes? She slipped out of her pumps and left them beside his, running up the steps and down to the beach after him.

By the time she reached him he was standing in the surf. Although the dry sand had been warmed by the sun, by late September, the ocean temperature was always a crapshoot, though it wasn't unusual for it to be as warm or even warmer than August. Whether or not it was, it apparently didn't bother Rex, as he was in it past his ankles, his sunglasses on, his jacket shoved back by his hands buried in his pockets. Obviously, he was deep in thought about something, and Charlotte wondered if it could be about her. In a way, she hoped he was. She aimed toward him.

On anyone else a suit and tie with rolled trousers and bare feet might have seemed silly, but not on Rex. With his broad shoulders, with his shirt molded to his chest by the breeze, his thick hair ruffling, Charlotte thought him impossibly gorgeous. And herself, a probable idiot. Something happened to her when she was around him, and that kiss in the car—and what she said to him after because of it—had only made her seem like a fool. She stepped onto the dampened sand and into the surf. *Tolerable*, she thought, tapping her toes. When she went up to him she hoped he'd think the same of her.

"Rex," she said, the cool breeze sending her hair flying around her. "I didn't mean what I said. Please, let me apologize."

He turned to look at her, his shades adding to his unreadable expression. *He really has a beautiful mouth*, Charlotte thought with a shiver, recalling his kiss. Or was it just the chill salt air? Either way she folded her arms over her, her thin silk shirt rippling in the wind.

"Here," he said, pulling off his jacket. He slipped it over her shoulders, his elegant scent enveloping her, his hands lingering just a few seconds longer than necessary. Then he turned back to the ocean, those hands once again in his pockets.

"Thank you," Charlotte said, pulling the jacket tighter. They let the sound of the rolling waves speak for them the next minute or so.

"You know, all I've seen of the New Jersey shore was what I could see from either the window of a plane or a casino in Atlantic City," Rex said. He picked up a broken oyster shell, skipping it across the surf before it got caught by the curl of a wave. "It's so different when you see it up close. It's really lovely."

The tide rushed in, swirling around their ankles. "Yes it is," Charlotte said. "I don't know where I'd be if I didn't have this place. It's always brought me a sense of clarity."

"So it was your grandmother's . . ."

"Yes," she said. "Where she spent her retirement."

"I can see that," he said. "Somehow it makes perfect sense."

She wasn't sure what he meant by that, but then again there were so many things about Rex Renaud she didn't understand, including her feelings about him. In so many ways he represented all she hated about men and their selfish ambitions. But in so many other ways she was inexplicably drawn. And that was the most confusing part of all.

He turned to walk, beckoning for her to join him. Like a gentleman, he took the side closest to the surf, crossing through a short tidal pool and half dozen or so gulls breaking open clams on the jetty rocks. They walked in silence, passing the scattered fishermen and strollers enjoying the sunny day. He hadn't accepted her apology, so it still loomed between them, making their silence all the more deafening.

"Rex, I am sorry for what I said. For the way I acted. Can you forgive me?"

He stopped, turning to her. "I shouldn't have ever gone off with that girl. She was too young and I was just being stupid and vain. Out of all the things I've told you about what happened, I want you to know that above everything else."

"And I'm sorry, too," she said. "For the cheap shot. Please forgive me."

"But I deserved it. I shouldn't have kissed you. And now I need to apologize to you." He nodded his head. "I'm so very sorry."

She was flabbergasted. Because somehow she knew apology wasn't anything that came to him easily and was likely even more rare. "Are you now."

"*Oui*," he said, smiling briefly. He reached out to her, his thumb tracing a line down her jaw. "I want you to like me. If only for a little while. It'll make things easier."

She laughed, incredulous. "As if this situation needs more complications."

He looked to the water and back. "You said this place brings you clarity. So perhaps I've had a bit of my own. We're attracted to each other, Charlotte. We've both admitted to it. But whether or not we act on it anymore really doesn't matter because it's out there." He stretched out his arms as if holding a rifle. "Boom!" he said, pulling the imaginary trigger. "Now our elephant's dead."

"Aw, that's a shame," Charlotte said. "I really like elephants."

He waved her off. "Oh, I just shot a bullet over her head. See? She's still there." He pointed toward the street and where Lucy still loomed. "I just chased her off."

"Well that's good. But the problem is, she *is* still there."

"Though not *between* us anymore," he said. "She's out in the open."

"So what do we do about it?"

"I'll leave that up to you," he said. "When you decide, I'll be right here waiting."

"Hm . . ." she mused, crossing her arms as she turned to walk back. "Ought to be an interesting next couple of days. But it's not like we should lack for conversation. There's still your little problem."

"*Oui*, there's that," Rex said, chucking another oyster shell into the water. He fell in step beside her. "If anything, what's between us will teach me tolerance. Strengthen me to not go chasing after *les filles* in the future."

She slanted a glance at him. "I'm not sure I know how to take that."

He laughed. "Let me put it this way. Resisting you will no doubt drain my very reserves."

"Let's try to stay on topic." She had to. Because resisting him would be just as daunting. "So if you're innocent—and I do believe you—why would she accuse you? What's in it for her? Do you think she's just out to get your money?"

"That would make sense if it were just the girl behind it. With the way she looks, why would she pick on me? Not to seem smug, but there are too many old letches out there that'd be easier targets." He looked at her, as if obvious. "I don't think I'm quite in that category. Not yet, anyway."

Absolutely not. "So you don't think she's acting alone."

"I thought that the moment she started screaming. I should have realized it when she got so insistent about my ripping her panties." His mouth crooked. "To tell the truth, even though I've heard the request before it's always been, how shall we say . . . spontaneous."

"Yes, okay, all right," Charlotte said, not really wanting the details. "Any ideas who might be behind her?"

"You mean if there's anyone out there who would like to see me ruined?" He laughed with honest mirth. "The queue would probably stretch around the world. Including a few women whose panties I *have* ripped."

"Way too much information," Charlotte said, veering toward the water.

Rex pulled her back before the surf broke halfway up her leg. "The thing is, I have no idea. I'm well aware there are people who hate me, but to do this?" He just shook his head.

"I think the congresswoman should be at the top of the list for taking your phone, but at this point that seems incidental. One may have nothing to do with the other."

"Yet I can't help thinking everything that happened that night is somehow connected." He threw a frustrated hand in the air. "Lilith should have had that bill up for a vote a long time ago. Why didn't she just do it? I don't understand."

"Why do people do anything? Really, it's all for the same reasons. It's all about power, I guess. Or sex. Money." She looked at him. "Even love."

"In which case at least three out of four are involved."

"Who knows? Maybe it was love." The wind gusted, and she pulled the jacket closer. "Haven't you ever been in love, Rex? It can make you do strange things sometimes."

He looked at her, smiling vaguely. "I'm sure it can. Are you speaking from experience?"

"I'm not sure if I've ever been was in love. Perhaps I thought I was. The only thing I do know is that men most definitely make me crazy. I'm still trying to figure them out."

He switched sides with her as the swells started getting rougher. "You might call it your life's work."

"You might," she said. "You know I really am sorry about what I said before. I think sometime I get a little too wrapped up in my own dogma."

"Or not deep enough into it. True feminism encompasses either sex, doesn't it? All it really means is working toward the advancement of women."

"That's right," Charlotte said. "Though that statement's definitely in the minority with how most men feel. At least in my experience."

Before long they were back at the top of the beach, both sharing a little laugh over the value of their shoes versus the economic strata of her neighborhood.

"Some of these homes are legacies from the time the average middle-class worker could afford a vacation house," Charlotte said. "Now you'd need at least six figures a year."

"You mean lunch money?" he said, at which Charlotte shot him a smirk. "If that's true, it also means you'll have to do a whole lot better than those Louboutins if you expect your shoes to be stolen."

"Okay," she said, looping her fingers into her shoes. "Next time I'll leave Hermès." They walked up the driveway, Charlotte stopping at the garage door. "We should get our stuff out of the . . ." She trailed off.

"Car," he finished, his gaze locking onto hers.

All at once she was flooded with trepidation. *What now?* she thought. They'd get their clothes out of the car and then go inside and there'd they be, in this suddenly tiny little house with the two of them and the elephant once again, crammed between them.

"She's not here," Rex said, reading her mind. "Remember? We shot that bullet over her hear. She took off."

But it was only a warning shot, Charlotte knew. She was still there but just off to the side, still watching, still waiting.

They got their bags and went inside, both dropping them to the kitchen floor.

"Charlotte," Rex said, turning toward her, right back where they were before.

Chapter Eight

Egg MacGuffin

"CHARLOTTE . . ." REX said, his rumbling baritone prickling her skin with the very sound of her name. He gripped her shoulders, looking into her eyes. "I need to ask you something."

They were alone now—really alone, the vacant street, the closed door, the emptiness of the house, all working to seal them in. Charlotte fell into his gaze, the jacket still around her feeling as close as it could get to his actual embrace.

"What?" she whispered, her heart pounding in her ears.

His hand slid lightly down her arm and he smiled a bit sheepishly "Charlotte," he said, "I'm ready to gnaw the furniture. Can we please go get something to eat?"

"Is that it?" She sighed. Although whether it was from

relief or disappointment, she couldn't say. In all actuality, she wanted to smack him. "Oh. Sure."

He eyed her with trepidation. "What, were you expecting—"

"I don't know what I was expecting." She pulled off his jacket, tossing it at him. "Damn you and your goddamned sexy voice. I'll bet you can read a menu and make it sound like pornography."

He stared at her a moment, then burst into laughter. "Right now even a piece of toast sounds pretty decadent to me. But if you're expecting more . . ." He leaned in, kissing her lightly on each cheek. "Just let me know and I'll be happy to oblige."

Charlotte pulled back, peeved. "Goddamned Frenchmen. I know too many of them. And they all give me a pain in the ass."

He tilted his head, scoping her *derrière*. "And a fine little *cul* it is."

She threw him a scowl, grabbing her overnighter.

"Hey." He looked around. "What time is it?"

She glanced at his wrist. "Didn't I see you wearing a Hublot in Boston?"

"You don't wear a thirty-thousand-dollar watch to go begging for money."

"But five-thousand-dollar cuff links are all right?"

He lifted that Gallic nose in indignation. "How do you suppose I was to close my cuffs?"

"The clock's just over your head, above the sink," she said. "Sheesh."

He turned. "Two o'clock! No wonder I'm starving."

"Just give me ten minutes to clean up." She brushed the front of her skirt. "I think I'm still covered in all the vacuuming I didn't get a chance to do this week."

"Explain this *vacuuming*," he said, eyes narrowing in faux curiosity. "Is it some kind of a native term?"

"Oh Jesus Christ . . ." She sighed, shaking her head. "If you'd like to crawl out of that socioeconomic bubble for a bit, there's a bathroom right behind you, though I'm sure not as elegant as you're used to."

"Yes, I've noticed the distinct lack of a bidet, but I've been known to slum now and then." He set his own bag on the table, rummaging through it. "I'll survive."

"I sincerely hope so. When I'm through there's a nice little café not far from here we can walk to. You remember walking, right?" She left for the upstairs.

My God, she thought. *I can't imagine what he's thinking.*

MON DIEU, *I can't imagine what she's thinking.* Rex peeked around the kitchen archway, watching that gorgeous little *cul* traipse up the stairs.

Screw thinking. What the hell was he going to *do*? He left for the bathroom, unable to think of anything beyond the visceral at the moment, leaning over the toilet as he drained himself of the morning's bad coffee. From the upstairs he heard Charlotte turn on the shower, and he was half tempted to run up and jump in with her. Then his belly rumbled and he remembered how much harder it was to run this engine on an empty tank.

Goddamn—he was *starving*.

What a day it had been. And it was hardly past two p.m. So far he'd woken up in jail, stood before a judge, dropped five mil on a bond, was nearly brained with a brick, got kicked out of Philadelphia on the threat of being blown up, outran a tail—all to land in some godforsaken town on the New Jersey coast, complete with voyeuristic cops and a six-story high wooden elephant. He shook and flushed. Not his usual morning. But then again, there was that hot little *avocate* and some stellar scotch tossed into the mix, just to make things interesting.

Christ almighty, he could still taste her on his lips. A rather nice taste at that.

He turned to the sink and set the water running, washing his face and wetting down his hair. He opened his shaving kit and found his toothbrush, and scrubbing his teeth, brought himself back to a semblance of normal.

Normal. Is that what this was?

Normal on his last trip stateside was the Hay-Adams in D.C., drinking Stoli martinis and banging the congresswoman in the elevator.

Between floors, of course.

Oui, now *that* was normal. Or at least it had been. Until everything suddenly went wrong. And he sure as hell wasn't going to find out how that happened holed up in some off-season tourist town. He slipped off his tie and opened his collar, reflexively checking his hip pocket. "*Merde.*" He'd really like to get who stole his goddamned phone so he could break their fucking neck.

And he would, too. After he found a way out of here. And for that he needed to make a phone call.

From upstairs, he could hear Charlotte's shower just shutting off. He left for the kitchen and the landline on the wall. Did it work? Or was it just some relic from a World War II war bride? He picked it up—a tone hummed in his ear. He started to dial, then stopped halfway. Maybe he was just being paranoid, but since the cops had already come to the house, maybe they were listening as well. This was America, after all. He set the receiver back on the hook.

Better to find a pay phone somewhere or get one of those cheap phones they kept behind the counter at the 7-Eleven. Paranoid or not, he was charged with a felony and out on bail, and that was a sticky situation no matter what country he was in.

No watch, no phone. He felt almost naked—and without the benefits. He glanced at the wall clock. Two-fifteen. Had he been in Marseille he'd just be finishing off a salad and a nice Grenache, with either a board member or his latest *objet d'affection*, if she still had his attention from the night before.

Was that what Charlotte was? He heard her moving things around upstairs, imagining her stepping into her panties and slinging those luscious *seins* into her bra. Shame. He'd like them better out of it. He'd like them heavy in his hands where he could caress and squeeze them, lower his mouth to them, run his tongue over . . .

He cleared his throat. And moved away from where he could hear her and toward the next room. After just one kiss, Rex quickly learned Charlotte wasn't the type to be toyed with, no matter how much she shivered and sighed. And no matter how much he wanted to make her do it again.

He entered through an archway into a large room, all arranged in a simple chic style. A dining area on one side, the living room with overstuffed cane furniture on the other, a screened-in porch just out the front door, hardwood flooring with the occasional rugs scattered around. And off to one side the stairs, and Charlotte just coming down them.

"I hope I didn't make you wait too long," she said. She wore no makeup, her damp hair piled in the back of her head into a kind of curly froth, her shoes low leather sandals that matched the color of her simple sleeveless dress. "I know you're probably as hungry as I am, so I just threw myself together so we could go eat."

Rex perched on the edge of the sofa, pleased with what he saw. "If that's how you throw yourself together I'd sure like to see when you make the effort. You look lovely."

"Oh stop," she said, blushing slightly as she grabbed a sweater out of the closet. "I already know you're hot for me, so save it."

Yet her blithe attempt to blow him off only irked him. He latched hold of her hand as she passed. "I wouldn't say it if I didn't mean it."

"Yeah, well . . ." She slipped away from him and toward the kitchen. "If you really meant it, you wouldn't have to say it."

"What kind of sense does that make?" he asked, going after her. "Christ, he really must have been a dick, right?"

She fumbled with something in her purse, not looking up. "Aren't they all?"

"I'd like to meet that asshole who took you for granted," he said, slipping his arms around her. "All you'd have to do is ask and I'd pound him right into the ground. And you know why?"

"No," she said, looking up. "Why don't you tell me?"

He kissed her forehead. "Because, damnit, I'm starting to find out I *like* you." He tipped her chin with his finger. "So be honest. Is that going to ruin our relationship?"

She stared at him a moment, then she laughed, slapping his chest. "Oh my God, let's go eat, okay? I've so had it with dicks for a while."

"Hey," he said, following her out.

THEY WALKED TO a little café a few blocks away, which had about a half-dozen tables outside. Away from the beach the temperature was warmer, Charlotte slinging her sweater along the back of her chair, Rex grateful he'd left his jacket at the house. With his tie off and the few top buttons of his shirt open he felt quite the libertine, as usually his stateside visits were all work and no play—no matter the degree of his indulgences—warranting his usual business attire. But there in the salt air and afternoon sun, sated by a tolerable bottle of local wine and an asparagus omelette, Rex felt able to breathe for the first time in over twenty-four hours. And it wasn't only because he was starting to form a plan. It was also because of the woman sitting next to him, and the not-so-placating admission he'd just made. For all their blathering and fussing, he really *did* like her.

And because of that, he also needed to find out if her could trust her.

They sat facing the street, cars and pedestrians crossing and cruising past them, as Rex eyed the dinosaur on the corner. Not the kind that Charlotte accused him of being, but one of the more recent kind.

"I have to make a call," he said, sipping his wine.

Charlotte grabbed her purse, saying around a mouthful of omelette, "You con huse ma hone."

"What?" He leaned in, grinning wickedly. "Swallow, *chere*."

She did, her brow arching. "I said, you can use my phone."

"No." He slung his arm over her shoulder, leaning in. "Not for this."

"Who are you calling?"

"My boss."

"Oh. *Him*." She retrieved her phone, holding it out. "You can still use it. Go ahead."

He wrapped his hand around it, guiding it back to her purse. In the split-second he had to figure, he pondered again whether to tell her. Ultimately he knew he'd have to. "Thanks, but no. I'm contemplating something illegal, and I'd rather not leave a trail."

"You *are*?" Her face lit up. "What? Can I help?"

He was surprised how relieved he was at her reaction. "You just might," he said, his finger twirling a curl at her neck. "I need you to cover for me while I dash down to Washington."

"You—you want to go down to D.C.?" When he nodded, she stared at him, aghast. "But that's jumping bail. It's bad enough we're here in Margate, but at least the cops know about it. Why would you deliberately jeopardize your case? Do you want to be thrown into jail?"

"No, I want to find out why I was arrested to begin with."

"But why would you think the answer's in D.C.?"

"Because that's where all the players are."

Charlotte was mystified. "So you're thinking it was the lobbyist or the congresswoman who set you up?"

Rex dug into his pocket for change. He couldn't remember the last time he used a pay telephone, let alone an American one. "It could be either one of them, but I'm not going to find out from up here."

"But what's the point?" Charlotte said. "As bad as it seems now, maybe you won't need to prove your innocence. This is turning out to be a classic case of he said/she said. If there's no forensic evidence, then the charges have no teeth. That'll come out in the investigation."

"The point is why did it happen in the first place?" He rubbed his chin, his beard bristling. "The only thing that connects me to Washington is that dredging bill. What other reason would anyone have to discredit me or Mercier or both? But I only have until Thursday to find out who is out to nail me and why."

"Because after Thursday Congress clears out of town until after the November elections."

"*Oui.*"

Charlotte set down her fork. "Or, more specifically, the congresswoman?"

"That's about as specific as it gets." He took a sip of wine, his gut roiling with that realization.

Charlotte gripped his arm. "So to prove your innocence you'll need to confront the congresswoman—"

"—who's down in Washington and has a fifty/fifty chance of losing her seat."

"And if she does, that'll make her a lame duck, then the bill and—"

"—the mystery dies with her." He lifted his wine in salute. "*Exactement.*"

"Oh God." She backed up. "Don't tell me we're finishing each other's sentences."

"It appears so." He took one more sip of wine and got up. "I'll be right back."

The pay phone was outside a pawnshop and Western Union, looking as neglected and forlorn as those dinosaurs of the pre–cell phone age typically did. As with the house phone and all similarly abandoned instruments, Rex wanted to make sure it still worked, so he picked up the receiver, listening for a dial tone. He heard one so he dropped in a couple of coins and dialed, knowing full well Marcel wouldn't answer a strange number. And since he couldn't text him to let him know who it was, Rex knew he'd have to leave a voice message.

"Call me back ASAP."

He hung up to wait. In less than a minute, the pay phone rang.

Rex picked it up at half a ring. "*Allo?*"

"Don't give me '*allo*' motherfucker," Marcel said. "Where are you?"

"*Mon frangin*, your voice is music to my ears."

"Too bad I can't say the same. Christ, how the hell did you get yourself arrested? And why aren't you calling me on your own phone? It couldn't have taken you this long to get out of jail. Come on, I'm busy."

Busy getting laid, he knew. Son of a bitch was on his honeymoon off the coast of New England while Rex rotted away for *la firme*. "It did take that long. And my phone's missing."

"Fucking *flics*. I'll get it cleared."

"No—don't!" Rex said, much too quickly. *Merde.*

"Christ! Okay! But why not?"

Should he tell him how he taped the congresswoman? Should he say what his suspicions were behind this whole thing? Or should he just let it ride until he knew for sure? Rex let his instinct decide for the latter. Better to play it off for now.

"I have some files on it I can't afford to lose, that's all. I'm sure they'll find it sooner or later."

Marcel paused. "You're hiding something from me, but I'll let it go for now. But I'll have it traced."

"It won't work. I shut it off when I gave it over. But that's not the larger issue anyway. Someone is trying to frame me for whatever reason. But I'm not going to find out up here in this bourgeois Riviera. I need to get down to D.C. And I need you to get me a car that can't be traced."

"I'm no expert on American law, but didn't you just post a five-million-dollar bond?"

"Which is why I have to do this under the radar. Can you get me a car or what?"

"Can't you get your own?"

Jesus, talk about dicks . . . "No, because they're watching us. Even sent the goddamned cops over to the house."

"Us? Whose house are you at?"

Fuck. Rex pinched his eyelids. "My lawyer's."

"So you called Legal. Though I don't know how good they are at criminal bullshit. But I heard that Bélanger once clerked for a district—"

"I didn't call Legal. I got my own lawyer."

"Who? Do I know him?"

"Her." He may as well tell him. "Charlotte Andreko."

Rex could almost hear his head exploding. "*Her?* Why in the holy fuck would you pick that crazy *salope?*"

Was that his own nails cutting into his palm? He forced himself to stay calm. He needed Marcel to help him and besides, he couldn't smash his face from here. "Can you think of a better person to defend me on a sexual assault charge than a feminist lawyer? Especially one who's a partner in a firm in the city where I've been charged?"

"Okay, I get it. I also get the big, juicy *lolos.*"

"You know I haven't forgotten that sucker punch in Boston. You still have one coming."

"All right already. Where are you?"

"Not too far from Atlantic City. At least I can see it from the beach."

Silence, then, "Get back to me in a couple of hours."

"Don't take too long." Rex said. "I don't have much time."

Rex heard something bang in the background. "Neither do I. Call me in two. *Ciao*."

When Rex returned to the table Charlotte was staring straight ahead, her chin propped in her palm. "The congresswoman," she said, not waiting for him to sit, "she's in love with you."

"What are you talking about?" he said, even though he did.

She looked at him directly. "I'm talking about Lilith Millwater."

"In love with me . . ." *Merde*. He flicked his hand. "What difference does that make?"

"What difference?" She looked flabbergasted. "She's *in love* with you."

"*Non*," he said, continuing *en français*, "I was fucking her. She was fucking me. It was servicing. That's all there was to it."

She looked up, answering in kind. "You're wrong. It makes all the difference in the world. Women never just fuck. They're always emotionally invested in one way or another. It could be because they're unhappy, or they need the attention, or yeah, maybe they're in love. But it's always something."

"Right. She liked my cock and I wanted the bill passed. A simple barter system."

"But what if she stole your phone and listened to your recording of you hooking up with that lobbyist? My God, it'd be like a double whammy. An insult to injury. Rex, if she *is* in love with you, it would destroy her."

His jaw tightened. "Wouldn't that be the intention?"

"What?" She seemed incredulous. "Let me wrap my head around this. I thought you taped your conversation with her for your *own* protection, because who trusts politicians these days? But it never was for that, was it? You'd blackmail her if necessary, wouldn't you?"

He laughed softly, hardly believing his ears. "Wouldn't you? What kind of lawyer would you be if you didn't throw every wrench in your toolbox?"

"It's not the same thing," she said, slowly rising. "You don't hit them below the belt."

"But why not? That's the softest spot."

Charlotte stared at him. "God, you can be cold. It's like you throw a switch and you turn into this iceman. How do you sleep at night?"

He picked what was left of his wine, downing it. "Like a baby."

She turned, hurrying down the street.

Chapter Nine

Filling in the Blanks

"CHARLOTTE, LET ME explain!" *Merde.* Now he really screwed it. He went after her.

When she stopped at a traffic light, Rex caught up with her. She turned to him before he could speak.

"You must forgive me," she said, looking back to the street. "As you may have noticed, I have a tendency to say the first thing on my mind. It's a bad habit and why I don't have many friends. You owe me no explanation."

"Of course I do." The light changed and they continued on. "You're my lawyer, so you need to know the facts. Why do you think I recorded her to begin with?"

"That's easy. To throw her words back in her face."

"And why would you think I'd have to?" This was the part that sent his blood pressure through the roof. "I've come to realize she doesn't give a damn about the bill or the thousands of jobs it could create, even though that's what she's been campaigning on. She doesn't give a damn because she's a shark, Charlotte. She's such a shark she makes you look like a fucking jellyfish."

That got her attention. "Gee, thanks."

"I'm serious. She hates her husband, her kids are grown and off on their own careers, and she's in real danger of losing her seat because she's been accused of not hating Washington enough. So she's keeping this bill in limbo just so she can show her voters how hard she's fighting for them, as well as show the party bosses how much she hates Washington by letting it die."

"Yet you were fucking her."

"*Oui*. I was taking one for the team."

Charlotte looked at him, incredulous. "That's disgusting."

"You do what you have to do."

She considered that a moment. "Then she's using you."

"She thinks she is."

Her lawyerly radar was on, her face lighting. "So by recording her, you're really calling in your marker?"

"Exactly."

They came to another light and she paused, her face creasing. "But she's still in love with you, you know."

"Right. That's the vig."

It changed, and they continued on. "The what?"

"The vig. The juice. The slice I take for doing her the favor." She wanted the iceman? Oh boy, was she getting him. "The part that sinks the knife when I drive it home."

That stopped her cold. "But that's horrible."

"She taught me the Washington rules, Charlotte. I'm just playing by them."

She walked faster. "I don't want to hear any more. I've been hired to defend you against a charge, and your liaisons are none of my business. As far as I'm concerned, the two have nothing to do with each other. I'm sorry I stuck my nose in your affairs. It won't happen again."

Hearing that hardly placated him. He didn't want her being so civil. He wanted her coming at him in a huff and screaming with jealousy, and not like so many woman of his acquaintance, cavalier and dismissive of their relations. Because deep down he actually hoped she *was* jealous, and not this outraged feminist, blindly defending a woman who'd cut her down as quick as breathing. He didn't want Charlotte living by the rules she adopted for herself. He wanted to be the exception to them.

Ahead lay the beach, Charlotte aiming for the pavilion at the foot of the strand. The wind was freshening the closer they came, and it was a good thing she'd slipped on her sweater as he didn't have a jacket to lend her. Somehow he wished he had, if he could offer her some kind of peace offering, no matter how insignificant. A distance now gaped between them, and the fact that it bothered him startled Rex considerably.

When the street ended they stepped up to the pavilion, Charlotte crossing it to the railing at the entrance to the beach. As she looked toward the ocean, Rex came up beside her, leaning back so he could face her.

"Charlotte," he said, his finger brushing her arm.

She glanced to it before turning her gaze back to the

water. "Seriously, Rex, I don't need to hear any more about your affair."

"To call it an affair would be like calling McDonald's haute cuisine," he said. "I'd come to Washington, I'd get the latest story on the bill, we'd have some drinks, and then I'd—"

"Please," Charlotte said, turning toward him. "No play-by-play. The only reason I mentioned it in the first place was because it'll complicate things."

He straightened. "It seems it already has."

"Apparently. Now you have a jealous woman behind this whole thing."

"I wasn't talking about the congresswoman," he said, taking her by the shoulders. "I was talking about you."

"Me?" She palmed her chest. "Do you think I'm jealous?"

"Are you?"

She huffed. "No, of course not."

"Then what is it?" He swept his hand over the top of her head, smoothing her flying strands. "Because it feels like more to me."

She seemed surprised. At least he hoped she was. "Maybe it is. But I don't want it to be."

"Maybe I don't give a damn what you want," he said, his mouth falling to hers.

Perhaps that was the last thing Charlotte expected, Rex kissing her, but he didn't care. After just a couple of hours he already missed the taste of her, the feel of her in his arms. He couldn't remember the last time he reacted to anyone this way, maybe he never had. He pulled her closer, hardly caring if anyone was watching or if he was a grown man making a fool of himself. When she sighed and deepened their kiss, he turned to pin her against the rail, his body pressing against hers.

"I want you, Charlotte . . ." he murmured against her lips. "I want you very badly."

"Maybe I don't give a damn what you want," she whispered back, nipping the corner of his mouth.

He growled, "I could take you right here . . ."

"Do you always take what you want?" she said, her hips shifting in a tantalizing pass.

"*Oui*," he wanted her to know. "Though it usually comes willingly. I choose my targets carefully, you see."

"Is that what I am?" Charlotte's blue eyes sparked fire. "A target? An objective?"

"*Oui*," he said without hesitation. "I go after what I want and I don't stop until I get it." He kissed her once more, then pulled back, caressing her cheek. "Are you gotten, Charlotte? Or is that exceedingly bad English?"

"*Oui à la fois*," she said, toying with a button on his shirt. "And God help me—I don't want to be. In fact, you're scaring the crap out of me."

"*Très bien*," he said, kissing her again. "That's what I expect from all my conquests. How do you think I've gotten as far as I have?"

"I'm not joking, Rex. You do something to me. Do you think I react this way to all of my clients?"

"Since most of your clients are women . . ." He broke into a wicked grin. "Why, you saucy little thing, you."

She turned six shades of red. "Oh—*stop*," she whispered. "I'm serious."

"Believe me, I know," he said, throwing his arm over her shoulders as they walked back to the street. "Your demons are mine, *ma belle*. I find you very, very hard to resist, too."

He felt her laughing as she tipped her head against him. "Oh, if only you knew what was going through my mind now."

"Are you still thinking of Lilith?" He kissed her temple. "Oh, *merde*, I'd still like to meet that guy who messed you up."

Her arm tightened around his waist. "Then you're jealous, too?"

"Aha!" he said, pointing at her. "You *were* jealous."

"Only because I had a reason to be. You, *mon ami*, don't." A tiny derisive sound came from the back of her throat. "I wouldn't be surprised if she coerced that lobbyist just to get your attention."

Rex stopped. "What are you saying?"

"You mean you hadn't thought of that?"

"It's obvious someone had, but Lilith?" He wouldn't put it past her to steal his phone, but this added a whole other dimension.

What possible reason would the congresswoman have in alienating Rex? Their relationship, if it could be called that, had been centered around the dredging bill, their coupling hardly more than a pleasant way to settle the day's work, much like the old-school backroom boys would use a glass of scotch and a cigar to seal the deal.

It hadn't entered his mind to look for anything deeper, and if Lilith had ever shown any strains of jealousy, it was only because she was protecting her turf. Rex well knew that information was the lifeblood of D.C., and it didn't hurt having the ear—and the cock—of the chief operating officer of one of the biggest privately held corporations in the world. But *son of a bitch*, why would she have to do something like that? Didn't she trust him? As if he didn't know. In Washington *trust* was a currency at ten thousand percent inflation, as worthless as a day-old newspaper.

"It's a possibility," Rex finally admitted. "Though the girl would owe her big-time."

They stopped at a corner to wait for the light to change, his arm still around her. "And for what?" Charlotte said. "What would induce a young woman to compromise herself like that? The victim would always take a character hit. She'll always be seen as complicit in some way."

He eyed her skeptically. "Always? Do you really think so?"

Charlotte looked miffed, slipping from his arms. "All right then, we'll say *usually*. But she'll still bear the brunt of the stigma. People will always view her through the sexual lens of the crime. They'll picture her with her skirt hiked up around her waist and naked beneath, not screaming or shaking in terror. That's why so many women never report it."

"And it'll only get worse when her story turns out to be false."

"Exactly," Charlotte said, apparently appeased as she

allowed Rex's arm around her again. The light changed and they crossed. "She must have been paid one hell of a sack of money. Did she seem like the type?"

"I hardly remember. Do you think I was actually listening to what she was saying? I was looking at her *lolos*."

Charlotte peered at him, moving away. "Do you have any idea how chauvinistic that just sounded?"

Christ, she's a prickly woman. He slipped his arm around her waist. "Yes, though it just proves how little attention I actually paid to her. Now *you*, on the other hand . . ." He caressed her hip. "I listen to every word that comes out of that smart mouth of yours."

"I'm not sure how I should interpret that," she said, lifting her chin.

"It means you most definitely have my attention." Then he kissed her, right there on the street, amid the traffic with the pedestrians having to move around them, making a spectacle of himself for all of Margate to see. Not that he cared. He was quickly discovering Charlotte was like a blast of sea spray, too much champagne, closing a billion-dollar deal. But as intoxicating as she was, he also needed to remember he had too much to do and so little time to accomplish it, and Charlotte was too smart and intuitive to treat lightly. He needed her and her expertise to extricate himself from this mess, but if he let things get too complicated between them, well . . . he didn't want to think about it. All he wanted to think about was *now*.

"I have to get a few things," he said as they walked toward the boulevard. "Does there happen to be a men's store around here?"

"Burberry? No," she said, casting him a wary glance. "But I think we may be able to find something within walking distance."

"Good, because as much as I'd like to be out of my clothes around you, I still have to deal with the world."

She squeezed his hand. "Don't I know."

A short statement with more implications than she realized. He stopped in front of a bakery, clutching her in front of him as he caught her reflection in the window. "The congresswoman's in D.C., *ma petit*. You know I'm not going to find out what's behind all this from up here. I have to make a call in a couple of hours about picking up a car in Atlantic City, then I'm taking it down there to see her."

"But how can you be sure she's even there?"

"She has to be. Congress recesses after Thursday, and as I mentioned before, that's her last chance to get the bill out for a vote."

"Yes," she said dryly. "She has to at least *pretend* like she's trying."

"As I said before, I don't write the rules. I only play by them."

She peered back at him, her reflection hovering over a row of éclairs. "Have you ever thought of running for office? You'd make a damned good politician."

"Ha! I've heard that before. But what would be the profit in it?" He leaned in, whispering, "Have I mentioned you look good enough to eat?"

"Have *I* mentioned the poll that said Frenchwomen prefer chocolate over sex?"

He was horrified. "Where'd you read that—the *Onion*?"

"The *New York Times*, I think. It was very scientific." She tapped at the window. "We're stopping here on the way back. I want that éclair."

He kissed her neck. "And I want you," he said, one hand sliding to the underside of her breast.

"Don't worry," she whispered. "It'll be a friendly competition."

They walked on, coming to a row of shops on Ventnor Avenue, Rex finding a store that sold men's furnishings, surprising him how upscale it was. He bought underwear, two pairs of Jack Donnelly khakis, four Lacoste polos, socks, a belt, a pair of Top-Siders, and a gray tweed sport jacket from which he snipped the tags and slipped right on.

"Planning on staying a month?" Charlotte asked.

"I only planned on staying overnight. The rest of my things are on the plane, and it's not like they'll let me get within a klick of it."

"I know how you feel," she said wryly. "The rest of my things are at my chateau."

The extremely obliging shop owner beamed at Rex from over the piled items. "And how do you wish to pay for this, sir?" he asked, teeth gleaming.

Rex slid a black metal card across the counter. The man stared at it, eyes widened in awe. "I've heard of these," he murmured, pinching it off the wood. He held it reverently between his fingers. "Though I never actually saw one."

"Is there something wrong?" Rex said.

"Oh no!" the man said, alarmed. "Everything's perfect. Please—it'll just take a minute."

"Show-off," Charlotte said to Rex.

He arched a brow. "I have no idea what you're talking about."

"No, I expect you don't," she said, rising from the chair where she'd been waiting. "I don't suppose it's often you float down to earth and mix with the little people."

"I'll have you know I used to be one of those little people," he said, turning toward her.

He could see the bare outline of her nipples beneath her dress, the fabric shifting tantalizingly as she came up to him. "And how many eons ago was that?"

"I was born into them," he said, Charlotte drawing him out again. She could make him tell her things he'd never said to anyone, and he had to be careful of that. So he tossed a wrench as he usually did when someone got too close. He traced his finger over the hem of her bodice. "Back then my car seat had to suffer the indignity of a Benz instead of a Bentley."

Charlotte squinted at him, properly thrown, before she caught the joke. "Oh, how horrible for you. I'll bet you had to go from a golden spoon right down to silver."

"You know me so well," he said, his finger trailing up to her chin. "Why don't we duck over there into that dressing room again, so I can get to know you a bit better?"

"Your card, sir," the shop owner said, his smile ready to crack the plaster off the walls. "Would you like some assistance carrying your purchases to the car?"

Rex asked him if they could be held while he did a bit more shopping, and the man readily agreed, though he seemed puzzled why any more shopping was actually necessary. As did Charlotte as they walked out the door.

"What else?" She smiled suggestively. "Besides éclairs, I mean."

"I need to get a phone," he said as they stood on the sidewalk.

"There's a Verizon right over there," she said, pointing down the block. "See?"

"I'm looking for the throwaway kind. Is there a convenience store around here?"

"Now I get the black AmEx. What are you really, a drug lord?"

"*Non*, just a businessman, remember?"

"How could I forget."

"But now I'm also a cautious one."

She looked to the other end of the block. "There's a store down there." She slipped her arm in hers. "Come on, Bentley. After we're through there, I know a place where we can hook up with some black ops."

Rex pulled her close, whispering in her ear, "*Ma chérie—tu es complètement givrée.*"

THE FIRST THING Rex did when he got back to the house was call Marcel. This time he picked up on the first ring. "*Allo?*"

"Turning adventurous, are you?" Rex said. "You didn't even wait to make sure it was me."

"Who the fuck else could it be, calling precisely two hours later?" Marcel said. "Okay, are you ready?"

"Go ahead," Rex said pen poised over a Chinese take-out menu.

"A black Lincoln will be parked in Caesar's garage, fourth floor, slot 450. It's keyless entry and the code is 58292. There will be a fob under the passenger side mat once you get in."

"You said *will be*," Rex said. "When is that?"

Marcel sighed. "Well, that's the thing. You wanted untraceable so we ordered one with diplomat plates."

Rex couldn't help being impressed. "No shit. Where'd you get that—*non*, don't tell me. I don't want to know."

"Don't worry, it's legal. I just called in a favor. The thing is, it won't be there until five tomorrow morning."

That'd cut into his time in Washington, but then again . . . it would give him a whole night with Charlotte. "I think I can manage that."

"Work it into your schedule. Because if you don't pick it up by five-fifteen we'll assume you're not coming, and it'll be gone. And one more thing," Marcel said. "You'll only have it for twenty-four hours. Seems someone's on holiday, and they'll be back to claim it. And you don't get it back to the same spot by five the next morning it'll be reported stolen, and I won't be able to help you."

"I thought you said it was legal?"

"It *is* legal, but shades of gray, *mon ami*. Just get it back to the same spot at Caesar's by five Thursday morning and all will be right with the world. Can I reach you at this number?"

"*Oui*. It's my new thirty-dollar phone. At least until I get my old one back."

"So, do you have a plan?"

"Of course I do." *Liar.*

"Well, good luck with that. Keep in touch. *Ciao*." He rang off.

Rex glanced at the time: 6:02. *A plan*. Eleven hours to think about what the hell that was and what he was going to do once he got to Washington. *A plan*. And four hours more after that once he was in motion.

Out in the living room, Charlotte was trying to remain unobtrusive, on the sofa with her legs crossed, scrolling through her phone. Should he tell her it wasn't working? That he was almost more aware of her than he was of his own hands? He flexed his fingers, imagining smoothing them down her naked body, her skin rippling under his trace.

"Charlotte?" he said, heading toward her, the Chinese take-out menu in his hand. He looked to it, then to her.

For this, he most definitely had a plan.

He heard a soft thud as she set the phone down atop a glass table. "What?"

Rex sat down next to her, angling himself so he could gauge her reaction. Should he tell her? *Need-to-know basis*. For now, he'd play it safe. "I'll be leaving tomorrow morning very early for Washington."

She stared at him a moment before saying, "You know how I feel about that."

"I do, but I have to go." He took her hand. "I'll only have twenty-four hours to do what I have to do, so I'll be up and back before you'll even know I'm gone. The thing is, I'll need you to cover for me. Will you?"

She slipped her hand from his. "I don't really have a choice, do I? I'm supposed to be responsible for you." Then she shot him a look a warning. "But remember, if you get caught I go down, too."

The prospect was unthinkable. "I'm fully aware of the consequences. But I'd turn myself in before I'd let that happen."

"What would you say?" She pushed herself up. "That you snuck out while I was sleeping?"

He caught her hand before she could walk away. "That's one lie I couldn't tell," he said, rising to pull her into his arms. "Especially since you'll be spending the night under me."

He kissed her, hard and without mercy. *Mais oui*, he most *definitely* had a plan . . .

Chapter Ten

Hors D'oeuvres

"KEEP THE CHANGE and thanks," Charlotte said, exchanging a fifty-dollar bill for one heavy bag of Chinese takeout.

The delivery man smiled wide. "Thank *you*," he said and she closed the door, carrying the food into the kitchen. She grabbed a roll of paper towels and from the refrigerator, a liter of Evian, and . . . She considered the three-quarters full bottle of Pinot Noir. Would a California red go with Chinese food, especially when served with a side of Frenchman? She wasn't sure, but she grabbed it anyway, dropping two paper cups into the bag.

What the hell was she doing?

Oh right, she could be so cavalier about it now. After what she had done—correction—what she had done *to her* just a little while ago. But as wonderful and insane as it had been, it was only a precursor to the Main Event coming up next. Was she ready for that? Would she ever be? Because really, this was Rex she was referring to. *Rex*. All six-foot-two of dark-haired, inky-eyed Frenchman, he of the five-thousand-dollar cuff links, black AmEx, and private jet, who nearly made her swoon each time he had kissed her.

Who would be the first man she'd been with in over two years.

So why'd she have to pick one who was setting them both up to get thrown in jail?

Charlotte set the food down and took a quick swig of Pinot, before taking all of it upstairs to her bedroom.

Along the way she passed the bathroom and the sound of Rex just turning on the shower, the silhouette of his ripped torso visible through the curtain. She had just come from perching on the sink, filing her nails as he shaved, entranced as she watched him scrape his razor up his oh-so-angular jaw. It wasn't even a question whether he had wanted her there or not. She just shoved aside a few bottles and climbed up, Rex kissing her before he bent to splash his face and slather his cheeks with shaving foam. But as innocent as it looked it was really pretty darn bad, as he, an accused felon, and she, his attorney, flouted nearly every rule of professional propriety. And it was about to get much worse.

And *oh boy*, Charlotte shivered as she set the bag and bottles on her night table, *did bad ever feel as good?*

Especially as she recalled what had happened just before that. When she had taken him upstairs to show him the rest of the house. When he had stopped her at the threshold of the bedroom.

"What's this?" he asked.

"Where I sleep," she answered.

He slipped his arm around her waist, caressing her cheek, "Is it anything else?"

She wanted him, so badly she ached in her bones. Which would probably blow to hell every shred of advice she ever had given to her clients—*Don't set yourself up! Watch the sexual innuendo! Be professional at all times! If you want to be equal, treat everyone equally!*—but at this moment, with Rex just a heartbeat away, she was far from caring. He said he wanted her, and goddamnit—he was about to get her.

"It's where you're going to have sex with me," she said.

He kissed her, laughing against her mouth. "My God, the mademoiselle has the second sight." Then he lifted her into his arms, and took her to the bed.

He set her at the foot of it and leaning over her, kissed her with an intensity she'd never known before, and with a tenderness that surprised her. As she propped her arms back and arched her neck, he trailed kisses down the curve of it to her collarbone, sliding the strap of her dress over her shoulder, then kissing the spot where it had been.

"This is for you—this is all for you," he whispered, kissing a trail to the slope of her breast. "You have a beautiful body, and I want to make you more aware of it than you've ever been."

"Oh yeah?" she said, Rex slowly leaning her back against the bed. "How're you going to do that? I mean, should I do . . ." She took a deep breath, smiling shyly. "I guess I'm just not very good at this. Men have always—"

"*Tais-toi*," he said, silencing her with a kiss. He braced himself on his elbows above her. "I know you're nervous, Charlotte, but I don't want you to be, not with me anyway." He kissed her again, light and quick. "Forget all those *enculés* you've been with before."

"Believe me I have, but it's not only that. I think I've just forgotten how to . . . Or maybe I've never known in the first place. Or . . ." She felt like crawling under the bed.

"Has it been a long time? Is that it?" he said, smoothing her unruly hair.

"Oh God, does it show?" Maybe she *would* crawl under the bed. "Men haven't exactly been my friends lately."

"I'm not surprised." And when she gasped, he kissed her again. "Strong women repel weak men. Only strong men understand them. And you, *ma belle*, are a strong woman."

"Who's attracting an equally strong man, I suppose?" she said. "A little backdoor self-adulation, Rex?"

He laughed, teeth and eyes gleaming, sliding down to growl against her breasts. She whooped, grabbing him by his hair. "Stop!"

"You're adorable, you know that?" he said, nipping her breast through the fabric as he slipped even further to the floor. He got down on his knees, his hands just under her dress on either side of her thighs. "But you have too much going on here, impeding my progress. We're going to have to do something about that."

"Oh yeah?" she said, wriggling against him. "What?"

His dark hair was mussed from her tousling, his chin alluringly shaded. She could catch a glimpse of his chest from the three opened buttons of his shirt, hardly able to wait before she could strip it from him. But for now it seemed all about her as he slid her dress up, Charlotte lifting her behind, and in one swift motion, it was off.

"The Great Unveiling," he said, openly admiring her bra and panties. "*C'est magnifique*. And I don't only mean this beautiful body. You're a work of art, Charlotte. And if any of those men couldn't see that, they didn't deserve you, the fucking assholes." He tossed her dress in the air, biting her belly.

She whooped again, feeling every neuron inside her come alive, wondering whether another man's touch had ever felt like this. But with Rex's lips suddenly on hers and opening them, with his tongue searching every cavernous corner of her mouth, *thinking* suddenly became an impossibility. She gave herself over to the sensual, letting the electric force of this man bring her body back to life.

His hand fell to her breast as hers trailed to the small of his back. He slid his palm over a nipple, lightly circling it until it rose, stiffly peaking under her bra. She groaned.

"Save your groaning," he said. "You'll need your breath for what's yet to come." He pulled back, his dark eyes gleaming wickedly. "Which of course, will be you."

"Will I?" she said, hooking two fingers into the front of his shirt. "Won't you join me?" She yanked, pulling him to her.

"Later," he said, pinching the clasp at the center of her

bra. "Right now I've something else to attend to." With one swift flick he unsnapped it, her breasts tumbling into his waiting hands.

"*Merde—tu as des seins magnifiques . . .*" he whispered, his hand lightly brushing its heavy underside. He traced a finger around her areola, leaving her skin pebbling in its wake. He lowered his mouth to her.

"Oh!" Charlotte squeaked, arching into him, electricity jolting through her. She clasped onto him, her arms sliding down his back.

"Gorgeous breasts . . ." he murmured, licking, sucking, his hand kneading the other, its nipple peaking into stiffness. "You're so beautiful, I . . ." He circled her areola with his tongue, until she squeaked again, his mouth exploring and nipping and pulling hard, leaving a trail of marks. "*Tu me donnes envie de . . .*"

"*Quoi?*" she murmured. "What do you want to do?"

"Everything," he said. "Everything and more until I can't move and you're begging me not to stop." He moved to her other breast, his tongue circling and exploring every inch, leaving more intimate brands before he slid up to capture her mouth. His lips claimed hers so thoroughly she felt his kiss right down to her toes.

"Oh God—*Rex* . . ." she purred, curling toward him, "it's not fair. I want to see you, too. I want to feel your skin against me."

"Not yet," he said, his hand falling to her hip, his thumb slipping under the elastic of her panties. "I promise your chance," he said, "but not now."

"No," she said, her hand on his. "I'm afraid I must

insist. Before you go any further . . ." Her knee glanced the obvious evidence of his arousal. "I'd like to see a bit more of what fills your beautiful shirts so extraordinarily." She flicked open another button. "May I?"

He smiled. "Well, when you put it that way . . ." He pushed up. "Go ahead."

So she did, opening each button in quick succession, the dark hairs of his chest slowly coming into view. She reached the waistband of his trousers and slowly pulled his shirt from them, glancing up to see him following her movements. When she unbuttoned the last one she reached up and pushed his shirt back, Rex falling back on his heels to finish the job for her. As he did Charlotte got exactly what she asked for, The Great Unveiling of a man formed to perfection. She raised her hand, grazing it over him.

"What are you d-doing," he said with a flinch.

Charlotte ignored him, skimming her fingers down the hard planes of his chest to his rippled abs, lingering there a bit before she trailed to the buckle of his belt.

He snatched her hand. "Now I'm saying it—*no*."

"But why?" she said, her finger looping inside the leather strap to pull it from the metal.

He grabbed both her hands and pulled her arms above her head, the soft hairs of his chest lightly brushing her breasts. "Because I'm the one who's supposed to be driving you insane, not the other way around." Then he kissed her hard and slid down to his knees, bringing her legs together before he latched hold of her panties and slipped them from her.

"Jesus," he whispered, his gaze fixed.

"Oh no," she said, clamping hold of the coverlet, bunching it between her fingers. With her dress off, her bra dangling off her shoulders, and now her underpants gone, she stiffened with a sudden attack of self-consciousness. No doubt brought on by the vision of perfection above her. "Seems I'm a bit exposed," she murmured.

"You're lovely," he said hoarsely. His finger glided up the expertly manicured strip of blonde coils centered atop her pussy. "Christ, you're sure a curly little thing, *n'est-ce pas?*" He smoothed where she'd been waxed. "So hot, your *chatte rasée.*"

Charlotte shuddered from his touch, her eyes fluttering. "I s-swim a lot."

"Kind of like a landing strip," he said, his thumb ruffling the curly patch.

She bucked, the slight pressure jolting her. "Don't tease me—please. I'm sure you've seen it before."

"Oh Charlotte," he murmured, spreading her legs as he slid his hand between them, "teasing you is all I want to do." He kissed her belly, and slipped a finger inside.

"Ohh-ohh . . ." she whimpered, nearly sliding off the bed.

"*Ta chatte est tellement mouillée . . .*" he whispered, kissing his way across her belly to her thigh. He slid his finger in and out, his thumb flicking her rock-hard clit. Charlotte squirmed, writhing against his hand, tiny sparks shooting behind her eyes. His tongue went from hot to cool as he blew against her wet skin, her forehead breaking out in a sweat when his trailing slipped to the inside of her thigh.

"Oh Rex . . . Rex . . ." she moaned, twisting atop the coverlet as his tongue trailed closer and closer to her most sensitive spot. Her hips swiveled with the cadence of his finger thrusting in and out, pleasure tremors beginning to rumble deep inside. She threw back her head, reveling in this slow, steady bliss, waiting for that easy roll of release. That is until his finger withdrew and his tongue suddenly stopped trailing, just above her clit.

"Rex . . . ?" she said, lifting her head.

He grasped her hips, and dove in.

"*Rex!*" she yelped, his tongue savaging her, licking, sucking, devouring, his finger stroking her mercilessly. Her hips lifted as she bucked against his mouth, Rex palming her belly to keep her steady. Within seconds she felt herself rising, but it was no ordinary roll of release. It was lightning fast and deliciously violent, a hard, wickedly jolting explosion of pleasure that sent Charlotte clutching Rex's back, her head thrown back in a silent scream so relentless she nearly lost her breath.

Rex slid up her body to capture her mouth, his finger still circling her clit. "That's it *belle*—come for me. Come as hard for me as I'll come for you." He kissed her, biting her lip as she was still coming, still gasping for breath when he cupped his hands under her *derrière*, gathered her into his arms.

"Oh Rex . . ." She sighed, kissing his neck. "That was wonderful—*you* were wonderful."

"Then will you do something for me?" he said. "Just a little thing?"

"What's that?" she said, the backs of her fingers smoothing his cheek.

A few moments passed before he spoke again, his eyes visibly tracing her, as if taking a scan for memory. "I would like to see you. I would like to see *all* of you." Then he looked at her with trepidation, as uneasily as she'd ever seen him. "Would you do that for me?"

She was mystified. "But can't you see me now? Or do you . . ." All at once she couldn't speak. Because all at once she knew exactly what he was asking for. And it thrilled her.

She kicked off her shoes and got up, Rex sliding past her to sit on the edge of the bed, Charlotte rolling her shoulders until her bra slid down her arms and off. Now fully naked she reached back, plucking the clips from her hair until her wild, wiry curls fell down her back, Rex watching in silent fascination as she tousled it.

"Is this what you want?" she said, stepping into the spread of his legs.

"*Oui*," he said, transfixed, his hands propped on either side of him. He looked into her eyes, continuing in his own language. "You're so beautiful. May I touch you?"

She couldn't help laughing, answering in the same. "Isn't that what you've been doing for the last few minutes? Why is it any different now?"

"Because that was for you. This time it's only for me." He looked almost ashamed to admit it. "Do you mind?"

The idea that her mere body, something she never

thought of as exceptional, could produce such a response in him was exciting beyond every erotic thought she'd ever had. "Mind?" she continued *en français*, raking her fingers through his thick hair. "If that's the way you feel, then believe me, Rex, it won't only be for you. Oh, hardly." She moved closer, placing her hands on his shoulders.

Within a breath his hands were feathering over her shoulders and down her sides, his touch light and tentative as he murmured, "*Si belle . . . si belle*," his thumbs curving down her breasts to barely wisp across her nipples. They skipped around her areolas, slowly circling, the pinked flesh pebbling beneath. "*J'adore les seins belle*," he murmured, his eyes hooding.

Charlotte sighed, wavering until Rex steadied her, his hands slipping down to her waist to grasp it lightly. Her breath hitched as his fingers skimmed across her navel, his hands trailing to her hips to send rolling waves of heat through her body. He trailed further, reaching around to the slope of her *derrière*, lingering as his thumbs stroked the sides of her thighs. Charlotte leaned into his touch, swaying slightly as he smoothed her pebbling skin up and down. The combination of heat and chill was making her dizzy and she sighed again, Rex slowly bringing his hands around her thighs to the flat of her belly.

"Charlotte . . ." he whispered, his dark eyes fixed on her, "you are so very, very lovely." Then his thumb dropped to her still-hardened clit and all at once she was coming, her hips shaking in his grasp.

"Rex . . ." she groaned, clutching his shoulders as she fought to stay upright. He held on to her, his fingers tightening around her hips, his eyes never leaving hers as one glorious spasm after another racked through her body. When they finally stopped he clasped her to him, his cheek against her belly.

"Oh my . . ." she said breathlessly, "that was unexpected. See what you do to me? I thought that was supposed to be for you."

He kissed her stomach, laughing against it. "Who said it wasn't? Do you have any idea how hot it is to watch a woman coming? I want to throw you to the bed right now and shove myself inside you."

She bent to him, saying against his lips. "Then why don't you? I'm right here—naked and waiting."

He sucked in a breath and flipped her to the bed, his hand at his fly as he spread her legs with his.

"Oh damn!" She stopped him, her hand pressing against his chest. "I just called for the Chinese food—remember? They ought to be here any second."

"*Fils de pute,*" he muttered, launching a streak of French curses into the air. He straightened, pulling her with him. "Come with me," he said, grabbing her robe from a hook on the wall. "I'm going to shave and shower," he said, helping her into it, "and you can sit with me while we wait for the food." He turned her around, kissing her quickly. "When it comes we'll leave it on the bedside table because I know I'll be starving after."

She eyed him coyly. "After *what*?"

His eyes gleamed wickedly. "*My* turn."

And now, there sat the Chinese food, waiting for him. She glanced from the bag to where his shower water was still raining. It gave her an idea. She dropped her robe to the floor, and left for the bathroom.

When she shoved the shower curtain aside he turned, water and soap suds runneling down the muscled sinks and angles of his body. He looked like something out of a glossy magazine and Charlotte's stomach flipped, especially when it trailed to what was hardening against his exquisite thigh. His mouth curved. "What took you so long?" he said, hand extended.

"Well, there was that food to wait for . . ." She took his hand, stepping inside. He shoved the curtain back and she turned to him, falling to her knees.

REX STARTED HARDENING the moment he heard her step across the threshold. Within seconds she was before him, his raging erection in her hand.

"Holy shit . . ." she whispered, gaping, "you *are* goddamned T-Rex." Then she opened her mouth and took him straight down her throat.

Rex slammed back against the wall, the water raining over them. He needed it to cool the fire racing through him as she cradled his balls, her mouth doing its absolute best to drive him out of his mind. He fisted his hand into her hair until it coiled in silken tangles around his fingers.

"Charlotte, *chérie*." He clenched his eyes as a gasp escaped him, his hips shifting as her tongue flicked the tip of his cock in agonizingly quick repetition, her hand encircling him just below, pumping, stroking. She gave him a good suck before letting go, trailing her tongue down the hot length of his shaft to his balls. She opened her mouth, closing it over them.

"Goddamnit woman . . ." he growled, his knee hitting the shower wall, but if it hurt he didn't notice. He was too caught up in the motions of this gorgeous *femme*, watching in wonder as her tongue licked a fiery trail back to the head of his cock.

She sucked as if she just invented the word. As if she were taking him someplace he'd never been, but why would he give a damn about the destination when the journey was already this good? Each lusciously erotic motion built upon the other until all at once everything surged forward and his jaw dropped, pleasure colliding so recklessly inside him he—

Did he scream? He wasn't sure. Because if he had he couldn't hear it past the fireworks going off in his head. His hips jerked and he was coming in endless waves, Charlotte draining every milliliter of pleasure out of him until he was gasping like a landed fish, spent and absolutely boneless.

"Jesus Christ . . ." he murmured when he finally stilled, Rex catching a wariness in Charlotte's eyes. As if she were waiting for his assessment, as a schoolgirl would after the first demonstration of a lesson. But Charlotte hardly seemed a student. Her skill was masterful and he felt a sudden jealousy toward anyone who'd ever gotten the benefit of it. As she rose he slipped his hands to her cheeks and kissed her, still reeling from the small miracle she'd performed on him.

After a few moments he broke their kiss, saying, "Where the fuck did you learn to give head like that?"

Her mouth crooked. "Like it?"

"*Like* it?" He kissed her until she was just as boneless as he. "My cock nearly exploded."

"I'll take that as a good thing." She slipped her arms around him. "So what now?"

"We eat," he said, reaching back to turn off the shower. "*Food.*"

Chapter Eleven

Main Course

"OPEN YOUR MOUTH, *chérie*." When she did he plopped in a fried wonton. "Can you tell which one that is?"

Charlotte chewed. She had no idea. "Shrimp?"

"No—crab. But seriously, does it matter?" Rex clamped his chopsticks around another. "How about one more?"

She fell back against the pillows, her hand flat against her belly. "I'm so full now if I eat one more thing I'll collapse the mattress."

He set the carton to the bedside table and shifted under the sheet, arching his arm over her. "I can think of an infinitely better way to do that."

She walked her fingers up his bare chest until they curved around his cheek. "Can you now?"

"*Oui*. If you'll let me. Will you?"

Funny he should ask. Anyone could observe the obviousness of the situation. There they were, naked under sheets illuminated by soft lamplight, feeding each other Chinese takeout as each basked in the afterglow. Charlotte knew it hardly mattered how separately their pleasure had been meted out, as both had been benefactors and beneficiaries. And the fact that his desire—as well as her own—had hardly been slaked, was so evident the air fairly pulsated with lust. All anyone needed to do was glance at Rex's eyes to see the longing in them, to see Charlotte reflecting his back. So why suddenly did their potential joining give her pause? She laughed to herself. That, too, ought to be as plain as day.

This is Rex Renaud we're talking about. International business leader. Confidant to presidents and prime ministers. Man of the world.

Industrial gigolo.

Yes, there is that. . .

He brushed the hair from her eyes. "Have I told you how lovely you look, my gorgeous little secret weapon?"

As well as suave, debonair, and ruthless to the core. She wondered if all his conquests were brought to their knees this quickly. And if so, when was her expiration date? Her best guess was court time, Friday morning. If she even lasted that long. Though chances were she would because didn't great men need diversions too? And the fact she could service both his legal and carnal needs was an absolute testament to his efficiency, as well as his fiscal sense.

If not his heart.

But hearts didn't matter in this game as a heart would be a definite liability. And knowing that, she needed to put her own aside and remind herself how much good she could do with his two million. How many of those so-called hammers he accused her of carrying she could buy to bust through the glass ceiling. How many men similar to Rex she could bring to heel.

So was it just his money she wanted? Of course it was, she reminded herself. Yes, she was attracted to him, but she'd never get any further than that, no matter how tenderly he looked at her, no matter how sharp his wit, no matter if he was just as coldblooded as she was often accused of being. He was her diversion too, and she shouldn't forget it, no matter how extraordinary he made her feel, inside and out.

"Charlotte," he whispered, sinking lower, "did you hear me?"

She shifted toward him, her legs entwining with his. "How could I forget? You said I was lovely."

"That wasn't all." His lips brushed hers and she opened to him, his tongue slipping inside to claim every corner of her mouth. When she sighed he tilted his head and deepened his kiss, his hands cradling her cheeks as his chest slid to hers, bare skin to bare skin. She sighed, raising her arms over her head to grasp the spindles of the headboard. "Charlotte, didn't I ask you something, too?"

"I think you did," she whispered against his mouth. "But for the life of me I can't remember what it was right now."

He laughed softly, kissing her neck. "Very good, *ma belle*, very good."

He reached past her, grasping both her wrists in one hand. When he did her breasts tightened and flattened out, her nipples hardening as they pressed against his chest. He leaned over, taking one in his mouth. He suckled one then the other, sharping them to taut peaks. Charlotte groaned as he kissed his way down the valley between them, spreading her legs with his.

"I want to be inside you, Charlotte," he said, moving atop her, a fevered look in his eyes. "Is it what you want, too?"

"Oh God yes," she said breathlessly, any reservations she might have had a few minutes prior evaporating.

He let go of her hands and reached to the bedside table, retrieving a condom. In expert time, he was ready and poised at her entrance. "*Tu es très belle*," he murmured. "*Tu me donnes envie de te bourrer.*" He kissed her, lingering at her mouth. "It's been a long time for you?"

"Yes," it embarrassed her to say. She hoped he couldn't decipher the real truth in that statement. Which was, she admitted, "I've never been that lucky with men."

"Well, that's good, *chérie*, don't you know?" He kissed her cheek, the sensitive spot behind her ear, her neck. "Your luck with men has led you to me. And for that, I'm grateful as hell." He raised up, easing himself in.

He wasn't halfway in before she huffed, arching her neck, her hands falling to his hips. It wasn't as if he'd hurt her. The feeling was more curious than that. It was more like her insides were a wool sweater and he was stretching her back to normal. Still, he must have sensed something amiss as he paused.

"Are you all right, *ma p'tit*?" he said, nuzzling her neck. "If you're not I'll pull out."

"Don't you dare," she said, squeezing his hip. "You, uh, just take some getting used to."

"I appreciate your candor," he said, easing in some more. "Because if you want some more . . ." He eased all the way in, his eyes closing in bliss, before he stilled again. "You feel fucking incredible."

"I'm so happy you're pleased," she said, sliding her hands down his rock-hard ass. "But I bet you say that to all *les filles*." Then as a thought struck her, she couldn't help laughing.

"What's so funny?" he said, flinching as she stroked him.

"I was just thinking where we were not even twenty-four hours ago. How I was spitting my venom at you at the police station. How I wanted to see you rot there." She laughed again, looking at him. "And now here we are. I wouldn't have believed it then."

He looked down on her, his cock deep inside her, his eyes heavy and lidded. "Do you want to know what I was thinking then?"

"Oh yes," she said honestly.

"I was thinking how much I wanted to do—*this*," he said, giving three hard thrusts.

She jolted, groaning. "That is so—typical," she said, stretched sufficiently to savor the invasion. "You're arrested and charged with a felony, then someone with tits walks in and the only thing you think of is your cock."

He leaned on one arm, tracing her lips with his thumb. "I wasn't only thinking of my cock, *ma belle*. I was thinking of it in relation to you."

"Only because I was there. I'm sure if anyone else with tits showed up, you'd have the same reaction."

"Oh hardly," he said. "It was only because of—"

"Because men only think with their—"

"Jesus Christ! *C'est des conneries*—do you hear yourself?" He pulled himself from her and rolled to his back. "There I am with my *bite* inside you and you're debating whether I find you desirable? *C'est incroyable!*" He threw his hands in the air with an unmistakably Gallic huff. "You've had trouble with men? No wonder they don't all run away screaming."

Charlotte couldn't move, mortified. She couldn't have been more startled if he'd thrown a bucket of ice water over her head. "I was only—"

"*Ta gueule!*" he cried, silencing her with a string of French curses. He huffed again, then sat up, looming over her, his hair tousled from his raking, his eyes jet-black and seething. "Charlotte." He took a breath. "Listen to me. You are one of the funniest, smartest, savviest women—no—*people* I know, not to mention how goddamned hot you are. But *mon Dieu*, you're so insecure—how can you say you're a feminist when you still measure your worth against anyone who happens to have a cock?"

She turned away. "You're wrong."

"Am I? That's why you give head like a call girl, and you probably don't even enjoy it. It's because you know it makes your victims vulnerable. And it lets you beat them at their own game."

She whipped around to glare at him. "Is that what my lovers are? Victims?"

"That's what you turn them into. You're on top, and that's the only way you want it."

"Oh, so I'm just supposed to be passive?" she said, her eyes stinging. "Just lay back and let the guy go to town on me? Like you did before—" She flipped her hand toward the end of the bed.

"No," he said softly, incredulous. "That was *me* bringing pleasure to *you*. That was to show you how much I—" He slammed his hand against the headboard, rattling it. "Goddamnit, Charlotte! Who the fuck fucked with your head! How could you be so normal otherwise, but pull your panties down and you turn into a crazy woman."

That was about all she could stand. "You go to hell," she said, bolting from the bed.

He was on her in an instant, pinning her to the wall before she could run out of the room. "Charlotte," he said from behind, "*ne me laisse pas. S'il vous plaît.*" He kissed her neck, saying softly in her ear, "I only said those things because I want to understand you. I want to know what's behind all this anger. Please tell me, *belle*. I want to know."

It *was* anger. The realization came to her suddenly, as all epiphanies usually did. What else could it be? But how could she admit it? Least of all, to Rex. He'd see her as weak, then where would she be?

"I don't know," she finally said, her fingers clenching.

"Sure you do," he said, his hands closing over hers. "It just hurts too much to examine it." He turned her in his arms. "You just have to let yourself think about it, not ignore it every time a situation brings you too close to confronting it. Believe me, I know how you feel. I used to let the anger get to me, too."

What comfort it was just talking to him. Something which she could never allow herself to get used to. As if he'd ever give her the chance. "And now you just get even?"

He smiled. "You ought to try it sometime. It's the best hard-on in the world. Next to this." He kissed her, gathering her up until she wrapped her legs around him. When she did, he drove himself inside her.

"Oh God," she groaned, flinging her arms around his neck as he kissed her, first with tenderness, then with heat. "I'm so sorry," she said when he allowed her to speak. "You were right, everything you said."

"I always am," he said, stepping back so Charlotte's shoulders lay against the wall, angling himself in deeper. "I'm going to fuck you now, Charlotte. And when I do we're going to enjoy it just for what it is. No games. No one-upmanship."

"Oh Rex," she said, sighing from the feel of him inside her. "If we could do that then I guess it'd be a first for both of us."

He grinned with wicked pleasure. "*C'est ma fille*," he said, ramming her hard. "My sassy little *chienne*." And from there, it was just a matter of degrees.

He held on to her, one arm under her *cul* as the other he braced against the wall, as Rex thrust into her without mercy, Charlotte crying, *"Plus fort—plus fort!"* Harder, harder, *"Plus fite—plus fite!"* Faster, faster. Until he whirled her around to set her atop the dresser, bottles and assorted paraphernalia flying to the floor.

"How is it, *ma belle*?" he asked, Charlotte loving the feel of him, the intimacy of his press into her. He smoothed his hand down her hip. "I don't want to hurt you."

"You can't possibly hurt me," she said, "not after these two long years. Please . . ." She raised up against him, curling her arm around his neck. "Please please please just fuck me."

So he did, wordless and with even more intensity, Charlotte threading her fingers into his hair. She tilted her head, feeling wanton, Rex's gaze fixed on her so tightly it almost scared her. He was too handsome, too flawless—why, even the tiny mole high on his cheekbone suited him to perfection. As was his advice, matching her own feeble commands. "Fuck me . . ." she ordered. "Just fuck me." She grasped him by the shoulders and wrapped her legs around him, pulling him in deeper. Much to her surprise, and just like he had asked her, she was enjoying every thrust just for what it was.

Incredibly so.

Rex groaned. *"Coquette,"* he whispered, and shoving a stack of towels aside, bore down, slamming her hard. He looked to their left, spying her Louboutins. "We'll have to try it with those on."

"Got a thing for shoes—do you?" She huffed, tossing her head to the side. "Oh—you typical *man*."

"There's nothing typical about me," he growled, grinding his hips. "As for you . . ." He smiled. "You're nothing short of extraordinary."

"Yes I am," she said, and he kissed her soundly, lingering. When he finally let her speak she added, "But how can you possibly know?"

He smoothed her hair. "I wouldn't have asked for you if I didn't think so."

She sighed, sliding her bare feet down his hips as he worked his magic. She lifted her hips, matching her rhythm to his. The sensation was like riding a wave, each swell a slow-building pleasure, leaving her loosened as well as emboldened.

"How's do I feel?" she murmured, her hands at his hips. "Do I feel as incredible for you as you do for me?"

He looked up at her, breathless, his mouth slightly opened, his eyes a glimpse into an entirely different world. "They need to invent a new word for how you feel to me," he said in a gravelly baritone. He kissed her hard, his hand sliding to her breast, his fingers kneading it until she sighed from their hot, possessive feel.

From there the waves increased, climbing higher, stretching further, until their undulations rose with a tidal force. As he relentlessly pushed her on, Charlotte felt a charge building within her, jolting her with each impact. She gripped his shoulders and he pulled her into his arms, Rex kissing her over and over as he drew her close, his heart beating soundly against hers.

"I want to come—but not before you," he whispered, his eyes fixed on her. "I want to watch you lose control." He gripped her tighter, saying against her mouth, "I want to see you lose it because of me."

"Oh God oh God . . ." she moaned, his cock buried so thoroughly inside her it seemed to fill every inch of her body. She dropped her head to his shoulder, damp from his exertion, her own breath heating her as she panted against his neck. Suddenly his hand slid between them, his fingers trailing to the intimate folds of her skin to its most sensitive spot and she jolted, sparks flying behind her eyes.

All at once Charlotte threw her head back, a wail rising up from her throat as she went rigid with the force of her release. Rex closed his eyes, finally letting loose, Charlotte's cries sending him over the edge.

A few moments later Rex opened his eyes, smiling as looked down on her. "*Bonsoir*," he said, tracing a finger down her cheek.

"*Ça va?*" she answered, lifting up to brush her lips against him.

"Oh, *très bien*," he said. "Just finished making love to this beautiful woman. You ought to see her." He smoothed back her hair. "Gorgeous."

"Yeah?" She laughed, wriggling against him, aftershocks roiling through her from his half-flaccid cock, still within her. "Well, you ought to see who I've just been with. As a matter of fact . . ." She looked askance a moment. "I think you're him."

"And don't you forget it," he said, pulling himself from her as he stood up. He rolled the condom from him and tossed it in the trash, returning to kiss her just below her belly. "If I could, I'd fuck you as you are right now. Just to see that look on your face again as you were coming around me." He slid even lower. "As a matter of fact . . ."

He spread her legs and in one swift motion sank a finger into her. Charlotte yelped, grabbing his hand, her first reaction to push it away. She was still too sensitive, still feeling the afterburn from the last rocketing orgasm he had given her. But he gave her no quarter, and inside a minute she was coming more violently than she ever had before. Rex pulled out as her hips lifted off the dresser and a spasm of pleasure ripped through her, his thumb shifting to her clit as he watched her go over the edge.

"Lovely," he said, carrying her to the bed.

As she lay there panting, she said, "I will pay you back for that, rest assured."

"And don't think I won't hold you to your word." He climbed in beside her, kissing her neck, then long and languorously on the mouth. Then he propped his arm up and leaned over her, tracing her collarbone with his finger. "Sex with you is sure interesting."

She eyed him warily. "Isn't *interesting* just a code word for *terrible*?"

"Perhaps, but I mean it just as it sounds. It *is* interesting."

She pushed herself up, facing him. "You're going to have to explain that."

He waved his hand between them. "Look at us. Here we are, naked, your *chatte* no doubt still vibrating, while you've given me the best workout in a week."

A wave of heat streaked through her. She slid her leg up, restoring herself to partial modesty. "Well, that's putting it bluntly."

"*Non*, don't do that," he said, nudging her knee down. "Why are you hiding yourself from me? Don't you think we're beyond that?"

"Okay, if that's the way you feel." Charlotte rolled to her back, twisting her body like a centerfold. "Is this interesting enough for you?"

"It's certainly interesting me," he said, throwing a leg over her. "Now, this is what I'm talking about." He swept his hand between them. "What *we've* been talking about. It's the fact we *do* talk, before, during and after sex. We're talking now—even after. And that's something I never do." He leaned down, kissing her tenderly. "Something I've never *wanted* to do."

She looked up, twirling a lock of hair. "You mean you usually just get up and leave?" She tsked. "That's typical."

"Well, it's either that, or roll over and collapse."

"Yeah, that's a close second." She peered at him. "Why do men do that?"

He laughed, propping himself up on his elbow. "Usually because they're exhausted, but more than likely, because they've accomplished what they've come to do."

"*Come* being the operative word," she said dryly.

"You have no idea how true that is. Like in that old David Bowie song—*wham bam thank you ma'am*. And when they're done? It's either get out or go to sleep."

She was almost afraid to ask. "Is it like that with me, too?"

"Hardly." Then his mouth crooked with a mix of amusement and candor. "Charlotte, now that you've calmed down, sex with you is, well . . . *fun*."

She wasn't sure what to think of that, not that he gave her much time to ponder it, kissing her again. Coming from Rex Renaud, though, she supposed it would be a compliment of the highest order, and something she shouldn't take lightly. She curled into him, resting her head on his shoulder. "Well, thank you, Rex," she said. "That's the best thing you've said to me all day. I *think*."

"You're the best thing that's happened to me all day." Then he winced. "Such a shame I have to leave you so soon."

"Not a shame at all," Charlotte said as she rolled off the bed. "Because I'll be going with you."

Chapter Twelve

Dessert

"OH NO. FORGET it," Rex said, sliding to his side of the bed. "You're not going to D.C. Absolutely not."

"I think you should reconsider," Charlotte said, grabbing a carton of chicken fried rice. "You know? I think this stuff tastes better cold." She held it. "Want some?"

"*Non, merci,*" he said. "And don't try to be so blasé about it. You're still not going. You need to stay here and cover for me. If you're not here, then we both look suspicious."

"But if only one of us is here, then it's worse." She abandoned the chopsticks and switched back to a plastic spoon. "No, I'm thinking it's better if we both go. All or nothing."

He glanced into her carton, bypassing it for the bed-side table and a spring roll. "I'd like to hear how you'd justify that."

"Well, for starters," she said around a mouthful of rice, "if the cops happen to come around and I'm the only one here, don't you think they're going to think it strange?"

"*Beurk*." He winced, dropping the spring roll after only one bite. "These most definitely do not benefit from sitting on the nightstand for an hour. Pass me the sweet and sour pork."

She did, but only after stealing a piece of pork. "Look, we were out all day with the car parked in the garage. I mean the cops even *saw* where we parked it. So if any-one's keeping an eye on us, they're already used to that scenario."

He considered that. "So what if they're waiting for us to leave again, and they don't see us come out?"

"Then they'll just think we're in here doing what we just did because that's what you wanted them to—oops." She looked down, a lump of scrambled egg landing atop her left breast. As she went to pluck it off, Rex brushed her hand aside.

"Allow me," he said, bending into her. He cupped his hand around her breast and licked it off. "There," he said, "all cleaned up."

"You know," she said, "if you can make coffee, I'll hire you."

He gave her a quick kiss. "*Ma beauté*, for you, I'll work for free. I'm thinking the perks more than make up for the long hours."

"Long hours?"

"*Oui*. I mean, look at the time." He clamped onto a wedge of pineapple. "We've already been at it two-three hours now, and we've hardly begun." Rex sat back, drawing a leg up, his chopsticks clicking around the candied vegetables.

"You know, you wield a mean pair of chopsticks," she said, glancing over. "Where'd you learn to do that?"

He dumped some brown rice atop the pork. "We have an office in Shanghai," he said. "And whenever I'm there I always try to drop in at this place near Taizing Lu. They serve up a *shengjianbao* so *fantastique* it'll make the eyes roll back in your head." He used his chopsticks for emphasis. "You would love it, really. As a matter of fact—"

"I think you're trying to distract me," she said, setting down the fried rice. "There was a point I was trying to make, you know."

"Oh?" *Click-click.* "And that was?"

"Look. You need to see the congresswoman, right?"

"*Oui.* I'm crashing her lunch with Representative Hitchell."

She knew it was illogical, but that irked her. She never even saw the woman, but she couldn't get the image of those two going at it out of her mind. "Really. Where?"

He frowned into the carton. "Here, *belle*, this is getting nasty." he said, handing it to her. "Pass me the lo mein."

"Where for lunch . . . ?"

"The Hay-Adams." He prodded her shoulder. "The lo mein, *chérie.*"

She passed it to him. "That's a hotel, isn't it? Near the White House?"

"Yes, it is." He took a quick sip of wine, then wound

the chopsticks around a few noodles, dropping them into his mouth. "I'm a bit partial to their Cobb salad." He dropped his gaze to the lo mein, frowning again. "Unlike this."

"And I'll bet you had many an occasion to eat it."

"Well, I usually stay there when I'm in Washington, and it's where Lilith and I would . . . meet." He looked over. "I believe you're looking a bit green, Charlotte."

"Me? Nah." She turned to the bedside table and plucked a spring roll from a bag of them. "It's just interesting you're meeting the congresswoman at the hotel you used to, well . . ." She bit into the roll, chewing with purpose.

"Hey." He set down his carton and turned to her. "As I told you before, there's nothing between us and there never was. Ever."

"If you say so," she said, still chewing.

He huffed. "I'd like to kiss you, Charlotte, so swallow." His mouth crooked. "I know you know how to do *that*."

She did. "Very funny." He slipped his arm around her neck and drew her in, his mouth falling to hers.

He tasted of lo mein and Pinot, a mix of salty and sharp, and oh, how close that came to the real Rex. But what *was* the real Rex? Had she any idea? Could he really be like the side he'd shown her here tonight, the one that made her stand back and take a good look at herself, or the other, the methodically cool calculator who used sex as a business tool? She really couldn't be sure. She needed to break through his shell as he'd broken through hers, but for right now . . . All she knew was she was starting to crave the way his kisses tasted, whether they were salty or sharp or too sweet for her own good. He broke their kiss, looking down on her, the hand resting just below her breasts, gently stroking her.

"You feel good in my arms," he said, his face uncharacteristically relaxed.

What a nice thing to say. "I feel good being in them." And totally unexpected. Like her reply.

He ran his finger down her nose, shivering her. "Ever since we first met in Boston, I told myself that on my next trip to the U.S. I was going to call you. Look." He turned to the bedside table, reaching for his billfold. He slid a card from it, handing it to her.

"Oh my," she said. It was her business card. "How did you get this? I don't recall giving it to you. I surely never would have in Boston."

"You gave it to one of our lawyers," he said. "I saw it on top of one of their portfolios and slipped it away when he wasn't looking."

"You did?" She laughed, taken aback. "But why?"

"Well, I was damned sure you'd never give it to me. You were hating anything with a Y chromosome that day. But you impressed me." He took the card from her, tucking it back into his billfold.

"I wondered how you were able to get in touch with me last night. Gee." She thought a moment. "Has it only been since yesterday?"

"And here we are," he said as she leaned back against the pillows. He kissed her again, his leg sliding over hers. She could feel him ratcheting up again, and she wasn't quite ready for that, especially after what he'd just said. Could he possibly be more serious about her than she thought? Was he even capable of that? The idea both thrilled and terrified her. Rex was so different from all the men she'd ever known, yet so understanding of what she was about she could picture herself falling for him. Even so, something was lingering beneath his surface that still gave her pause, something she could quite put her finger on. Though one thing was for sure. He nipped the corner of her mouth. He sure knew his way around a kiss. She gripped his shoulders, her toes tingling as his hand slid down her leg. Quite a contradiction for a man who could be as ruthless as he was romantic.

"Um, Rex?" she said.

"*Oui, ma belle?*" he murmured, his arms caging her, his eyes hooded.

She held up her hand, fingers still pinching the half-bitten spring roll. "I'd really like to get rid of this."

"*Merde.* What are you still doing with that? *C'est dégueulasse.*"

"I'll remind you the Chinese takeout was your idea."

He glanced to each of their bedside tables, both overflowing with half-eaten cartons and trays. "I think it's served its purpose." His face screwed. "I'm most definitely not hungry."

"Not even for dessert?" Charlotte said. "There's still those éclairs downstairs."

His face lit. "Oh. Those." He turned to her. "The ones I'm supposed to eat off your belly?"

"Yes, those." She climbed from the bed and slipped

into her robe, plucking the big take-out bag from the floor. "Let me get rid of this, and I'll be back with dessert. I have coffee if you'd like me to make some."

He waved her off. "*Non*, it'll only keep me up and I really need to get some sleep." He glanced to her, his smile wicked. "Then again . . ."

She shoved the cartons into the bag. "I'll see if there's any more wine," she said, going to his side of the table. He slid his empty containers into the bag, then reached for his phone, scrolling before he clasped it to his ear.

"Don't be long," he said.

But then he flashed her a look that didn't quite say, *Will you excuse me?* but the intent was clear enough. Perhaps it was because asking for privacy after being naked together for three hours could be a bit awkward. Charlotte nearly laughed at the irony. Perhaps that little gesture was a big part of why she still held this strange liaison with the very mysterious Rex at arm's length. In her head, at least, and most certainly in her heart. But then again, he sat at the helm of one of the world's biggest corporations. She glanced back as he tended to a bit of business, the sheet molding his body. Yet there he was, naked in her bed. *I kind of like that*, she thought, leaving for downstairs.

The downstairs she entered into was dark except for the light thrown in from the street, and she paused, letting her eyes adjust. She hadn't been down the shore in weeks and she'd forgotten how the autumn darkened it, being so used to it being lit late into the evening in the summer. Still, after a few moments, she didn't see any use in turning on the lights until the bathroom. She padded into the kitchen, setting the bag on the table before she went to empty her bladder, the sensitivity from Rex's intimate invasion duly noted. When she finished she caught a glimpse of herself in the mirror as she brushed her teeth and ruffled her hair into submission. Never had she looked more thoroughly tossed. *I kind of like that, too*, she thought, turning out the light.

She noticed when she went to the kitchen the take-out bag had fallen over, disgorging its contents all over the table. "Damnit," she muttered, shoving the leaky cartons back in. No sense dumping it into the kitchen trash to ferment, especially since she didn't plan on being there the next day. She gathered it all up to take it to the garbage can outside.

But before she opened the door she noticed something odd out on the street. A couple doors down a car was parked on the curb opposite. She knew most everyone on both sides of the street, at least for half the short block down, and all except for the Gabaldis were summer residents. And although it was common to see people down on weekends at least until Thanksgiving, no one would be down on a Tuesday, and certainly not the occupants of the house where it sat, as they had a long driveway. She dropped the bag in the trash next to the refrigerator, and crept around to the living room for a closer look.

The living room had a side window that gave a clear view of the block and Charlotte hunkered down, trotting half bent up to it, sliding the curtain aside just enough to peek through. After a moment she could see what looked like a very expensive-looking car, with one person in the driver's seat, and although she couldn't quite tell, possibly another one sitting in the back, almost as if they were being chauffeured. Which was certainly strange, at least in this part of town. Although her street harbored a few professionals like herself, no one came close to that type of wealth. She let the curtain drop and crept back upstairs.

"*Bonsoir*," Rex said, just finishing his conversation as she made it back to the bedroom. He tossed the phone to the table as she scurried in. "What are you doing?" he asked, eyeing her curiously.

"Shut off the light," she said, finger pointing to the lamp at his side. She did the same to hers. "Keep down and come here," she said, scrambling to the French doors that led to a small second-floor porch. She edged the curtain aside. "Look. There—just down the street."

He came up beside her, opening the curtain a bit more. "Do you mean that car?"

"That's right. And there's someone in it."

He looked closer. "The cops?"

"Driving *that*? Take a better look at that car. I sincerely doubt it."

He leaned in. "There's someone in the backseat, too." He made a decidedly derisive sound in his throat. "What the hell—"

Just then the car surged forward and made a U-turn, taking off up the street, not turning on its headlights until it was nearly a block away.

Charlotte clutched Rex's arm. "What the hell was that?"

He was still staring into the street. "You're not staying here by yourself tomorrow," he said quietly.

"So I'm going with you to D.C.," she said, not as question.

He turned to her, looking very grave. "Apparently someone is watching us, and it's fairly obvious it's not *les flics*. Not unless they pay the police really, really good in this town."

"In that car? I really don't think so. What was that anyway?"

"A Rolls."

"A Rolls-Royce?" She almost laughed. "Does anyone really drive them these days? I thought they were something you just saw in old James Bond movies."

"No, believe me, people still do drive them." He slid a hand down her arm. "Though not in your tax bracket, I'm afraid. So," he said, looking past her. "Where's the éclairs?"

"How can you think about éclairs when there's someone outside stalking us. For all I know it could be one of those crazy lunatics that wanted to bomb me in Philly."

"Wrong side, *chérie*. The only ones who could afford to stalk you in that car would be sending you flowers instead."

She huffed. "Then it must be one of your mobster friends."

Rex grasped her by the shoulders. "The only mobsters I consort with are the Washington kind, so I sincerely doubt we'll be gunned down by anyone from the backseat of their Rolls. Especially with the chauffeur watching."

"Then who was that?"

"I'm not sure, though I have my suspicions."

"Yeah? Who?" she asked.

"*Chérie*, rest assured, I'm going to find out." His eyes narrowed. "For now know that whoever *is* out there, they're not looking for you. They're looking for me."

"And that's supposed to make me feel better?" she said.

"Perhaps not. But you'll be happy to know it's enough to convince me you're not staying here by yourself. You're coming with me." He kissed her forehead. "And that makes me happy, too."

She laid her head against his chest. Although she couldn't help feeling antsy about being watched, it did give her a measure of comfort that Rex was concerned enough to take her with him. "Let me go get the éclairs then."

"*Non*," he said, walking her back to the bed, slipping the robe from her shoulder as they went. "Just let me take care of a few things, then we'll have something altogether different for dessert." He kissed her forehead, leaving for the bathroom.

She tossed her robe to the chair and climbed in, noticing he had taken his phone with him. Apparently, that car was concerning him much more than he was letting on. In a way, it gave her a charge that it worried him enough not to want to leave her alone. Not that his concern completely overrode the fact he was giving her something to worry about in the first place. Who the hell was tracking him down—and to her house? Obviously there were many things in his life she wasn't privy to, but *Christ almighty*! She hunkered down in the bed. How weird was it that although he'd no doubt be inside her very shortly, for Rex Renaud, that was by far the very least of his intimate connections.

VIVIANE MERCIER WAS at it again. He raked back his hair with an exhausted sigh. When the hell would she finally give up?

It had to be her. Who else did he know that rode around in a chauffeured Rolls-Royce? Still, it made no sense to worry Charlotte until he was sure what she was up to. Which could be almost anything.

Rex knew she wouldn't answer his call, not with this cheap pay-go phone number, so he'd send her a text instead:

I don't know what your game is, but I'm on to you. See you soon, chérie.

He kind of liked the look of that. Seemed much more sinister. Which was how she liked to operate. He also knew she wouldn't answer his text either, but he hit send anyway, then went to take a piss. If the Mercier matriarch was part of this fiasco, then maybe things were finally starting to make sense. But she was only point A to a very distant point B. The real trick would be in figuring out what—or who—was the connector. And that would prove very complicated indeed.

He flushed the toilet, bracing his hand against the wall. Jesus Christ, when would she ever give up? A lesser mortal would've been crushed by the weight of that vendetta a long time ago, but there she was, still carrying it around. When would she ever find peace? When would she ever leave him alone to find his?

He was a businessman, for Christ's sake. He was supposed to sit behind a desk, consult with his board members. Take conference calls. Drink martinis at lunch. Give speeches at consortiums and conventions in Paris and New York. Pore over reports. Vacation on the Riviera. He loved what he did, right down to the very last spreadsheet. And he'd been told he was very, very good at it. Which was only logical. It was what he was raised to be. It's what Marcel was born to do. Why didn't she just leave them be and let them do it?

Though when had anything gone according to plan?

He turned to the sink, washing his hands and splashing his face with cold water. If it had, he'd be married by now to a beautiful but empty-headed woman, who'd run his home and bear him a boy and a girl, a woman he'd shower with diamonds and Prada so she'd look good on his arm at corporate galas. Be an asset to his image, an icon to all the other corporate wives, and the object of envy to his friends. No independent thinking wanted or required. Well, as long as her independent thoughts aligned with his.

He leaned into the sink, brushing his teeth before he dried his face and shut off the light. When he went back to the bedroom she was waiting for him in the dark, the pale light from the street gilding her. She didn't look or act or think like anyone he'd long been told to look for and, he suspected, she never would. Perhaps like music and art and poetry, the beauty was in the perception. And for now, his was making him smile.

"So I'm going with you to D.C.," she said, her hair a fluffy blonde cloud around her head and shoulders. The sheet was tucked up to her armpits as she sat against the headboard. He could see the outline of her breasts beneath it.

"*Oui*," he said, waiting for the other shoe to drop as he slid in next to her. "Your point being . . . ?"

"Well, since you were going without me, you must have had an alternate plan for transportation. I'm sure you weren't thinking of driving my car."

"*Non*. We'll have a car waiting for us in Atlantic City. A very special one."

"Well, speaking of special things, I have a special friend in Washington who may be able to help us," Charlotte said.

"Oh?" he said, sliding next to her against the headboard. He wasn't sure he liked the *special friend* designation. "Who's that?"

"Trent Webster. He's a congressman from New Jersey. Do you know him?"

"I've heard of Secretary of State Webster. Are they related?"

"Trent's his son."

Rex thought a moment. "I met another of the secretary's sons once. Alex Webster. At a party or reception someplace—Princeton, I think."

"That's his oldest brother. He runs the family's banking empire. And you're right. The family's from Princeton, though Trent's in South Jersey. That's how I got to know him, from the charity work he does in Camden, a poor city across the river from Philadelphia. I'm sure Trent can shed the light on something. The whole family's really well connected. Plus he owes me."

"For what?" he said, a shard of jealously ripping through him. He well recalled hearing what a rake Alex was. He was sure Trent wasn't far behind.

Charlotte laughed. "Oh, just more of that pro bono work you're so fond of. I also hold the bar in New Jersey."

"Is there no end to your talents?" Rex said. If there was, then *that* would surprise him.

"Well, I don't know," she said, moving toward him. Rex brought his legs up and she straddled him, her arms around his neck. "Shall we find out?"

"Surprise me," he said, kissing her.

In no time he was more than ready for her, as a few more of his kisses, a few deft strokes, as well as her fingers torturously sheathing him with a condom, made her ready for him.

"*Mon Dieu . . .*" he groaned, Charlotte impaling herself atop him. She leaned back against his legs, allowing Rex to bury himself to the hilt. "*Merde,* you feel *fantastique,*" he whispered, sliding his hands up her sides, his thumbs just under her breasts. "Are you comfortable?"

"Give me a moment," she said, her eyes fluttering as she positioned herself. She groaned, swiveling her hips slightly, sending little electric shocks through his groin. She ran her hand through her hair, biting her lip. "Mmmm . . . you're one big boy, T-Rex."

"And you're one luscious girl," he said, slowly lifting her up and setting her down, leaning in to lick the tip of her breast. But mostly he just sat back and let her fuck him, Charlotte's swiveling and writhing atop his cock sending glorious sensations through his body.

"Oh God, Rex, you feel so good," she whispered, grinding, lifting herself up and down. "But then you always feel good."

"Is that so," he said, sliding his finger to her slickened clit, massaging her until it was rock-hard and throbbing. "Does this feel good too?"

Her answer was a groan long and low, her climax building until all at once her body went rigid with pleasure. As she tightened around him Rex found his own bliss, streams and streams of it as he emptied himself deep inside her. Before long she slumped against him, sated, kissing his cheek.

When they were through, she turned on her side. "Good night," she whispered, her hair spreading threaded gold across his pillow.

"*Bon nuit, ma belle,*" he whispered back, spooning against her. It'd been a long time since he'd spent the whole night with a woman, curling his arm around her.

And knowing what was out there waiting for him, he hoped it wouldn't end too soon.

Chapter Thirteen

Diplomatic Pouch

"Wake up, Charlotte," Rex whispered in her ear. "It's time to get up."

She snuffled and rolled to her stomach, pulling the covers up to her chin. The house was quiet except for the sound of the furnace igniting downstairs, and the soft crash of the surf beyond the street. And, it shocked her to realize, the soft breathing of the man sharing her bed. *Rex*, she thought. Rex Renaud. *I thought I couldn't stand him.*

That was yesterday and a lifetime ago.

She turned to him. He lay on his back with his eyes closed, dark lashes fanning his cheeks, his beard rising. She felt a tingling deep down inside her, especially when she looked to the long, hard expanse of his chest, trailing lower and lower to where the covers stopped just below his navel and tangled around his legs. His eyes opened as he raised his arms over his head.

"*Bonjour*," he said, flexing, his tendons cording.

"*Bonjour*," she whispered back. The tingling returned.

He rolled to his side and she burrowed into his warmth, his arm wrapping around her belly. She could feel him hardening against her, and she wanted him to take her right now, no foreplay, just to sink himself inside her. But she knew he wouldn't, the gentleman that he was, unless she gave him some kind of indication. So she decided to aim for discretion, reaching around to grab his cock.

She sucked in a breath. *Oh my.* There was just something about the first thing in the morning.

She rolled to her stomach again. He rolled to his bedside table. She heard a packet tear and before she knew it, he was atop her from behind and spreading her legs, slipping himself in.

"You have such a beautiful ass," he said *en français*, murmuring French endearments as he slowly filled her.

Charlotte clutched her pillow, biting her lip as he moved inside her, the feeling so exquisite she couldn't help moving with him. He grabbed his pillow and slid it under her belly, angling her higher as he fell in deeper. It was all she needed and she came swiftly and with long, rolling undulations, like the ocean outside the windows. Feeling her climax, he followed, his breath coming in soft, quick, gasps before it leveled out into a slow exhale, his hips resting against her.

He rolled to his side, taking her with him. Still joined,

he kissed her between her shoulder blades, holding her close. "*Mon Dieu*," he whispered, yawning, "that was nice."

She rubbed his thigh. "That's because I love to fuck you."

Charlotte started, her heart leaping in her chest. Did she really just say that? She must have been half asleep. Why oh why would she use *that* word in a sentence?

"What?" he said, yawning again. "Did you say something?"

He didn't even *hear* her? Well, she wasn't about to say it again. "No."

Then he yawned one more time and pulling himself from her, left for the bathroom.

She grabbed her robe and went to the downstairs bathroom, leaning against the kitchen sink when she was done. "Huh," was all she could say, staring into incredulity. She didn't know whether to go sit in the garage, make coffee, or hit him over the head with a frying pan.

Then she heard the bathroom door open. "Charlotte. Are you down there?"

"Yes," she said, huffing.

"Come here, *s'il vous plaît.*"

She didn't know why, but she did, going to where he stood at the bathroom door. When she got there he pulled her in.

"What?" she said.

He held her head between his hands and kissed her. "I love to fuck you, too, you know."

After a moment, she said, "Well, that's good."

He kissed her again. "Do you have any idea how adorable you are?" he said, untying her robe.

"No. Why don't you tell me?"

He reached into the shower, turning it on. "I'll tell you later. Do you know what time it is?" he said, sliding her robe to the floor.

Actually, she didn't. "I give up. What time?"

He stepped into the shower, Charlotte following. "Well, you should feel rested and relaxed."

It surprised her to notice she did. As she should. They went to bed at what—eight-thirty? He stepped aside so she could move into the shower, the spray flattening her curls. "I guess I do."

He squeezed a dollop of shampoo in his hand and scrubbed it into her hair. "Then it shouldn't upset you too much to know it's three."

"Oh my God—that's absolutely obscene," she said, grabbing the soap to rub it across his chest. "You know what?" she said, trailing the soap lower. "So is this."

"Isn't it though," he said, angling her back under the water. "Then it's a good thing we already got *that* out of the way."

"You're so efficient," she said, trailing even lower, and he growled, taking the soap from her.

"But I hear women are very different from men—in that respect." He slid the bar down her torso. "That their opportunities are limitless."

"Oh!" she squeaked, her eyes widening.

A little while later they had temporarily retreated to their separate corners to dress, Charlotte picking out what she thought was a classically feminine dress with a flared skirt, coupled with silk sweater and three-inch pumps. Rex wore one of the two suits he had brought with him, this one a gray pinstripe with a midnight-blue tie.

"Dashing," Charlotte said as she stood behind him at the dresser mirror, smoothing his shoulders as he tied his tie. "You've quite a flair for these things."

He harrumphed, closing his jacket. "I have a man in London and another in Paris I pay ridiculously well to make me look however I do."

"Tell them I admire their work." She swiveled around to him and half sat on the dresser, reaching up to straighten his tie. "You're quite the fashion icon."

His gaze fell to her. "You don't look so bad yourself. As a matter of fact . . ." He pulled her to him, turning her around so they both faced the mirror. "We both cut quite the figure, don't we?"

"We do," she said, to her instant regret. She wished he wouldn't say things like that. They reeked of permanence, and she didn't want to end up wistfully recalling scenes like this long after they had ended.

Apparently, Rex felt the same way as he flashed her a textbook smile, patting her shoulders before he stepped away. "Well, then. We should get on our way. I'm going to rely on your local knowledge to get us to Atlantic City without a car."

"Which is easy, but we'll have to walk a bit," she said, slipping into a tan trench coat. "And because of that mysterious Rolls last night, I suggest we start off on the beach."

"That's all right, I don't mind the sand at all. Then he

stood back, assessing her. "The trench coat adds a definite touch of intrigue."

"Well, this is a covert operation," she said. "Don't you have one?"

"Sadly, no," he said, tucking his phone in his inner pocket. Then he grinned. "But we will have an invisible car."

"Now *that*," she said as she led the way out, "I can't wait to see."

Once downstairs Charlotte led him to the back of the living room where there was another pair of French doors out to the backyard. She pulled the curtain aside to a night clouded over, perfect for stealing through the dark. "We'll cut through the neighbors' yards to get to the beach a block over. Do you mind?"

"I think I can manage it," he said. "Are you ready?"

"Just a second." She trotted to the kitchen, returning with a string-tied white box. "To go with our coffee later," she said, holding the éclairs aloft.

His brow narrowed. "Not the scenario I had in mind for them."

"And it's too late for that now," she said, moving past him toward the door. "Besides, I'm hungry and they're not getting any fresher. But don't worry. I'll let you feed them to me."

"In public? *Chérie*, you're more adventurous than I thought." He came closer, his hand on her shoulder. "Seriously, Charlotte, I don't want you to worry about that car we saw last night."

She was trying to put it out of her head, but apparently

it still showed. "I'm trying not to, but it was so weird. Don't you think?"

"It *was* strange, and I'm working on it."

And why was that? "Do you think you know who it was?"

He paused a moment, seeming to weigh whether or not to tell her. "I have my suspicions." Then he pulled her into his arms. "And if you were just this beautiful woman I'm finding I want to know more and more about every day, I'd tell you. But seeing that you're also a lawyer, well . . ." He paused again, this time, his eyes darkening. "Don't take this the wrong way, but Charlotte, I know how tenacious you are. And I don't want to make accusations until I know for certain. As an attorney, you operate on facts, and I'd rather wait and learn a bit more. Is that all right?"

"That's fine," she said, pulling back. "Because I wouldn't lie for you or anyone. That's not the way I roll."

"I realize that. And I'd never want you to."

"So knowing how our relationship has"—how should she put this?—"*changed*, do you still want me as your lawyer?"

"Oh, *oui*," he said, his embrace tightening a bit. "Even more than I did before. Just know for now, you have nothing to be afraid of. And as soon as I learn more, I'll tell you everything." He kissed her cheek. "Does that make you feel better?"

She smiled, feeling somewhat relieved. "It does but even so, I'm glad you're taking me with you."

"And I'm happy you're coming." He kissed her forehead. "In fact, I always am. Let's go."

They entered into a sandy yard scattered with pea gravel, outdoor furniture still waiting for its winter bundling of plastic. All around them the houses sat dark, both from vacancy and the early hour, and without seeing anything stirring, they crept through a couple of unfenced yards and into the street one block over. At the head of the beach, Charlotte kicked off her shoes.

"Aren't you going to take off yours? Roll up your pants?" she asked, pumps dangling from her fingers.

"My heels aren't three inches," he said, stepping over the short seawall and into the sand. "Plus my legs aren't half as gorgeous as yours."

"I think your legs are dead sexy," she said, taking the hand he offered as he helped her over the seawall. "See, it all depends on perspective."

He eyed her up and down. "I know exactly what you mean."

He kept her hand as they walked across the sand to where the surf hardened had it, the mottled clouds settling an eerie cast upon the water. The beach was quiet and deserted, sunrise still a few hours away, the ocean a sonorous blanket of rippling dark. They walked along, not saying much, until Charlotte broke the silence.

"So," she said. "What's the plan?"

"Ha," he laughed mirthlessly. "You act as if I had one. All I know is I have to get to Lilith and find out what she knows, not to mention I'd like to get my phone back. I've got half my life on that thing."

"Christ," she said. "Haven't you ever heard of iCloud?"

He slanted her a glance. "Haven't you ever heard of

hackers? I don't *cloud* my information, *ma p'tit*. I keep it close to my chest."

She let go of his hand. "Excuse me for thinking you're running a shipping company and not Interpol."

"They're much the same thing," he said, pulling her back beside him. "I don't think you realize just what Mercier does, what it encompasses. There's only one shipping company that can come close to Mercier. Their name is Richette."

"I've heard of them. You see their containers being trucked down the turnpike."

He slanted her a glance. "Along with quite a few Merciers, I'm sure. But they're publicly traded. We're private—still run by the same family for over a hundred and fifty years. We have a hundred ports in over forty countries, employing over one hundred thousand people. We ship oil, food, medicine, lumber—anything you want or need. A company like that can make or break countries. Or the governments who try to run them. With that kind of power the head of a company is always open to sabotage."

"Why, is someone out to get Marcel?"

"Not personally," he said. "Just what he controls."

She thought a moment, then looked up in realization. "Someone's looking to take over the company, aren't they?"

Rex nodded gravely. "It's starting to look more and more like it. The directors have been rumbling lately about going public because they still see Marcel as incapable. But they'd do well not to underestimate him. He *is* brilliant. So much like his father, who expanded the company beyond his predecessors' wildest expectations. You may have heard, though, his father had a stroke a few years back."

"Yes, I did. That's when Marcel's brother, Andy, stepped in to take over as CEO, right?"

"*Oui.* But only until Marcel could find his footing. He's almost there now, and probably this marriage is just the stability he needs. But a lot happened when he was running around. Mercier was almost swallowed up in a hostile takeover, and if it weren't for André's quick thinking and skill with negotiation, it would've happened. You see the dirty little family secret is his mother, Viviane Mercier, was behind it."

Charlotte stared at him. "His *mother?* How could she do that to her own son? Oh wait. Was it because her husband left her for another woman?"

He waved her off. "*Merde*—that's a simplistic American justification. It goes much deeper and much further back. Their first mistake wasn't taking her serious enough as a director. Viviane's a shrewd, shrewd woman, and she didn't take kindly to being passed over as CEO, not for her then twenty-three-year-old son." He stopped, turning to her, his eyes even darker in the thin light. "You see there are people out there who haven't forgotten what almost happened. People who see Marcel as still vulnerable."

"Leaving him open for it happening again." Then it hit her. "That was his mother in the Rolls last night, wasn't it." When he didn't answer, she knew she was right. "Rex, please. You can trust me, really you can."

Rex stopped, turning to look at her, weighing again, no doubt "I know I can," he finally said, touching her cheek. "But I'm only guessing about this. I didn't actually see her, so I can't know for sure. But if it is her, then it'll be up to me to protect Marcel again."

"Wait a minute." She thought she misheard. "What do you mean—*again*?"

"It was me André came to see at Richette," he said. "I was the COO at the time. Marcel's mother had approached us along with a couple of Mercier directors. But then André offered me a deal that would not only make me very rich, but would also tip the balance of Mercier shares to thwart his mother's scheme."

"So you double-crossed her." She stared at him a moment before she laughed. "God, she must hate you."

He laughed as well, though a bit harshly. "There are a lot of people who do. And that's why I've been thinking this dredging bill's passage is the link to this mess. Because if it passes, we can expand, and then Mercier only becomes more valuable. So if someone is truly out to discredit me, it could be the whole scenario starting up all over again."

Maybe it was the sloping surface, or maybe because her shoes were in her hand, but up until then she hadn't quite realized how large and imposing Rex really was. As was the enormity of what he was saying. "You do realize this complicates everything. Between us, I mean."

"Because it means I'll have to trust you." His hands slid up her arms. "Can I?"

"Of course." She knew she could do the same with him.

"*C'est bon.*" He pulled her closer, his thumb smoothing her jawline. "Because I think I'm going to have to."

He kissed her, but it was a kiss different than any of the others he'd given her, and that made it all the more intimate. This wasn't a kiss of lust or even longing. This went deeper than all the physical places he had taken her. Charlotte knew this closed and secretive man had never given this kind of kiss to anyone. This opened a door to his inner workings. And quite possibly to his heart.

"You can," she said, her hand over his.

"*Ma belle* Charlotte," he said, kissing her again. "Thank you. You don't know how much that means to me."

She set her hand to his cheek. "Just tell me what to do."

He threw his arm over her shoulder and glanced toward the dunes, shivering a bit from the wind. "How about getting us the hell off this beach?"

She snaked her hand under his jacket and around him. "Follow me."

From there they walked another couple of blocks to a bus stop, riding it into Atlantic City, to arrive just after four-thirty.

"Caesar's is just up the street," Charlotte said. "I know a little coffee joint around the corner. Let's grab a couple of cups and have our éclairs." Soon after they were sitting on a bench facing the casino sipping coffee, pastries in hand.

"A shame," Rex said, staring at it. "I had such plans."

"That's the lovely thing about plans," Charlotte said,

biting into her. "You can always make more. Along with éclairs."

"A shame, nonetheless." His was gone in two bites. "Come on, let's go into the casino. I'm running low on cash and I need some pocket money."

"What? Your big, black AmEx run out of gas? I thought you one-percenters didn't believe in folding money."

He downed the last of his coffee, tossing it into a nearby trash can. "*Merde*, that tasted like shit. I could never get used to coffee in a paper cup. Listen *avocate*, first rule of thumb—paper money, no paper trail."

"Ah, now I get it." She stood, bending at the waist. "I bow to your superior conspiratorial skills. Lead on, Dreyfus."

"*Jeune fille sarcastique*," he muttered, grabbing her hand.

They wandered into the casino from the boardwalk, the floor subdued on the weekday morning. Most of the pits were closed except for a select few blackjack, roulette, and craps, the meandering cocktail waitresses serving more coffee to the pit bosses and clerks than drinks to the players.

"You know it's getting close to five o'clock," Charlotte warned as they strolled past the craps pits. "Don't we have to pick the car up by five-fifteen?"

"This won't take long," he said, scanning the floor, by-passing craps as it fed into the roulette wheels.

"Why am I not surprised you're not a craps man," Charlotte said. "Roulette, of course. *Si français*."

"And so wrong," he said, aiming for the blackjack pits. He picked the only hundred-dollar table open and walked up to it, just as the dealer stifled a yawn. He threw a bill down, standing behind the chair.

"Aren't you going to sit down?" Charlotte whispered from behind.

He set the single black chip to the table. "It won't take that long."

Five minutes later they were walking to the cashier's window with a short stack of purple chips. "Holy shit, Rex—how much did you win?"

He gave it a quick count. "Only sixty-five hundred dollars. I could've won more if we had more time, but how much do you need?"

She eyed him suspiciously. "Are you a counter?"

"You're joking, right? I'm almost offended."

"An evasive answer if I ever heard one. You know, you're quite good at that." She waved her hand in front of her face. "Never mind anyway. I don't want to know or before long I'll be representing myself at my own trial." They stepped up to the window.

He walked away with mostly hundreds and a selection of smaller bills. "Here," Rex said, passing her a fold of cash. "We don't want to keep all our eggs in one basket."

"Christ." She shoved the wad in her purse. "You're like an ATM, aren't you? Oh hurry—there's the elevator." They ran, catching it.

"Push four," he said, the door closing.

They exited to a mostly empty floor lit by pale neon. Outside the sun hadn't yet risen and a chill permeated the open structure, aided by the elevation and the cool ocean breezes. With a couple of cars slowly working toward the exit and hollow sound of their heels clicking against the tire-scarred concrete, Charlotte couldn't help seeing the whole milieu as a bit sinister. She tightened the belt at her waist, crossing her arms over her chest.

"Chickening out?" Rex said, glancing toward her.

"What?" She glared at him. "No. It's just cold in here."

"Not that cold," he said flatly, checking the numbers painted on each space: "402, 403, 404—it must be on the other side. Come on."

They didn't even walk halfway there before they found it, a sleek black Lincoln looking right out of the showroom. He went to the back of the car.

"Diplomatic plates, huh?" Charlotte whispered.

"*Oui*," he whispered back.

She nodded her head slowly. "So that's the invisible car."

"*Précisément*." He checked his phone, then punched the entry code into the door. The lock clicked open. Reaching in, he found the fob under the passenger side floor mat and opened the other door for Charlotte.

Rex slipped the seat belt over him and hit the ignition, the car roaring to life. "Let's get the fuck out of here."

"Roger that," Charlotte said, strapping herself in.

Chapter Fourteen

Everyday Folk

SOMEWHERE PAST THE Maryland border, Rex pulled into one of those down-homey restaurants normally seen near interstate exits. The huge parking lot was crowded with people in transit, businessmen and the usual assortment of big-chain denizens, including truckers, RVers, screaming children, and a healthy dose of the Great Unwashed. As they climbed from the car, Charlotte could almost swear there was a look of horror on Rex's face.

"*Mon Dieu. M'épargner le commun des mortels,*" he muttered, wincing.

"You insufferable snob." Charlotte slipped her arm in his, slapping it. "Seriously, their breakfasts aren't bad."

His Gallic nose lifted. "I'm not a *snob,*" he said pointedly. "I'm only bemoaning the sad decline of the average American." He winced again. "Deplorable."

"You wouldn't know an average American if he bit you in your Guccis."

He put an arm around her as a trio of kids ran past. "I don't know why you couldn't have waited until Washington. I know a place in Georgetown that serves a great kippers and eggs."

"Because we've been in the car for over two and a half hours, and that's all my bladder will stand." He pulled the door open and they entered into a huge space that looked like the inside of a barn, filled with overflowing displays of knickknacks in every genre imaginable. She pointed toward the back. "I'm going to the ladies' room. If you don't have to go, amuse yourself with this"—she grabbed a book from a display of them and shoved it at him—"until I get back."

He glanced at it. "*Uncle Jack's Bathroom Reader*?" She thought he might gag. She left for the bathroom.

As she washed her hands, Charlotte noted that although they'd had a significant breakthrough on the beach, he'd really told her nothing about what he planned to do once they got to Washington. Did he really expect to walk into the dining room at the Hay-Adams and confront Lilith Millwater right there, out in the open? Charlotte was sure the congresswoman fully expected Rex to remain cloistered in Philadelphia after his arrest, but then again . . . She couldn't help smiling as she dried her hands. If the congresswoman did, she hardly knew him at all. Then all at once she sobered. But if she didn't . . .

She found Rex exiting the men's room as she came out, every remaining strand of his beach-blown hair smoothed back to perfection. He reached for her hand. "Well, the best thing I can say about that experience is at least I didn't have to tip anyone."

"There is that," Charlotte said as they approached the hostess.

A few minutes later Charlotte sipped coffee as Rex considered a plate of biscuits and apple butter. "I recognize the biscuits, but what's that?" he asked, glaring at the dark sauce.

"Apple butter," Charlotte answered, breaking off a piece of biscuit and smearing a dollop of apple butter on it. "Try it, it's pretty good. Quintessentially American."

He eyed the biscuit suspiciously, but took it, popping it into his mouth. He shrugged, chewing. "*Pas mal*," he admitted, reaching for his coffee. "At least this is in porcelain."

"Thank God for the little things." She broke off a piece of biscuit for herself. "Anyway, I was thinking. You can't just show up at lunch at the hotel. If you walk into the dining room the congresswoman's going to bolt as soon as she sees you. That is, if she's there at all."

"I know," he said. "I've thought of that, too. I'm assuming she thinks my getting arrested has somehow lessened the imperative of the situation." He met her gaze with renewed fervor. "It hasn't. Not by a long shot."

"No doubt." She took another sip and another bite, preparing herself for what she knew she had to say. "That's why I think you need to hit her in her soft spot. Play on her"—she sipped more coffee—"feelings for you."

His eyes didn't leave hers. "Seems we're thinking

along the same lines. I thought perhaps we could meet in a room at the hotel. The same suite we always met in." He broke off a piece of biscuit, toying with it between his fingers. "That'll mean something to her. Should lessen her suspicions. Especially when she realizes I put my bail in jeopardy just to get to her."

"I think she'll find that quite romantic," she said after a moment.

He paused as well. "How do you feel about it?"

"Why should I feel anything? You already told me—you do what you need to do."

He dolloped apple butter atop the biscuit, his face passive. "Whatever it takes, right?"

Why was he doing this to her? Why was he *always* doing this to her? She leaned into him, calling his bluff. "Rex, if you feel you need to have sex with her to get what you need, then go for it. Don't inject me into the situation. I hold no illusions about what's between us."

He dropped the biscuit into his mouth. "What *is* between us?"

"Your cock," she said, wanting to bruise him. "I suppose that's it."

"Really?" He trained his eyes on hers, languidly sympathetic. "Is that all, *belle*?"

She could see now why he was so successful. All he had to do was unleash that soothing baritone and he could defuse any situation, no matter how volatile. At least it worked that way with her. But there was one it hadn't quite worked on, and she'd do well to remember that's why she was here. And what she was hired for.

"No, of course not." She sighed, shaking her head. "You really are quite the bastard, aren't you?"

"It's what you find so attractive about me, isn't it?" His mouth crooked ever so slightly, but his smile was as brilliant as ever. "I aim to please."

"I think you have the pleasing part down to a science, at least as far as I'm concerned—ah, here's the eggs."

A few bites later, Rex said, "You know damn well as I do I'm not going to have sex with her, Charlotte. I wouldn't have even . . ." His gaze caught hers before it arrowed back to his plate. "Even if you and I hadn't gotten together." He looked up, using his fork to make a point. "And don't go making any more of your cogent observations. The fact is, if Lilith is in love with me as you say, it's of her own invention. As far as I'm concerned, it was just business. I never gave her any reason to think more of it than what it was."

She shoved potatoes around her plate. "And what was it?"

He shrugged. "Mutual masturbation."

"Oh." She went to take a bite of poached egg, then returned it to the plate. "You do that with all your business associates?"

"Only the female ones," he said. Then his mouth crooked. "But then again, I'm pretty good at fucking the male ones, too." He leaned in. "Except they never know it."

Charlotte set down her fork. "Rex, I—"

"Charlotte." He slid his hand over hers. "If you don't know by now what we have between us is different, then there's nothing I can say to convince you. *Chérie*, we both have a sexual past. Mine is spectacularly colorful, and there's nothing I can do to change that."

"Not asking you to," she said. "Nor will I apologize for mine. All I'm saying is just do what you have to do and don't let this"—she flipped her hand between them—"stand in your way to getting it done." She sipped her coffee, looking askance.

He regarded her, knifing eggs onto his fork. "You do that a lot, you know."

"Do what?" She had no idea.

"This flipping thing with your hand." He demonstrated, waggling his between them. "When you don't want to say something aloud. You wave your hand instead."

"Seriously? Like for what?"

"As in the word you don't want to call us."

"Oh?" She pressed her hand into her lap. "What word is that?"

"*Les amoureux.*" He leaned forward, his eyes smoldering. "Lovers." He lifted her palm to his mouth, kissing it.

"Rex!" She yanked her hand back. "Don't go all French on me now, jeez," she said, quickly sipping her coffee.

He answered *en français*, "I'd like to go French all over you right now, right on this table, right in front of all these . . ." He flipped his own hand. "Whatever they are." He laughed, low and throatily. "Wouldn't that shoot the apple butter right out of their quintessentially American asses?"

Charlotte slammed her cup down, coffee nearly shooting from her quintessentially American nose.

AT A LITTLE past ten Rex pulled off the gridlocked interstate and into the vehicular hell known as Washington, D.C.

"Well, that wasn't too bad," he said, the city of white looming in the distance. "We're only an hour or so off schedule."

"Not too bad for D.C.," Charlotte remarked. "I was stuck on the exit ramp once for two hours."

"Oh?" Rex was instantly curious. "Have much occasion to come down to D.C.?"

"I used to. Not so much anymore." She flipped down the visor mirror, pulling a lipstick from her purse. "I used to date a D.C. lawyer. Worked for the State Department. We both went to Rutgers Law but I never knew him at the time. Hooked up with him at our ten-year reunion." She glided the lipstick over her lips, then pressed them together, snapping the cap back on. She shot him a glance. "What a dick he was."

They pulled up to a light, the corners thick with tourists and government workers. "Was he the one that messed with your head?"

She propped her chin in her hand, looking out the window. "He was one of them, that's for sure. The only good he ever did me was introducing me to Trent Webster."

Websters. Rex fumed. He thought it best to keep his opinions to himself about that family, the sons, at least.

"Anyway," she continued, "what's plan B if you can't get a room at the Hay?"

"I already have a room."

"You do? Oh." She seemed put off. "I didn't see you call."

"I didn't." The light changed and he still had to wait for a couple of tourists wearing shocking blue tricorns to cross. "My staff always reserves the same suite at the Hay whenever I'm in the U.S."

"Seriously? On the off chance you'll decide to go there?"

"Don't be too impressed. It's extremely hard to get a hotel room in D.C., especially during the workweek and when Congress is in session. And for the past year I've been coming down here every trip, ever since the bill was introduced."

Charlotte considered that. "It's a pretty important bill, isn't it?"

"Damned important. Mercier wants to start using the new larger container ships, but we can't if the harbor isn't dredged in Elizabeth. These new ships use solar power and half the fuel. They're crucial to our future bottom line."

"Because the U.S. really needs more cheap clothing and shitty small appliances. And fast, too," Charlotte opined.

Rex raised a brow. "The ships sails both ways, you know." *Christ, she was a prickly woman.*

They went a couple more blocks, then hit another light, idling again. He glanced over to his passenger who was trying to smooth that wild tangle of curly hair. Not that he thought she needed to. It looked just fine to him. Even better when she was under him, her hair spreading across his pillow, those long, luscious legs wrapped around him.

"Stop staring at my legs and get going," she said. "The light's changed."

"I wasn't staring at your legs," he said, accelerating.

"Yes, you were. I caught you."

"Then you were fantasizing. I was staring at your breasts."

She laughed. "That's even worse."

"Perhaps, but it's in an entirely different direction. If you're going to accuse me of staring you should at least be precise about it."

She turned to him, amazed. "That's the first entirely reasonable justification I've ever heard for ogling. Bravo."

"*Merci.*" He turned off the street and toward a portico, idling off to the side. "Well look at this. Here we are."

"How convenient. Hey, why'd you stop here?"

He turned to Charlotte, his hand at the door. "I'd like to remain as unobtrusive as possible. Since the suite has a standing reservation, I'll call right now and get your name listed on it. Just pick up the key and I'll meet you inside."

"You mean you want me to check in? As what? Your paramour?"

"Charlotte. Remember your place. As part of my legal team, of course. Paramours check in after seven p.m." He opened the door, leaning over for a quick kiss before he slipped out of the car.

Having Charlotte get the key afforded Rex time to answer his phone that had been vibrating in his pocket for at least a half hour. Not that he didn't trust Charlotte. In fact, after this morning, he was starting to find her opinion more and more important to him. But she was still straddling a fine line between lawyer and lover, and he didn't want to put her in a position where she'd have to make a choice between the two. He took out his phone as he crossed the street toward Lafayette Square, calling the hotel before he retrieved its message. *Marcel*. He dialed.

He picked up on the first ring. "*Ciao*. I take it you made it to D.C.?"

"As a matter of fact I did. Thanks for the car."

"Just make sure it's back in the same slot by tomorrow morning, five a.m. By the way, I have some bad news for you."

Rex sighed. Just what he needed. "What?"

"Seems someone found your phone and hacked it."

Enculé de ta mère. "Not entirely surprising. Do you know where it is?"

"The last location is Philadelphia. Any files on there I should be worried about?"

"All of them. But don't worry, I had Lee encrypt them." The year previous, Rex had hired the former Chinese hacker, considered the best in that shadowy business.

"He's the one who found out about it."

"That's why we pay him so well. But I have more sensitive material to worry about than a just bunch of spreadsheets. Like the kind that could save my ass."

Marcel paused. "I think you're about to tell me something you neglected to earlier."

Should he? He went with his gut. "I had my phone on

record practically the whole time I was at the fund-raiser. When I was talking to Lilith. And when I was with—"

"The girl?"

Rex sighed. "Yes."

"Hm." Marcel took a few moments to digest that. "Why didn't you tell me this earlier—no, don't answer that. I already know. Because you think you know this business better than me. You think you know it better than anyone. Because you're a smug, secretive son of a bitch. Because you think you're my goddamned mother. I already have one of those and that's one too many, you self-righteous bastard."

"Speaking of your mother—"

"What about my mother?"

Oh, he'd hit a soft spot there. Or rather a festering wound. Marcel hadn't forgotten how Viviane had tried to sell his birthright away, and Rex doubted if he ever would. "I think I saw her last night outside Charlotte's house."

"She's tailing you?"

"It's possible."

"Son of a bitch. What the hell does *that* mean?"

"That she may be at it again," Rex said.

He took another few moments to ruminate on that, and Rex couldn't help feeling sorry for him. "You gave me a lot of shit to think about," Marcel finally said. "I'll get back to you."

"Then I'd better go do what I came down here for."

"You do that. *Ciao.*"

Merde. He slipped the phone into his inner pocket. It

was a good thing he put two hundred dollars on it, or by now he'd soon be dropping quarters in a pay phone. He turned from the park, heading back to the hotel.

They'd both been the arbiters of each other's bad news, he and Marcel, giving each other an equally shitty day. Now he had to think about his phone being hacked. Christ—how could he have let this whole thing happen in the first place? The light changed and he trotted across the street. It happened because he got sloppy, thinking with his *dard* instead of just doing what he had to do, then going back to Marseille. But no, he let his ego get in the way. Let some pretty young thing stroke it as if that would keep the gray out of his hair or his kilometer under four minutes. He laughed to himself, the smug, secretive son of a bitch that he was. Might as well tell the clock to stop ticking.

Pretty presumptuous of him to think he could stop it. He was now forty, after all—*forty*. Hardly old, but not so young anymore either. Certainly old enough to know better. Because as rich as he was, sooner or later the girls would stop looking, and he'd either end up with a string of gold-diggers or face his decline as a lecherous old man.

Quite a future to look forward to. And with this charge, he was already well on his way to greet it. He entered the hotel, going straight to the elevator. After all this time, he could find the suite in the dark. It occurred to him dark was something he ought to get used to, as soon he'd be spending a lot of time in it, alone.

He grabbed his forehead. Jesus—where the hell were these thoughts coming from? He couldn't let what happened throw him off his game. If he let it get to him, if he gave up, he could never get back on top again, and he fought and clawed too hard and too long to get where he was and lose everything. He was Rex Renaud, for Christ's sake. Sought after, lusted after, envied and imitated. Suave and sophisticated, an international icon of business, a born leader of men. He needed to remember that. And something else.

It was all a lie. Right down to his roots.

He was the original manufactured man.

What was he really—the son of farmers? No, even that was too lofty. Of grape pickers, of people who never owned the fruits of their labors, though they always worked as hard as if they had. And it wasn't any different now with Marcel. Rex was still a grape picker, only with shinier packaging. *I'll get back to you.* Simple truths were in that simple statement. Marcel was the born leader of men. Rex was the born follower. And there was nothing he could ever do to change it. The elevator opened and he went to the suite and knocked. When the door opened, she was behind it.

"Well, hello there," she said, leaning into it.

Charlotte. *Mon Dieu.* Charlotte. The only bright light in this whole fiasco. *Ma belle* Charlotte. The *Parisienne*, born into the bar. And who was he? The grape picker, born to follow. He shut the door behind them, taking her in his arms.

"Charlotte," he said, smoothing her hair, sliding her coat from her shoulders. It fell to the floor as his mouth fell to hers. "Charlotte," he said, whispering it.

He didn't deserve her either. But oh God how he wanted her. Wanted it all. Wanted *everything* he never had a right to.

"I'm right here," she said, her arms around him inside his jacket. "What the matter? What happened? You seem upset."

"Crisis of conscience," he said, kissing her neck, her ear. "I just talked to Marcel. Someone found my phone and hacked it."

"Oh. Damn," she said. "But still. I get the crisis part, but where does the conscience come in?"

I don't have one. He held her out and looked at her, really looked at her. She was so beautiful, she made his chest ache. "I want to show you something, all right?"

"Sure," she said, eyeing him warily. "What is it?"

He let her go, and took her hand instead. "Come here."

They left the big living room and went into the bedroom just off it. On the side was a credenza. Solid cherry, about a meter and a half high, brass knobs on the doors. It was where he'd keep his wallet at night. Keys, if he had them. His portfolio. His watch. And jewelry, if he chose to wear it.

"This," he said, pointing to it.

"It's a . . . what do you call it—a credenza," she said.

"*Oui*, that's what it's called."

She stared at him, mystified. "And . . . ?"

He didn't answer. He just kissed her. Tilted her against it and kissed her with everything in him. "Charlotte," he said.

"What?" she whispered back, breathless, with as much longing as he had in him.

"Charlotte," he said, biting, nipping her neck, his hand sliding up her leg until he reached her panties. "*Je veux baiser. Je veux te ramoner grave. Tout de suite.*"

"Okay." She arched her neck as he turned her around, lifting her dress. "Okay, okay. Just let me . . ."

"*Non*—now." He kissed her neck, her ear. "Charlotte, let me . . ." He unzipped, opening himself.

"Okay. Okay." She bunched her dress around her and almost immediately he slid her panties down her legs and off.

"Charlotte." His hands on her hips, he tilted her up and drove himself in.

"My—God," she murmured, moaning from the impact, grasping on to the credenza to keep herself upright. "Oh Rex—Rex, that's so . . . ah . . ."

He pounded her mercilessly and without interval. She turned her head so he could kiss her, but he just looked away. There was nothing affectionate about what he was doing, just a long, hard, impersonal fornication against the credenza. In less than a minute he was gasping, ready to come.

"Rex—wait! You didn't—"

"Charlotte, *mon Dieu*, Charlotte!"

"Oh, damn. Rex. Go ahead and—I-I don't—" She straightened, her head back against his shoulder as her climax ripped through her. "Okay, I don't care . . ."

He grabbed her hips and shoved her forward, her

hands slapping against the credenza as his groin tightened and he was coming, a long, hard, vicious eruption he planted as deeply as he could inside her. When he was through he immediately pulled himself from her and she turned, letting her dress fall.

"Oh my God, Rex." She panted, slumping on her arms. "That was intense."

"I suppose it was," he said, cleaning himself with his handkerchief, zipping up.

"Hey, that was kind of hot," she said, slinking to him, her hand sliding up his chest. "I'm going to assume you were a good boy and had no communicable diseases. I'm on birth control and well . . ." She traced a finger to his cheek. "I have had you in my mouth."

He eyed her blankly. "*Oui*, you have."

"I do have a question though." Her laugh was like silk. "What was the big deal with the credenza? Why did you want to show it to me? I mean . . ." She laughed again. "That was really hot, but . . ."

All he knew was he wanted to hurt her. Hurt her as badly as all those people who thought they were better than him had hurt him through the years. "The credenza?" he said, tossing his hand toward it. "That's where I used to fuck the congresswoman. Right up against it. I'd lift her skirt and fuck her from the back."

"What . . . ?" she whispered, blanching. "*What?*"

Suddenly he felt dizzy. Like the world was tilting under his feet. "Charlotte—I'm sorry. I didn't—"

"You. *Motherfucker!*" She hauled off and cracked him across the face.

His head snapped to the side but otherwise, he just stood there, taking it. What did he expect? What else could he do? Charlotte grabbed her purse and ran from the room and out the door.

"*Sale de merde . . .*" he muttered, believing it.

Chapter Fifteen

Lafayette Squared

CHARLOTTE TOOK THE stairs out of the hotel because she needed to run, needed to move her body and not just stand placidly in the elevator. She threw open the door to the stairwell and tore down the steps, agile even in her pumps. When she reached the lobby she finally stopped running, walking as fast as her awareness of propriety would allow. Soon she was out of the hotel and crossing the street, heading toward Lafayette Square.

The morning was warmer now that the sun was out, and with summer holding on a bit longer in D.C., she could feel the sweat blooming on her chest, matching the dampness under her arms. She found a grouping of benches that faced away from the street and collapsed atop one, staring blindly at a pair of squirrels chasing each other up a tree. She pulled her purse into her lap, folding her arms atop it.

"What did I do to myself now?" she muttered, shoving her damp hair from her face.

It was bad enough she had very few girlfriends and none who were really close. Which was a shame because she could sure use another woman to talk to right now. How ironic was it then, for all of the defending of women she did, that there was no one there for her to lean on now when she needed it? But wasn't that typical? Because no one wanted anything to do with the rebels after the gates had been crashed. What was the first law of a revolution? Wasn't it kill all the lawyers?

But what would she tell a girlfriend anyway? That she was sleeping with a client and now he'd turned on her? A girlfriend would probably chastise her pretty good on that one, wouldn't she? What was that saying she once heard? *Don't look for meat where you make your bread and butter.* But that didn't apply to this case, did it? Not when he came looking for her. Tracked her down and trapped her, then flung her back like he probably did all the others. Just like the well-fed cat when it's done with a mouse.

My, she was up on her aphorisms today. She groaned. So much for original thinking. Then again, after what just happened, she couldn't form an original thought if she tried.

Rex had been right, at least partially, though she'd hate to admit it. Sure men had screwed her over. Just like she'd done herself, so many times before. With almost every man she'd ever been with. Except the one she decided to take seriously. The one she'd hoped to spend the rest of her life with. Perhaps therein lay the true irony of her situation, as well as the bitch of it.

So this was nobody's fault but her own. Except this time she almost hoped it could be different. Thought *he* was different. Yet the only thing he proved was that although the packaging could change, inside they were all the same. She dropped her head in her hands.

A little while later she heard his footsteps approaching, felt the wood sink as he sat beside her. Of course it was he. Who else would it be?

"Charlotte," he said.

She looked up. His tie was askew, eyes were bleary, the imprint of her hand still visible on his face. He was pale and rigid, and staring straight ahead. This wasn't the Rex she knew. But neither was that man she slapped a few minutes ago. Where was the old Rex? She wanted that man. "Why did you follow me down here?"

"To tell you what a bastard I am."

"I already know that, but it's refreshing to hear you admit it. Why don't you tell me something new instead."

"That I'm sorry I said those things to you? Would that work? Even if I know you won't forgive me?"

When she'd run down to the square she had no idea where she'd go, only that she needed to get away from him. To get away from those ridiculous feelings he stirred inside her, the deep-down ones he shoved to the surface. He was starting to make her think of the possibility of permanence, and what a fallacy *that* was. If there was one thing for certain, it was what you saw on the outside hardly hinted at what lay beneath. Men were little more than icebergs, cold, secretive creatures. And self-centered to their frigid core.

"Why should I?" she finally said. "What explanation could you possibly offer me?"

"None that'd justify it, I suppose. At least not for you." He clasped his hands on his knees, staring at the ground. "I don't know if I can explain it at all, besides the fact it was unspeakably cruel. Because what I did in that room"—he swallowed hard—"*before*, with the congress-woman, I did it just like that, every time I was with her. I never would have thought she would think of it with any more meaning than I did. It never even entered my mind. So when I was with you just now, I was trying to apply the same level of logic. To test myself, I suppose. To see if it could be the same disconnected way with you." He cleared his throat and straightened, turning toward her. "But it didn't work."

She had no idea what he was talking about, or how he was trying to justify what he did by saying it. "Why are you telling me this, Rex?"

"Marcel gave me something to think about when he told me my phone had been hacked. He was angry about my not telling him about the recording. He gave me a dressing-down over it." He looked at her. "Can you be-lieve that?"

She shrugged. "Well, he is your boss."

"Right. He wasn't about to let me forget it. And it gave me a glimpse into my life as it really is. How I'm really nothing more than his employee, no matter what I think of myself."

"I think you're a little bit more than that. You know you are. What would he be without you?"

"He'd still be Marcel Mercier. But what am I without that relation to him? The thought of that just kills me. As does all the people who know that, like Marcel, like Lilith, perhaps even you. And that's what got between us upstairs."

He looked back to the ground, his hands between his knees. "I know now because of my own stupidity I'm in this fiasco. I let my ego get in the way with that recording and with that girl. To prove I'm something more than I am. I wanted you and I always get what I want. But in the end, when you should have been gone, you were still there, seeing right through me. Charlotte." He looked at her, raking back his uncharacteristically tousled hair. "Do you know how hard it is taking that good of a look at yourself?"

She couldn't answer him. Maybe she hadn't gotten that far yet. "All I know is what I see when I look at you."

"A bastard, right? Well, I can't blame you for that. But please realize how sorry I am. And how I very much want your forgiveness."

That angered her. "And what difference would that make? Who am I anyway? Should I give you my forgiveness just so you could feel better? Because tell me the truth. What am I besides just another broad in your sweaty stable of them? Just another way to top off your evening after a long day of toeing the corporate line, right up there with a belt of scotch. Well, here's a news flash for you, Rex. You weren't any more than that for me either."

His gaze snapped to hers, his eyes darkening. "Oh, I sincerely doubt that."

"Ha!" She jabbed her finger at him. "That turning table hurts like a bitch, doesn't it? Find that hard to believe? Well, isn't that too bad. Because I know how to fuck my way around a deal, too."

His jaw tensed, twitching almost indiscernibly. "I'm sure your standards weren't ever that low."

"What standards?" She looked at him blankly. "It was just business, wasn't it? Isn't that what you said? Well, that's how I used it, too. Until I fell in love. She scoffed at it. "*Love*. What bullshit. It wasn't until I fell out of it that I really got smart. When I found out what my vagina was really good for." Then she glared at him. "I should have kept it that way."

He fell back hard against the bench, shoving his hands in his pockets. "I'm sending you back to Philadelphia. Or Margate or wherever the hell you want to go. But I'm also sending you back with a check for two million, no strings attached. Then take the money and screw as many men as you want with it." His gaze, full of acid, shifted to hers. "Literally or metaphorically, if it suits your purpose. All I ask is that you remember where it came from. That's what a bastard *I* am."

"So you're going to send me home," Charlotte said.

"*Oui*," he said, practically hissing it. "Take the train or fly first-class. Hire a limousine if you want, I don't give a fuck. I'd send you on my own plane but I believe they've impounded it."

"Yeah, I believe they have." Two more squirrels were

chasing each other, or maybe they were the same pair. These two were circling around and around a tree as they ran up it. What would happen when they got to the top? "And what if I don't want to go?"

He shook his head. "You're going. I don't want you here."

"Is that so." She had to hand it to him. Had she ever met anyone who could clamp hold of a situation better than he could? He had come to her with his tail between his legs, and now he was trying to get her on the defensive. The fact was, had she been any other woman, that tactic would probably have worked beautifully. But she wasn't any other woman.

"What if I don't give a damn what you want?" she finally said.

"Why are you arguing with me?"

"Because you're not listening to *me*," Charlotte said, poking him. "If I go back without you, then what will happen to me? I'm responsible for you, and I'm not getting fined or even worse for you or anyone. So I have to stay. For purely selfish reasons."

His mouth crooked. "You're throwing my own attitude back at me, aren't you?"

"Why would you think that? Or are you letting your ego get in the way again?"

He squinted at her. "What are you, some kind of a taskmaster?"

"You need one. You accused me of being messed up, but you're way more fucked up than I am."

He laughed softly. "Probably more than you realize."

"No, I can recognize it when I see it." She looked for the squirrels, but they were gone. "I've spent quite a bit of time on the crazy bench." She spread her hands. "See? I'm on it again."

"We both are. *Merde*." He laughed again, harsh and low. "So what do we do now?"

"What we came to do, I guess."

He fell silent for a few moments, his expression more earnest than she'd ever seen it. "Does that mean you forgive me?"

She supposed she did. "You know what was the worst part of what you did?"

"I don't know." He shrugged. "Everything?"

She looked to his mouth, loving the way it curved when he looked at her. It pained her to think of how many women he had kissed with it, and how possessive of him she suddenly felt. "You didn't kiss me. Not once. It was like I wasn't even there."

"You were there," he said adamantly. "You were all around me. And you're right—that was the worst part. Because I didn't want to."

"Do you want to now?" she said, aching for it.

He turned to her, sliding his arm over the back of the bench. "Oh *oui*. Very badly." He moved closer. "If you'll let me."

She couldn't wait. She leaned in, kissing him.

"Charlotte," he whispered against her mouth, "I'm so, so sorry."

"Just kiss me," she said, falling into the crook of his arm.

After a few moments he looked at her, his hand smoothing her cheek. "There's another thing I didn't do . . . back there in the room, *ma belle*." He sighed. "In the heat of the moment."

"I know." A little shiver raced through her. "My thighs are all sticky."

He laughed. "Only you can make that sound so decadent."

"It *is* decadent." She slid her hand down his chest. "I'm also sitting here without my underwear."

"Now, *that's* decadent. And very, very convenient."

"Why? Are you going to lift my dress right here?"

"Over there," he said, jutting his chin toward a tree. "Behind that quintessentially American oak. But seriously, Charlotte." He turned very serious. "I always use *un préservatif*, so I don't want you to worry about that. And always have. In fact, that's the first time I haven't used one since my fiancée."

"You were engaged?"

"*Oui*. Once, about five years ago." He shook his head. "It didn't work out."

"What happened? If I may ask."

He touched her cheek. "I'm starting to learn we can keep very few secrets from each other. Let's just say her nature didn't align with the nature of my job. She was very traditional. Home, family—hers was enormous. Children. She wanted a husband who left every morning from her breakfast table and returned promptly at six, for his slippers by the hearth and her *cassoulet*. I couldn't promise her that."

She leaned back into the crook of his arm, the morning sun feeling good on her face. "I know what you mean. My fiancé was a lot like that. Except he only wanted it for me."

"*You* were engaged?"

She turned to glance at him. "You sound surprised."

"*Non, non,* that's not what I mean. It's just coincidental that we both were, and now we're not." He squeezed her shoulder. "It was the D.C. lawyer, wasn't it?"

"Yes," she admitted. "I knew that he eventually wanted to get into politics, and that thrilled me. I had visions of us being this power couple, living in Georgetown, and I could run his campaign. It sounded all so exciting."

"So what happened?"

"What happened was he wanted all that for himself, but none of it for me. I wanted Bill and Hillary, and he wanted me home and having babies. The fact was he had the Bill part down, but unlike Hillary, I wasn't so forgiving."

"He cheated on you?"

"Constantly. I know that's not a big deal for your politicians at home, but I like my men monogamous. If that's what they're telling the world at least."

"You know, there are people back in my *région* who want me to get into politics. Been pressing for it, in fact."

"Have you considered it?"

"I've thought about it. I feel like I can do some good. But . . ." He waved his hand. "Who has time for that. This job takes everything out of me."

"But look where it's gotten you."

He turned sharply. "Maybe it hasn't been so bad," he

said, tracing a finger down her cheek, "if it could bring you and me together."

"Yes. Though I suppose we should get back to it."

"So you'll stay?"

"Hey, I wasn't the one who wanted me to leave."

"I'm glad." He kissed her again. "Then let's go. I need to text the congresswoman."

Charlotte stared at him. "You mean you haven't already?"

"And when did I have time to do that? Before I ran out here to break up your tantrum?"

"So now it's a *tantrum*?"

"Over *my* tantrum," he said, kissing her. "Now, shall we go back inside, *ma belle*? I believe we have work to do."

"All right," she said, rising with him. "But only because I left my underwear on the floor."

He smiled wickedly. "That's what I'm talking about."

Meet me in the room for dessert, chérie. You remember where it is, don't you?

"Oh my," Charlotte said, looking at the text on Rex's phone. "That's hitting her over the head."

"She likes it that way," he said.

"Do you think it'll work?"

"I'm relying on her lust for me to take the bait, and . . ." He pulled her close. "I'm relying on *your* lust for me to understand."

She stared at him, amazed. "What is that force you wield so effectively?"

"Testosterone," he said, hitting send.

Charlotte pulled her legs up on the sofa, checking the time on the mantel clock. "It's nearly twelve-thirty."

"Which means she ought to be sipping martinis with Hitchell right now." Rex got up from the sofa, preferring to pace back and forth. "Who knows how long their lunch will take. He doesn't like her any more than she likes him."

"Do you know anything about him?"

"Only that he's insisting on adding something to benefit his own business to the dredging bill, or he won't sign off on it." He paused at a mirror, straightening his tie. "And that he has a lot of money to throw around."

"And you talk about *my* having a tantrum." She propped her chin in her hand, leaning forward. "Welcome to Washington politics."

"Hardly, *belle*. Welcome to the way of the world. I'm not poor by any stretch of the imagination, but from what I've heard, he could give Marcel a run for his money. Which means he has unlimited funds."

"And how'd he get that way?"

"I know he has some connections to oil."

"He wouldn't happen to be from Texas, would he?"

"Very perceptive, *avocate*," he said. "Oil equals Texas, right?"

"In the U.S., more than likely. Oil interests plus Texas often drags big money behind it. It wouldn't be hard to figure out."

"All I know is we need him to sign off on the bill." His eyes darkened. "And that the first words out of Lilith's mouth better be that he has."

"And what're your first words going to be?" Charlotte asked.

"How about 'Why are you out to get me? Who's behind you? Where's my phone? Why are you such an ungrateful, greedy bitch?'"

"How about you just smack her with your new phone? That's a little more subtle."

"I haven't any plans to be subtle, *ma belle*. The obviousness of the situation won't allow it."

Charlotte shook her head. "So you'd really use the proof of her infidelity against her? Are you really that much of a cad?"

He laughed, as if she just paid him a compliment. "I'll leave it up to your own impression to answer that question. But as far as Lilith is concerned, it would work to my advantage if she thought the worst of me, don't you think?"

"I'd rather not think about it at all. Especially since the phone was hacked and the proof may not be there anyway."

"*Oui*," Rex said quietly, picking at a bowl of mixed nuts. He grabbed a handful, then tossed it back. "There is that." He began pacing again, feeling more antsy than ever. And that meant he wasn't in control, a state he never liked to find himself in. "If she's down with Hitchell, it'll be a while before she makes it up here. Are you hungry by any chance? If anything, I can use some coffee."

She eyed him dubiously. "Right, because anyone can see you need an accelerant. Shall we order room service?"

"Absolutely," he said, sliding the menu from the desk drawer.

They settled on a cheese plate, a plate of assorted meats, pâtés and breads, a baby greens salad, a bottle of sparkling water, and a large pot of coffee. Not ten minutes later, someone knocked.

"Well, that was quick," Charlotte said, going to the door. When she opened it, she started, standing back. "Oh!"

"Oh!" the congresswoman echoed. She shot a glance to the room number on the door. "I must have the wrong suite. I'm so sorry—"

"You could find this room blindfolded," Rex said, stepping forward. "In fact . . ." His mouth crooked in mirth. "I believe you have."

She stared at him, her guard up. "What's going on here?" Then looked to Charlotte. "And who the hell are you?"

He took the representative's arm and he pulled her into the room, closing the door behind her. "Lilith, meet my attorney, Charlotte Andreko. Charlotte, this is Representative Lilith Millwater."

"Representative Millwater," Charlotte said, folding her hands in front of her.

The congresswoman looked between the two of them, settling on Rex. "I thought you were supposed to be in Philadelphia? I thought you were arrested."

"Things changed," he said. "But that didn't seem to stop you from dashing up here from your lunch with Hitchell." He waggled his finger at her. "Main course before dessert, Madame Congresswoman. You should know that by now."

She reddened considerably, from either anger or embarrassment, or a combination of both. "His office called and said he wasn't coming, so I left."

"That's sincerely unfortunate," Rex said, closing in on her. "But we have a few issues that're even more pressing at the moment, such as what the hell's going on. But why don't we start with my phone? Where the fuck is it?"

She flinched. "What are you talking about?"

"My cell. My mobile. *Mon téléphone portable*," he said, his voice low and lethal. "Do you need me to say it in Urdu?"

"You don't have it? But I assumed that since it wasn't—" All at once she blanched. "I-I mean—I thought—"

"What, Lilith?" he said, coming closer. He grabbed her by the arms, looming over her "What are you trying to say?"

"Let me go," she said, stepping back. "I'll explain."

"Yes," Rex said. "Why don't you?"

She swallowed, visibly nervous as she pulled her shoulders back, trying to regain a semblance of composure. "I called in a favor from my husband. The cheating bastard owes me plenty. He's a judge, you know. So I asked him to have someone sneak into the property room and"—she coughed—"take your phone."

Now he was getting somewhere. "All right, Lilith, I can see your point. You wanted to erase that recording. But you must also know by now there was something else on there, something that can clear me of this ridiculous charge. So give it back to me and I'll forget the whole thing."

She seemed surprised. "Are you saying there was a recording of you and the girl?"

"Yes," he said, as if it was obvious. "You didn't hear it?"

She sighed, rubbing her forehead. "I didn't have a chance."

Rex stared at her. "What are you talking about?"

"She means she doesn't have your phone," Charlotte concluded. "Isn't that right, congresswoman?"

"Yes," she said. "Because it was gone before my husband could get to it."

Chapter Sixteen

Poli Ticking

REX FELT LIKE he'd been punched in the solar plexus. He grabbed Lilith's arm. "What do you mean it was gone?"

The congresswoman shook him loose. "I mean there was no record of it. It wasn't there."

"The police took your phone at the scene, didn't they?" Charlotte asked Rex.

"*Oui*," he said. "I saw it at the police station. When I got there they made me empty my pockets, then they photographed and fingerprinted me. That's when the arresting officer gave it to them and I signed for everything." He looked to Charlotte. "You even saw the receipt." He cursed roundly in a French Charlotte didn't understand, though she thoroughly understood the tone. "They told me I could pick it up later after I made bail." He turned to the Lilith, incensed. "And now you're saying it wasn't even there?"

"I'm saying whomever my husband sent found nothing," Lilith said, looking frantic. "And now we're both screwed—thanks to you."

Rex cornered the congresswoman, incensed. "You pushed me to make that recording. You could have sent that bill through a long time ago but *non*—you were enjoying my contributions too much to send it out for a vote."

"That's not true," she said, squeezing around him to the bar. She grabbed a bottle of vodka and a glass, pouring herself a double shot. "Believe me, I tried but it never had a chance," she said, tossing it back. "It was dead on arrival."

"What do you mean?" Rex said, going to her. "I was there when member after member of both parties were out on the floor praising the bill, crowing about how many jobs it would create. Then I come back two months later and suddenly everything's changed. Why?"

"How the hell do I know," she said, pouring another shot. "Because they all talk a good game about jobs, getting those sound bytes in for the commercials. But when it comes to spending any money, they're all a bunch of little girls."

"But you knew this was going to happen," Rex said, "and the last time I saw you, you assured me you could fight it. Wasn't that how you justified taking my money?"

"I tried, I really tried. And I came this close . . ." Lilith pinched her fingers together. "Hitchell assured me he'd make a deal. He promised me. But apparently he pulled his support when he didn't show up today, and well . . ."

She shrugged, wincing behind her glass. "There's nothing I can do about it."

"You bitch," he said, his hands clenching. "I'd like to say you used me, but you'll get yours when that recording comes out."

She slammed the glass to the bar. "Don't say that—don't even joke about it. If it does, I'm ruined. My political career is over."

"Well, start planning a new one, because I just found out the phone's been hacked."

"You can't be serious," she said, coming at him. "I assumed your password would protect it. That no one could get into it but you."

"Well obviously, someone wants to get at me," Rex said, "or why would they have taken it?"

She swallowed hard, staring at him. "Rex, I—"

A knock came at the door. "I'll get it," Charlotte said, opening it to room service.

Lilith slugged back the last of her vodka. "Oh what's the use." She turned to the door. "I'm going—"

"Oh no." He stepped in front of her. "Join us. Please.

"I don't think so," Lilith said. "I think this conversation's over."

"No, I think it's hardly begun," Charlotte said. She looked to the server, indicating the dining area at the other end of the long room. "Three plates, please." And back to the battling duo at the bar. "We're all in this together, so why don't you two quit nipping at each other and call a truce. If you do, maybe we can figure this thing out."

"Just listen to your girl," Lilith said, glaring at Charlotte. "You've got her well-trained."

"I'm not his *girl*," Charlotte said evenly. "I'm his lawyer."

"And I was his friendly local politician," she said, yanking at the hem of her tailored jacket. "But I was also a girl in his *service*"—she spun the word, her gaze dropping—"just as much as you are."

"*Dégage*." Rex's voice seethed. "Get out."

"Hey, you were the one who asked me here," Lilith said, grabbing the bottle again. "Get a good look at what your money buys you."

"I said get out!" Rex flung his hand toward the door. "If you don't get—"

"Stop it," Charlotte hissed. She hastily tipped the server, then hustled him out. "Jesus, he heard everything you said."

Lilith laughed. "Which is probably just more of the same bullshit that happens in this town every day."

"Oh sit the hell down—both of you," Charlotte said, taking a chair at the head of the table. She dragged a tray over, sliding chorizo onto her plate. She looked up. "I *said* . . ."

Rex slanted a glance at Lilith, then flipped his hand toward the table. "*S'il vous plaît*," he said tartly, indicating the way. She slammed the tumbler to the bar and sauntered over, Rex waiting for her to sit before he did. As hungry as he was before, he couldn't choke down a crumb, but the bottle of wine definitely looked inviting.

"That's better," Charlotte said, setting down her fork.

"Okay, if we can get past our mutual animosity maybe we can learn a few things." She looked to the congresswoman. "Rex said you were there when he heard the door open to the conference room. Did you follow him?"

She filled her water glass, taking a sip. "Yes."

"I suppose this may seem fairly obvious," Charlotte continued, "but why?"

She huffed, looking askance. "Because I was angry," Lilith said. "Wouldn't you be? He just made a fool out of me and taped me while he did it. And then he went right from me to some little K Street whore."

"Did you know her?" Charlotte asked.

Lilith paused, taking another sip of water. "I'd seen her around at parties. A couple months ago I saw them together—in the bar downstairs. She was just leaving him." She tossed Rex a scowl. "Or maybe I should say— she looked like she was running away."

"That's a *lie*," Rex said vehemently.

"Rex, please," Charlotte said. She looked back to Lilith. "Did you confront him then?"

"No, but I asked him later about it. That's how I found out—hey." She looked to Rex and back. "Maybe I ought to have my lawyer here, too."

"I'm the one with the sexual assault charge, remember?" Rex said. "Or would you like to one-up me with your little story about judicial corruption and attempted larceny?"

Lilith tossed him a filthy scowl before turning back to Charlotte. "You were saying . . . ?"

"So when you saw him leave the ballroom with her, you got angry. You were jealous."

"Well, wouldn't you be?" Lilith glared at her, incredulous. "Rex had always made time for me before whenever he was in the U.S., but this trip he wanted nothing to do with me. I wanted to know why."

"And why do you think that was, Lilith?" Rex asked.

She ignored him, addressing Charlotte. "I even arranged my schedule so we'd have time together, to talk about the bill if he wanted, but he turned me down flat. Instead, he went after that little whore. So sure, I followed. And caught them red-handed."

"Quite the voyeur, aren't you, *chérie*," Rex said. "You like to watch?"

"Unlike you," Lilith said. "You're a man of action. More like fuck anyone and anything."

Rex laughed. "Recognizing your own modus operandi?"

"This was different," she said.

"You mean *I* was different. From all the others in your retinue."

She glared at him. "I was in love with you."

"Really." He calmly sipped his wine. "How awful for you."

"Rex, *please*," Charlotte said sharply. Which surprised Rex considerably. She looked back to Lilith. "So he made a fool out of you, then left to go off with another woman. You were angry and humiliated. So you followed them."

"Yes," she said quietly, taking a gulp of water. "Maybe I shouldn't have but he really left me no choice."

"You wanted an explanation for his actions. You wanted to continue the conversation."

"Yes, I did." Lilith looked grateful for the clarification. "I think he owed it to me."

"That's understandable," Charlotte said. "So you went out the same door from the ballroom that they did?"

"Yes, into the hall. It was empty, so it was easy to hear. And I did hear . . ." Lilith looked out into space, almost as if she were replaying the scenario in her head.

"What?" Charlotte probed. "Talking? Chatting?"

"Yes."

"Were you sure it was Rex and the girl?"

"Oh yes," she said, sliding a heated glance toward Rex. "By this time I knew his voice very well . . . under those circumstances." She shook her head, sipping more water. "I could hear her, too. She was moaning and groaning."

Charlotte leaned in, whispering, "Like she was in pain?"

Lilith laughed. "Hardly."

Rex held his breath. *Mon Dieu.* Charlotte knew exactly what she was doing.

"So you opened the door?" Charlotte asked.

"Yes." Her eyes narrowed. "And there she was with her legs up on the table, pulling up her dress. Then he goes and rips her underwear off, and that's when she started screaming."

"And didn't stop until security heard her from the ballroom and came in, right?"

"I suppose . . ." Lilith said, looking to Charlotte with trepidation.

Charlotte got up, gripping the back of her chair as she

stared dead into Lilith. "So this looked pretty consensual to you."

"Wait a minute." Lilith's gaze shot back and forth between the two. "What just happened here?"

"What just happened is if you could repeat what you just said under oath, it would go a long way in exonerating Rex," Charlotte said.

"And why would I want to do that?" said Lilith. "It wouldn't be ten minutes before the press would find out we were sleeping together. It'd be political suicide."

"But you'll have to admit it if you're called to testify," Charlotte said.

"*Non*, she wouldn't," Rex said. "She conveniently ran off before security came. Because it'd be my word against hers."

Lilith glared at him. "You bet it is. And until you find that phone, maybe I didn't see a thing."

"But we could call you," Charlotte said, "and you'd have to testify."

"As a hostile witness. Where I'd deny everything, including being there." The congresswoman reached for the bottle of wine.

"Seem we're at an impasse," Rex said.

"No," said Charlotte. "You're at mutually assured destruction. Which means you two better start working together, or you're both going where you so do not want to go. Or does prison and political obscurity sound good?"

"Point taken," Lilith said, filling her glass. "But there's nothing I can do about it."

"Try looking at the larger issue," Charlotte said. "Like why the lobbyist is accusing him in the first place."

"How the hell should I know," Lilith said. "And at this point why should I care? More than likely he's just getting what he deserves."

"And who would think that besides you?" said Charlotte, coming around to her side of the table. "Because if you're the only one who feels that way, it doesn't look good for you."

Lilith slanted her a glance, swallowing hard. "If you think I'm teamed up with that little slut you have to be out of your mind."

"Then tell me who else might think it's a good idea?" Charlotte said. "Who even knows him in Washington without his connection to that dredging bill?"

"No one," said Rex. "There was only one reason why I ever came to Washington, and that was to see Lilith."

"Oh come on," Lilith said, tugging at her jacket again. "I'm sure an important man like you knows lots of Washington politicians."

"Party acquaintances," he said, easing toward her. "Face it, Lilith. All roads lead back to you."

She pursed her lips, fingering the glass. "I find that hard to believe. I couldn't possibly be privy to all your connections."

"Though I'm sure you know a few," Charlotte said. "If Rex's only connection to Washington was you and the dredging bill, who would benefit by taking him down?"

"Only one person I could think of," Rex said, "besides *ma p'tit chou* of course. Hitchell."

Charlotte looked to Lilith. "Did Hitchell give you any reason why he couldn't make your lunch today?"

She stiffened. "No. His office called my cell when I

was already at the table, and said he wouldn't be coming. Outside of that, he's scheduled to speak on the floor this afternoon at three. That's all I know."

Charlotte glanced to Rex before she said to Lilith, "Can you get me into the gallery?"

Lilith peered at her. "Why? To see Hitchell speak? What good would that do?"

"Maybe we'll find out what was so important he couldn't show up for your lunch," Charlotte said.

Suddenly Rex was very hungry. He broke off a chunk of bread, slathering it with Brie. "I'm going as well."

"No," Charlotte said. "If anyone recognizes you you could land back in jail."

"I'll take that chance," he said, adding pâté and chopped egg to his dish. "Besides, if Hitchell is behind this, then I'd really like to see his face when he sees me. Especially since I've never met the man in my life. If he recognizes me, that ought to speak volumes."

"You're taking a chance," Charlotte said, already looking resigned. "Not that I thought you'd actually sit here and wait for me to come back."

"You'd be right on that," he said. He slid more cheese and bread on his plate. There was nothing like inaction to kill his appetite, but giving him something to do always sent it soaring.

"I think you're both crazy," Lilith said, rising. "And if you're going over to the House, it sure as hell won't be on my ticket. I'm leaving." She grabbed her purse.

"Thank you, Lilith," Rex said, raising his glass in salute. "You've been most helpful."

"Oh go to hell," she said, slamming the door behind her.

"Now that was fascinating," Rex said, slathering more Brie. "But how are we going to get in the congressional gallery now?"

"The usual way. Through your congressman. Or in my case, an old friend," Charlotte said, stopping at a mirror to fluff her hair.

"And I think I know who that is." Rex scowled, tossing the bread to his plate, suddenly not so hungry anymore.

Rayburn House Office Building
Office of Representative Trent Webster (D-NJ)

"Is that Charlotte?"

He came out of his office, Charlotte stepping into her friend's outstretched arms. "Trent—how great to see you."

He grasped her hands, holding her out. "Let me get a good look at you." He grinned, a million-dollar smile. "You only get more gorgeous every time I see you."

"And you never change." Fact was, he didn't. Tall and athletic, a latter-day Jimmy Stewart in *Mr. Smith Goes to Washington*. Except Trent Webster was no small-town innocent. Princeton born and educated, he was as patrician as his pre-Revolutionary roots, and as down-to-earth as the soup kitchen he'd just come from working. As a true Washington insider, he was also the first person Charlotte would hit up for dirt in her old D.C. days, and she had no reason to believe it'd be any different now. "How the hell are you, Trent?"

"Stellar, in fact. So, what brings you to Washington?"

"I'm here with a client." She glanced back to where Rex was sitting, casting her a rather sinister glare. She learned into her friend, saying softly, "It's rather confidential. Can we talk in your office?"

"Sure." He looked to his secretary. "No calls for a few minutes, okay?" Then he stood aside, following them into his office.

When the door closed Charlotte said, "Trent, this is Rex Renaud. He's the—"

"*Directeur général délégué compagnie du* Mercier." The younger man offered his hand to one surprised Rex. "*Bonjour*, Monsieur Renaud. *Enchanté.*"

"*Enchanté*," Rex replied, looking a bit confused as he shook Trent's hand. "Have we met before?"

"No," Trent replied. "But I saw you speak at a forum on the EU last spring in New York. You were brilliant."

Go ahead and stroke it, Trent, Charlotte thought. *If anyone needs it now, he does.*

"Ah yes, I remember that," Rex said, smiling subtly. "I got stuck in traffic from the airport and I arrived late."

"But you were worth the wait. Please, have a seat," Trent said, his hand indicating two chairs in front of his desk. After everyone was seated, he continued. "So what can I do for you?"

"I'll cut to the chase," Charlotte said. "Do you know anything about a congressman from Texas by the name of Brendan Hitchell?"

"Hitchell . . ." He thought a moment. "From Texas, huh? Wait a minute—I think he's introducing a bill today.

Or at least he's trying to." He looked at Rex querulously. "How did you come to be acquainted with the Honorable Mr. Hitchell?"

"I haven't had the pleasure," Rex said, "but he's most definitely making himself known to me."

"Rex was hoping to see a bill get to the floor for a vote," Charlotte said. "H.R. 22186, I think it was."

"The harbor dredging bill, of course," said Trent. "That makes sense. Philadelphia is the other port competing for the same funding."

"Is that area part of your district?" Rex asked.

"No, but Philadelphia's just across the river from it, so it does mean jobs for my constituents." He winced, shaking his head. "And it's a shame, as they sure could use them. I'll assume you're interested in the funding for the harbor around Elizabeth, right?"

"It's where Mercier has a terminal," Rex said. "But Hitchell's been holding up the bill for so long, it now looks like it's dead."

Trent sat back with a wince. "So I've heard. But that's not surprising."

"Why do you say that?" said Charlotte.

"Because he's an old oilman from down in Texas, but lately he seems to be shifting into hydraulic fracturing—or what you probably know as fracking—up in Pennsylvania."

"And how do you know about this?" Charlotte asked.

"Because some of his wells are just across the river from my family's neighboring district. And people up there are saying all he needs is one drilling mishap, and it could contaminate the Delaware and water supply. Been protesting all over Hunterdon County lately. The environmentalists are freaking out."

"But I don't understand, Trent," Charlotte said. "What does this have to do with Hitchell holding up the dredging bill?"

"The rumor is he's wanting to expand a liquid natural gas pipeline to an export terminal downriver on the Delaware Bay," Trent said.

"To export all that LNG to Europe, I'd bet," Rex said.

Trent looked at him. "And that'd be a winning wager, my friend. That's where the big bucks are now. Curiously enough, he's eyeing an old gas liquefaction plant on the bay which also has a dock and pier."

"And because he'd be creating a few jobs, I imagine he'll be asking the government to back his business venture," Charlotte said. "Instead of funding that dredging bill you want."

"Damn," Trent said, "now what I heard this morning all makes sense. Though I can't verify it."

"What did you hear?" Rex said.

"That there's a company already as good as signed to transport all that LNG to Europe."

"Who?" Rex said.

"I'm sure you've heard of them," Trent said. "Richette."

"Jesus," Charlotte said. She looked to Rex. "They're making their move, aren't they?"

Suddenly Rex was on his feet. "I need to get over to the House. Do you have any passes for the gallery?"

"Why sure," Trent said, reaching into his desk.

Rex turned to Charlotte. "I have the distinct feeling Lilith will be conspicuously absent from the gallery."

"Oh Rex," she said, "you can't be serious. Do you really think she's mixed up with him?"

"Nothing surprises me anymore," Rex said, reaching for her hand. "Let's go."

"This sounds like it's gonna get good," Trent said, on his feet as well. "Just let me get my coat."

Chapter Seventeen

Mars in Transit

RICHETTE, REX MUSED. The very name of the *compagnie* curdled his blood. He should have suspected, as it was only a matter of time. Sooner or later they had to come calling. And they were sending Viviane Mercier as their ambassador.

Trent had taken them below to the subway system that ran beneath the D.C. legislative offices to the Capitol. While they rode the tram through the narrow corridor to the House chamber, Rex could sense her presence, more strongly than he had in years.

She's here, he thought, and although he had no concrete evidence to prove it, he could feel it in his bones. Perhaps when she delivered her little calling card in the Rolls, she was warning him they'd soon meet again. In a way, that gave him a measure of relief to know who he was dealing with. Still, it left him baffled why Viviane would make another attempt at a takeover, especially with Marcel at the helm of the company. Or was Richette simply calling in her marker, the one they never got around to cashing before André stepped in and ruined everything. Before Rex himself was complicit in helping him. Well, what did she expect? He knew a good deal when he saw it. Wasn't it she who first showed him the value of one?

Wasn't it she who had told him one never gave anything out of the goodness of their heart? That there was always a price to pay, no matter how grateful you were. Or how justified you were in receiving what you did in the first place.

Rex looked across the car to Charlotte, the tram's rush billowing her hair, the congressman's arm rimming the back of her seat as they engaged in easy conversation. He was glad he'd told her about Viviane, though it felt as odd as it felt liberating, never having been this close to anyone before. And because of that he also felt a sudden rage at this Trent's embrace, even though logic dictated it was nothing more than the casual familiarity of an old friend. Still, her cozying up with Trent almost felt traitorous on her part, as their familiarity grated on him, no matter how innocent it appeared. Although a bit on the young side, Trent was nonetheless not so terrible to look at, and if anyone were going to touch her that way, it ought to be him. And he wanted to, very badly. Wanted to kiss her and hold her in his arms. Almost how a soldier kisses his wife or lover good-bye before going to battle, knowing if he didn't come out alive, he'd come back changed. And he was indeed going to battle.

Still, it had been very nice having someone to confide in. There was just something about Charlotte that made it easy, as least for him, as he was dead sure any empathy outside her causes didn't come to her easily. They had already agreed not to let on to Trent the charges that had been leveled against him. It was enough to let him know Rex was there to see to the bill's passage, and anything beyond that was between him and Charlotte alone. He smiled. Another confidence they shared between them.

His gaze slid down her legs to where they crossed at the ankles. He knew firsthand how smooth they were, and he craved to slide his hand down them. And up to where she was always ready and waiting for him. At that he burned with sudden possession. That part of their liaison was still too new to be sated so quickly, and all at once he wanted her very badly. And wanted this Trent person's arm off her shoulder. *Now.*

He decided instead to look past their own car to the one behind it, watching a pair of children as they played a guessing game with their nanny. Perhaps watching that would defuse these incendiary feelings he was having toward Charlotte. She was making him think of life in the long term, the idea of which he had no business considering, especially since those ideas had gone so terribly wrong for the both of them.

"Have you guys eaten lunch yet?" said Trent. "We have some time if you'd like to stop in the dining room." He looked to Charlotte with familiarity. "I remember you being particularly partial to their bean soup."

"That was *Senate* bean soup, Mr. Congressman,"

Charlotte said. "Or are you thinking about trading up?" She arched a brow. "Again?"

"Ooh," he winced. "That was cold. You're never going to let me live that down, are you?"

An inside joke? Rex thought. *Grrrrrrrrrrr. . .*

"Rex?" Charlotte said. "Are you still hungry?"

"Not hungry, but *merci*," Rex said, reaching for his phone as it vibrated inside his inner pocket. He looked at it. Marcel. *Mon Dieu.* He was going to love this.

> *Have you arrived?*
> *Yes. And I think I'm on to something.*

That would surely get him.

Almost immediately, Marcel replied,

> *What?*
> *In a word, Richette.*

Then he added quickly,

> *I think they're at it again. And I think they got to Lilith.*
> *How?*

Should he tell him about Lilith? Oh what the hell.

> *I think they got to Lilith. She told me she tried to steal my phone back, but it was already gone. I'm not sure if I believe her.*

It was a minute or so before he answered.

Okay. Keep me posted. Ciao.

Rex stared at his phone. *That was it?* You'd think the mere mention of Richette would have sent Marcel through the roof. Never in a million years would he understand that family.

He looked up to find the congressman whispering something in Charlotte's ear. *Merde, do I need this annoyance now?* She was listening intently and nodding, then all of a sudden she burst into laughter.

Rex lifted his gaze briefly as he scrolled through his phone. "I know it may be difficult during the workweek, but have you two thought of retiring to someplace a bit more private?"

"Very funny, Rex," Charlotte said.

Trent cleared his throat, and shifted away.

Rex continued scrolling, not bothering to look up again. If he did he just might push that arrogant little *minot* from the tram.

Charlotte grabbed hold of a support pole and swung herself to Rex's side. "What was that all about?" she whispered.

"To what are you referring?" Rex calmly asked, still scrolling through.

"To this." She leaned in, as close as propriety would allow and whispered, "I'm still not wearing any underwear."

His eyes popped wide, his shorts already beginning

to tighten. He glared at her. "You are too. I saw you pick them up."

"They're in my purse," she said, opening it just enough so he could see the white of their lacy edging. "I was just going to put them on, then Lilith showed up."

"*Merde*," he whispered, staring at them.

Charlotte smiled. "How about that, huh?"

He shifted uncomfortably, glaring at her. "I will most definitely reward you for that later."

"Promise?" she said, brow arching.

"Oh," said Trent from across the car. "*Oh*. Now I get it." He looked to Rex. "Sorry, but honestly we're just friends."

Rex regarded him with Gallic indifference. "How fortunate you are."

The tram slowed to a stop. "Er . . . we're here," Trent said, quickly rising. He jumped to the platform. "Right this way."

Rex stood back, allowing Charlotte to exit first. As he followed, he let his hand slip from the seat grip to the slope of her *derrière*.

"Oh!" she squeaked.

"A very articulate way of putting it," he said, both of them following Trent up the escalator.

After a few twists and turns and a long hallway, they entered into the lower level of the Capitol, Trent taking them to security to receive their visitor's badges. "It'll be a little easier to get around with these, but security is pretty tight, so stick to the public areas." He turned to Rex, offering his hand. "Mr. Renaud—a pleasure."

"*Oui. Merci,*" he said, taking it.

Trent gave it a good shake, then let go. "I apologize for any misunderstanding."

Charlotte turned on him. "Trent, what the hell are you talking about?" She eyed him speculatively. "If you are talking about what I *think* you're talking about, remember who you're referring to."

He laughed. "Spoken so succinctly." He squeezed her shoulder. "I have to get to the chamber as there's some people I want to schmooze. See you soon." He waved, and was off.

After he left, Charlotte turned to Rex. "As for you . . ."

He pulled her aside. "We need to talk."

She huffed. "Rex, you must be joking. Trent and I are just old friends. As I told you, my fiancé introduced us, and we were never, ever an item." Then she sighed. "Okay, maybe we were, for about two weeks. After my engagement ended we did date for a little while, but I swear, it never went beyond flirtation and a few make-out sessions. I mean, I'm almost *seven* years older than he is. Not that it should matter, but honestly, I'm no cougar. I prefer to date men my own age. I never even slept with the man. But don't get me wrong. He tried, but I guess I just wasn't into—"

"Charlotte," he cut in. "*Mon Dieu*—it's like you're stuck in sixth gear and the brakes are out."

"Sorry," she said, shoving her hands into her coat pockets. "But you're annoyed with me and I don't want you to be. Sure, he was a bit attentive, but it didn't mean anything. And you shouldn't judge me, not with your rep. A little while ago I had to put up with one of your old girlfriends, didn't I? You didn't see me treat her in any other way than civil—"

"Christ! There you go again." He pulled her away even further, into the stairwell. "Charlotte, shut up already." Then he cupped her chin in his hand and kissed her.

"Mmmm—mmm," she muttered, tilting her head back as he opened her mouth with his tongue. It was a quick kiss but no less ardent, Charlotte leaning into him as his hand fell to the small of her back. Just as they finished a passerby gave a low whistle.

"Must be a liberal," Rex whispered against her lips.

"Nah, that's a conservative," Charlotte said. "Dark corners are their preferred milieu. Liberals are notoriously shameless."

He looked at her. "So what does that make us?"

"In dire need of one of those private places you suggested."

"Moderates. A dying breed." He kissed her again, then let her go. "Let's take care of business, then we'll go look for a nice dark corner. And it won't take as long as I anticipated."

"Didn't you want to talk to me about something?"

"Yes." He took a deep breath. "I don't have any proof besides a feeling I'm having, but I believe Viviane—Marcel's mother—may be here."

"You're joking." She looked over her shoulder, as if she were standing right behind them. "Because of what Trent said about Richette?"

"*Oui*. I'm almost thinking that if she is, it would confirm their involvement."

"As well as their attempt to take Mercier down." Panic streaked over her face. "And you with them." She gripped his arm. "Oh Rex, if that's true, then you've got to get out of here. If anyone recognizes you they'll be a bench warrant out for you for sure." Her eyes widened. "Or maybe that's just how they planned it." She tugged at him. "Come on."

He pulled back. "No. Not until I see for sure."

"Are you insane?" She stared at him as if he were. "How could you take that chance? If Richette is truly out to get you, she's their first line of offense. We have to leave—and *now*."

"And we will. But not before we get what we came here for." He led her back to the floor toward the stairwell.

"Rex—no," she said, pulling back.

He turned to her. "Charlotte, I'm not leaving until I see if she's here. Are you coming or would you rather wait out here?"

She winced. "Rex, please. I mean, really—do you want to get caught?"

He felt a perverse pleasure in Charlotte looking so pained. That level of anxiety must mean she cared for him a great deal. And that only emboldened him further. "Charlotte, *chérie*, I have to see this through so I'm going with or without you. But I'd really rather have you by my side." He reached out for her hand. "Will you come?"

She sighed, and after a moment, joined him. "My God, you really are an impossible man. You'll have us both in jail before long."

He tucked her arm into his. "Then let's hope for conjugal visits. Now let's go. It's almost three."

The gallery was filling up with individuals and tour groups, as the House members gathered onto the floor. Legislators on both sides mingled within their own party and occasionally with those across the aisle, the floor and podium teeming with aides, staffers, and press. Off to the side a congresswoman spoke with an easel to her left full of diagrams and charts, playing more for the C-SPAN camera than the few people who were paying attention. Rex and Charlotte took a seat in the top row not far from the doorway, affording Rex a higher vantage point. And, he knew, a quicker way out.

"Can you see Congressman Hitchell from here?" Charlotte asked.

He started looking as soon as he entered the chamber. "No. But it's almost three, so I imagine he'll be up there soon in front of the camera, where that congresswoman is now." He also scanned the gallery for Viviane, but as far as he could see, she hadn't arrived.

He thought back to the only other time he'd sat in the congressional gallery. It'd been the day Lilith had first brought H.R. 22186 to the floor. He had such high hopes for the bill passing, especially after they had sealed their mutual ambitions with a quick *baiser* atop her desk. Was that the price of his ambitions? If it was, then who had been the real whore? Even though the bill could be reintroduced in the next session, it took it failing to realize he didn't have the stomach for Washington politics any longer. He gripped Charlotte's hand and she smiled. Especially with who was sitting next to him now.

Then Viviane Mercier walked into the gallery.

His breath caught—how long had it been since he'd last seen her? Years, he knew, yet she was still as devastatingly beautiful as she'd ever been. She made her way down the steps to the first row, just as the congresswoman yielded to Representative Brendan Hitchell.

"She's here," Rex whispered.

Charlotte gripped his arm. "Where?"

"Front and center," Rex said, tilting his chin. "The one with the bright blue coat and dark hair."

"Good God," Charlotte whispered as Viviane turned to the left. "Who could deny Marcel's her son? He's her spitting image." She looked to Rex. "Okay, there's your answer. Now let's go."

"In a minute—there's Hitchell," Rex said, leaning forward.

Representative Hitchell shuffled his papers atop the podium and looked to his colleagues. "Let me begin by saying I believe in climate change."

"Oh boy, a heretical admission for the right, but a new hero for the liberals," Charlotte whispered.

"And because of that," Hitchell continued, "we're constantly on the lookout for fuels that even out or eliminate carbon emissions, especially for developing nations and even in Europe. And that's why I say if we introduce new technology we can solve these problems and bring about a cleaner world, and in the process . . ."

"Please, Rex, he's sucking all the oxygen out of the room," Charlotte said. "Let's get out of here before you get caught or I die of boredom."

Viviane took a seat, loosening her coat, but she was hardly settling in. Rex leaned forward, watching her.

"And because of that I'm introducing H.R. 12953," Hitchell continued. "The LNG Carbon Reduction Funding Bill, that will make the United States the largest producer of clean fuel in the world . . ."

She's not listening to Hitchell, Rex thought. *She's looking around, searching for someone.*

Charlotte noticed. "Five more seconds and she's going to see you."

"Just a second," Rex said. *Who are you looking for, Viviane? Are you looking for me? Just a couple millimeters more and—* She turned, looking dead into his eyes. Then just as quickly, she looked away. Like she couldn't quite believe what she saw.

He wasn't about to give her another chance.

Rex rose. "Let's go. *Now.*" He grabbed Charlotte's hand. "Hurry."

They trotted out the gallery as fast as they could, and were out on the street and chasing down a cab before Charlotte could catch her breath.

"Jesus—Rex! Hold up!" she cried, running to the curb, Rex already sliding into the taxi Once they were out in traffic, she turned to him, her chest heaving. "Damn, that was close. As it was, I could almost hear the jail door clanging shut."

He took her hand, kissing it. "It was kind of exciting though, don't you think?"

"Almost getting caught?" She shook her head. "You're crazy. What if she saw you?"

He was excited, the blood pumping, pounding in his veins. He hadn't felt this charged in as long as he could remember. "That's the thing. She did."

"What?" She looked horrified.

"And you know what? I don't think she quite believed what she saw."

"You'd better hope not, or there's going to be five million less dollars in your bank account."

He leaned back, throwing his arm over her. "Oh, the look on her face . . ."

"Rex, stop. Please," Charlotte said, an ironic twist to her voice. "You're scaring me."

He looked to her, astonished, tilting her back in his arms. "Scared? Of me? When all I really want to do is kiss you?"

She held him off, her hand to his chest. "I'll bet that's the least of it."

"How well you know me already," he said, his mouth lowering to hers.

As soon as they got back to the suite Rex was like a bull in rut. Only randier.

"Come here . . ." he growled, pulling her into the bedroom. He ripped back the sheets, then proceeded to strip every piece of clothing from her body.

"You know I can do that," she said, standing there as he kissed her cheek, her neck, as he opened her coat and slid it from her. "And probably faster, too."

"You're like opening up a piece of candy," he said, slipping off her sweater before he proceeded to unbutton her dress, sliding that off her, too, until she was only in her bra and pumps, a puddle of clothing at her feet.

He raked his gaze down her, his eyes heavy and lidded. "You weren't kidding about the panties, were you?"

"Told ja," she said, as if it was obvious.

He pinched his thumb and forefinger between her breasts and let her bra snap open, sliding it off her shoulders to the floor. After a moment of openly gaping he stood back to gape even more.

"Like what you see?" she said, hands to hips, thrusting her breasts forward.

He shook his head slightly, like coming out of a stupor. "*Merde*," he said, low and throatily, "get in the bed."

"I will," she said, crawling into it, "but I don't care what your kinks are. These are not coming with me." She kicked off her shoes, then propped herself against the headboard. "Now it's my turn," she said, openly gaping as well.

Rex slipped off his shoes and socks and unknotting his tie, yanked it off, removing the rest of his clothing in record time.

"You've done this before," Charlotte observed, bringing her legs up to her chin.

He was left with his boxer briefs and for a split second, Charlotte wished he'd leave them on. Much like what lingerie does for a woman, she savored the mystery beneath the form-fitting cotton and silk below his broad chest and tightly packed abs. After a few moments he slid them off and came toward her, cocked and loaded. He slipped in beside her, taking her in his arms.

"You know, I . . ." He sighed. "Look, *chérie*, it's up to you of course, but we kind of dispensed with the wrappings before, so it probably wouldn't matter if we did it *au naturel* now." He stroked her cheek with the back of his fingers. "But even so, I kind of did it without your permission before, so . . ."

She cocked a brow. "It's kind of late for that now, don't you think?"

"*Ma belle*," he murmured, laying her back against the pillows. "I just want you to be sure."

"I'm sure," she said, stretching out beneath him. "And I trust you. Any reason why I shouldn't?"

"*Mon Dieu*, Charlotte," he said, his kissing her as he lowed himself, "there's every reason in the world."

Her breath caught as he slipped himself inside her, the feeling of fullness almost overwhelming. She arched her back as he drove himself in, his hand slipping under her thigh as he pulled her leg up to bury himself to the hilt. "Charlotte . . ." he whispered, groaning as he sank himself deeper. She smoothed her hands lightly down his back, Rex shivering under her trace. "Charlotte . . ." he whispered, nipping the corner of her mouth. She shivered as well. How couldn't she?

Because it was becoming harder and harder to separate the woman she was to the outside world, to what she became when she was with him. She'd been hired as his lawyer, but her feelings for him were so much more personal now. Maybe she needed to forget the inclusive feel of his arms around her, the desire in his eyes when he looked at her, that sense of belonging to someone other than herself. Because she didn't belong to him. Whatever they were together, she knew it was only temporary, a faux security unlikely to become permanent.

Yet when she touched his cheek, he smiled.

She couldn't help smiling, too. There were worse things she could fool herself with, she supposed.

She tossed her head back and let his steady stroking take her higher and higher, his eyes blissful as he rolled them over the edge. For now it had to be enough. For whatever would come, she'd always remember this, the two of them joined, a perfect illusion of one.

Chapter Eighteen

Thicker than Blood

REX HAD FALLEN asleep almost immediately after, sliding off to spoon behind Charlotte, his arms tightly around her. She awoke to find she could hardly move, but why would she want to? How long had it been since she'd spent this much time in such close proximity to another human being? Too long, she knew. And she was going to miss it after he was gone, not so very long from now.

She could feel him breathing against her neck, the soft hairs of his chest against her back, the taut muscles of his thigh as it rested on hers. He had been in her and now he virtually surrounded her, his arm flung across her chest in a possessive clutch. He was warm and she felt safe, from what, she wasn't sure, but if it was out there she knew he'd keep whatever it was away.

She opened her eyes and fixed on his hand, or what

she could see of it lying loosely across her shoulder. For as much as she knew of him, these weren't the pampered hands of a businessman. There was something in his life that had caused those calluses below the curl of his fingers. Probably indicative of all his mysteries, like a tiny glimpse into a life she'd never know. And suddenly she wanted to, very badly.

She wasn't sure why she was feeling this way now. Maybe it was because of what happened just before, how excited he got over playing a little too close to the edge. It had almost seemed that he wanted Viviane to see him. Why was that? What lay between them besides the obvious fact of his betrayal? She'd have to ask him as up until now, they seemed to have been following the same tack. Maybe that was significant. Maybe that proved whatever he came here to accomplish, he had. And that saddened her that this thing, whatever it was, was playing out.

Strange that it had happened to begin with. When they first met, she had hated him on sight, as she did all his breed of corporate bulldog. They were her bread and butter and she ate them alive every day, but somehow she could tell Rex was different. He didn't stare past her and let his minions do the talking. He listened and spoke his own piece, then let her do the same. He was courteous and gracious, but that only made her suspicious, having seen that ploy before. He reminded her of an old saying: *The knife will enter so much easier when it's oiled*. But not once did she feel as if she'd been played. She came in with her demands, then left with more than she expected. *It's just good business*, he had said. Suddenly Rex shifted against her and she moved along with him. Was this good business, too? She had to wonder.

He kissed her neck and she rolled over to face him. "*Salut*," she whispered.

He yawned and raked back his hair, his eyes even more sensual in their somnolence. "*Bonjour*. I must have fallen asleep." He kissed her shoulder, looping his leg over her again. "*Pardon. Toutes mes excuses*. Do you forgive me?"

"I always do." She took his hand, smoothing the pads below his fingers. "Tell me, how does a desk jockey like you get calluses as thick as these?"

His mouth crooked as he threaded his fingers into hers. "Maybe because real jockeys have something in common with me."

"Like betting on the ponies?" she said, trailing a finger up his chest.

He grabbed her hand, kissing it. "Like riding them."

"You ride horses?" She had to stifle a laugh. "What—polo ponies? That would fit."

He took exception, his chin lifting. "I'll have you know I've been riding since before I could walk."

"On little tiny baby polo ponies," she said, curling into him. "With training wheels."

"*Non*," he said, trying not to laugh. "On big, strapping Percherons."

Charlotte thought a moment. "Aren't they draft horses? Work horses, I mean?"

"*Oui*. They pull things. Like wagons full of grapes."

He brushed back her hair, smoothing it down her neck. "I grew up on a vineyard, and I used to ride all around it."

"Did you now?" It thrilled her he was telling her this. "Is that where you live now?"

"Too far from the office. I live in a little house by the sea in Vallon des Auffes, a fishing port in Marseille. But I ride every chance I get."

"I've never been to Marseille. I'll have to come visit you next time I'm in France."

"*Chérie . . .*" he murmured, kissing the slope of her jaw, "but I'm here, right now, with you."

He certainly was. But for how long? And that was the truly scary part. Because she was starting to ask herself—could she fall in love with him? He slid down her body, kissing the hollow of her throat. "Yes, you are. It seems I can't get you out of my bed."

He laughed in that low, throaty baritone of his. "*Tu me rends fou. Qu'est-ce que je ferais sans toi?*" he whispered, his tongue trailing little circles around her breasts.

Now she was as surprised as he. What would he do without her? "*Je ne sais pas.*" She supposed he'd find out soon.

He lifted his head. "Don't you?" he continued *en français*.

"You'll wither and die," she said in kind. "You'll miss me so terribly you won't know what to do."

He rested his chin on her belly, looking up. "I don't know what to do now, my love." He grasped her hips, kissing his way from one hip to the other. "All I know is I want you badly, more than any other woman I've ever been with." He kissed her navel, his tongue trailing around it and down. "I want you now and every second of the day. And just like now, I can't get enough." He trailed lower and lower, until his tongue deftly flicked her clit.

She arched up, startled, still moist from where he had come inside her. The very idea was almost too erotic and she squirmed, her hands at his shoulders, his grasp only tightening.

"Don't move," he ordered, pressing her hips to the mattress, his tongue pleasuring her in such rapid succession her breath became uneven. His hands slipped around to her backside and he lifted her up, his fingers delving in between, one rimming her before sinking deep inside.

"Ahh!" She gasped, yanking his hair, her hips bucking with the force of her rising. Rex probed deeper and deeper while she rose even higher until all at once he let go and slid up and sank into her. Before she could take another breath she was going off again, her head thrown back in a wordless yowl. A moment later his face contorted and he joined her, going rigid as he climaxed deep inside her. When he was spent he collapsed atop her. Charlotte, indescribably sated, flinging her arms around him.

"My—God," he choked out, still *en français*, "that just about cost me my—"

"Shut up," she said in English, turning her head to kiss him, so deeply he growled from the back of his throat.

"*Coquette,*" he said, his eyes flaring. "A kiss like that demands another fuck but I regret I'm down and out for the duration."

"Good," she said, kissing him lightly. "I don't think I could survive it."

"Oh you would, you'd have to." He slipped from her, sliding to her side. "I couldn't bear it if you didn't," he said, caressing her cheek. "Not when I've finally found you."

She stared at him, barely able to speak. "Rex—what are you saying?"

He didn't answer. He just looked at her, his eyes dark and fathomless. Then he turned and climbed out of the bed. "Come here," he said, gathering her up.

He took her to the shower where they wordlessly soaped each other down. When they were finished they simply stood under the warm rain, locked in each other's arms.

"What do you want from me, *ma petit*?" he murmured against her mouth. "Am I saying what you want to hear, and if I am, why won't you believe me?"

"Why do you have to even say anything?" she said, laying her head against his shoulder. "Why make this more than what it is—what you *know* it is."

"And what's that?"

It pained her to admit it, but she was veering too close to dangerous territory to even hope it was more than what it was. "A wonderful way to pass the time until the inevitable takes over." She looked up. "You know that's all it is."

"No I don't. I can't tell the future like you." He regarded her, his eyes heavy-lidded and unreadable. "How about for now we don't waste any more time talking about it. I want you and I want to be with you, and I'm fairly certain you feel the same about me. Plus I have you naked in my arms. How can I ask for anything better?"

"I suppose you couldn't," she said, sliding her hands down his slippery back, storing the memory for later.

WHILE CHARLOTTE DRIED her hair Rex ordered big, thick steaks and pommes frites for dinner, along with a salad of mixed greens, a cheese plate with bread, an assortment of petite French pastries, and coffee.

"And a big bottle of Cabernet Sauvignon," he said, putting down the house phone. He padded over in the hotel robes they were both wearing, leaning into the jamb. "Do you think that's enough?"

"I think I'll explode if I even eat a third of it," she said, reapplying her mascara. "And that's coming off hardly touching the food we got for lunch. I'm starving."

"So am I. They said it shouldn't take that long." His mouth crooked. "They always take care of me fairly quickly."

"No doubt," she said, sliding on her lipstick. "As much coin as you probably drop here." She stood back, fluffing her hair.

"I could watch you do that all day, *ma belle*," he said.

She didn't follow. "Do what?"

He crossed his arms over his chest, watching her. "Making yourself beautiful for me."

"For you?" She laughed. "Oh sweetie, this is just maintenance. If I didn't, you wouldn't even want to see me in the dark."

He came up behind her, resting his hands on her hips. "Why is it the loveliest of women are always the most disparaging of themselves? *Chérie*, I only want to see you in the dark now," he said, kissing her neck. "Because that would make it night and that would mean you'd be under me."

She groaned, arching into him, his hands hot as they snaked under the robe to her breasts. It was almost incredible how much she craved him, even again, even if it were only his touch. But someone had to be sane in this relationship. She pulled away, going for her clothes.

"I'd better get dressed," she said, reaching for her bra.

"*Non*," he said, his hands at her waist. "Not yet."

"Oh really," she said, turning in her arms. "You are indeed a T-Rex. But I think we'll wait for dessert, okay?"

"*Très bien*." He leaned in, smiling wickedly as his hand slid to her belly. "Why do you think I got the French pastries?"

"Éclairs?"

"Oh, very astute, Charlotte."

Twenty minutes later they were at the dining room table tucking into their steaks, each large enough to feed a small country. Or so Charlotte thought. Not that she was complaining.

"God, this is awesome," she said, slicing into the beef. "This is just what I needed."

"Right," he said, as if it was obvious. "What woman doesn't need a big slab of beef now and then?"

"Or two," she said, eyeing him salaciously, "you big beefsteak, you." She chewed, savoring each bite.

He glanced at the clock. "It's eight now. I think we'll wait a couple hours and then we'll make our way back. How's that?"

She eyed him speculatively. "That's a good idea. I'm surprised she hasn't tracked us to the hotel by now."

"She doesn't have to." He set down his fork, reaching for the bottle of Cabernet. Charlotte pushed over her glass and he poured them each one. "She knows where to find me."

"You mean with me."

"*Oui*, and I expect she'll pay us a visit before too long."

The mere mention of Marcel's mother seemed to set his teeth on edge. "And how do you feel about that?"

He swirled the wine, regarding it, before he took a sip and set it down with a wince. "Well, what do you expect from Sonoma. Anyway, I would say we've been due for a confrontation for a long time now. She's never forgiven me for thwarting her Machiavellian ambitions and siding with her son."

Charlotte thought a minute. "But what about Andy? Wasn't he the one who came up with the plan?"

"You know, I think he's the only person in the world who gives her pause, though I seem to have come in a close second. We've both had to bear the brunt of her wrath." He picked up his knife and went back to the steak. "Though all she tried to do was break up his marriage. How much worse could you get than getting someone accused of sexual assault?"

"I don't know." She tossed her hand. "Murder?"

His brow arched. "Now who's going to volunteer for

that? Call me self-centered, but I can envision much worse scenarios than compromising yourself with me."

She grinned salaciously. "I'll attest to that."

"Exactly." He slid a piece of steak into his mouth, chewed, swallowed. "Anyway, what better way to get a bill killed than by having it benefit a sex fiend like me? Even a vague association would be anathema."

"But Lilith couldn't know that when she sponsored the bill."

"*Non*, of course not. I think she came into it with honest intentions. Remember, it would benefit her constituency as it would mean jobs, so it could only help her in the election. And that's precisely why someone got to her."

"Marcel's mother."

"That's what I'm thinking."

"So Lilith's not so innocent after all."

"Lilith is for Lilith, but I knew that going in."

"Metaphorically speaking, of course."

"*Chérie*," he said, coloring, using his fork for emphasis, "I will allow that one time and one time only."

"Hey, I'm only your straight man. You thought that up all on your own."

"Don't remind me. I'm usually much more obtuse than that."

Charlotte sipped the wine. "What are you talking about? This is good. But then again, I'm not a wine snob like you."

He took exception. "When France starts making cheese steaks and root beer then you can become as big a snob about them as I am about our wine."

"Not setting the bar too high, are you? Anyway, so what you're saying is that perhaps Viviane got to the congresswoman and bribed her to string you along and kill the bill."

"I was gone for two months, remember. Anything could've happened in that amount of time. Which was when either Viviane or Hitchell probably got to her."

"So he was always the fly in the ointment, wasn't he?"

"The *what*?"

"It's an old American expression."

"Oh. Like, *on n'apprend pas aux vieux singes à faire des grimaces.*"

"What's that?"

"You cannot teach old monkeys to make faces."

"That's a rip-off on you can't teach an old dog new tricks."

"Variations on a theme." He leaned into the table. "But we digress." He took one more sip, this time frowning. "*Mon Dieu*, that wine is *dégueulasse.*" He shoved the glass away, tippling it,

"Rex!" Charlotte cried, catching it before it fell over. "For Christ sake, it's not from Provence, but it's hardly Boone's Farm." She downed a good portion from her own glass. "I think it's very good, but then again, I wasn't born with your silver spoon."

He looked up sharply. "You have no idea what I was born with."

"No I don't," she said, irritated he was acting this way. "You've kept most information about yourself very well hidden. As a matter of fact, the only things I really know about you are you hate this wine, you ride Percherons, and you like to fuck me." She took another swallow. "Well, *I* like this wine, and as far as I'm concerned you probably think you're slumming."

"Is that so," he said, rising, turning toward the bar. He poured himself a finger of scotch then came around to Charlotte. "Would you like to know a little about my upbringing?"

"I think it would help to understand you a bit more."

He sat back at the table, his legs spread, his drink between them. "Do you think that's important?"

There was a strange kind of hunger in his eyes. "Yes, I do," she said.

"Why?"

Why was he pressing her? Was he trying to make her say she loved him? Because she couldn't, not now. Maybe never. "Maybe I'm just a little bit curious about what it's like to get everything you want right from the start."

"Is that what you think my life's been like?" He tossed back the shot. "Then let me enlighten you. My epicurean and oenological tastes come from a long line of sausage makers and grape pickers. *Les bouseux*, they're called back home—the cow pies. Then along about the later part of the twentieth century some members of the family decided to get ambitious and trade their clogs for boat shoes. So my father left the farm and went to the big city, to work for a shipping company called—"

"Mercier," Charlotte finished.

"Exactly," Rex said. "He was to start off as an ordinary seaman, the lowest of the low on a ship. But it was a good job, and it paid steady. And after a while, he'd have enough money for a nice big apartment in Marseille. So one morning before I left for school, I remember seeing him at the door with his suitcase, my mother in his arms. She was crying so hard he had to hold her up, and they spent a very long time kissing. After a while he came and told me to be a good boy and take care of my *maman*, then he kissed me and left. I was nine years old, and I never saw him again."

"What happened?" she said, transfixed.

He looked down into his glass. "About three months later he was helping to repair a winch when he got caught in it and it snapped his head off."

"Jesus . . ." Charlotte whispered.

"They sent his body home in a leak-proof box and the company gave my mother a pension for life. Everyone thought it was fair, especially since we wouldn't have to worry about money anymore. But that didn't stop my mother from hanging herself in the basement on the day the first check arrived."

She brushed her hand down his arm. "Is that when you went to live with your aunt?"

He set the glass to the table, sitting back. "She was responsible for me, but I never lived with her. She went back to Mercier and demanded they do more for me, since I was now an orphan. They thought they had done enough, but she was relentless, demanding they take care of my education. So the next thing I knew I was shipped off to boarding school, and a trust fund was set up in my name. I did so well I eventually went on to Cambridge, then Harvard for my MBA, finding out I had an unusual penchant for business. You see, *I* was the original wunderkind, way before they started calling Marcel that. By twenty-eight, I had risen up through the corporate ranks to become a vice-president in charge of finance for Andele Chemical. By thirty, I was chief operating officer for Sinclair Aero. Then a year later I was lured away to Richette. And that," he said, pulling her into his lap, "is the story of this simple boy's rise to riches."

"Oh, I'm sure there's much more to it than that," Charlotte said. "You're way too complicated for simplicity."

"You should know," he said, tilting her back in his arms.

IT WAS CLOSE to six-thirty by the time they made it back to the Margate beach up the street from Charlotte's house. The sun had nearly risen over the rim of the ocean, the horizon streaked with reds and golds.

"I'm glad I wore this coat," Charlotte said, walking faster. "It's pretty chilly out here."

Rex pulled her closer, his arm around her. "Thank God for body heat. Shall we throw a log in your fireplace?"

"There's a lot of seasoned wood out back. My grandmother was big on fires at holidays. Why, every Christmas we would—" She grabbed Rex's arm, stopping him. "Rex—look. Someone's sitting in my backyard."

He peered through the twilight. "What the hell?"

"Do you think it's someone from Philly?" she said as they picked up their pace. "Or maybe even the cops?"

"I don't know. But if it is the cops, we'll just say we spent the night in Atlantic City. There's no law against that, and they'll have me playing on camera."

"As well as that big wad of cash you still have in your pocket. Good idea."

Suddenly, he stopped. "Wait a minute. That's no cop."

"How do you know?" she said, squinting to see.

He looked at her wryly. "Not in those shoes."

Charlotte looked at him. "It's a woman?"

Rex took her hand as they approached the steps from the beach. "Come on."

By the time they turned the corner into the yard they could see a woman in a black coat and very high heels, her head covered in a scarf. She was just crushing out a cigarette when suddenly she saw them, her eyes a striking shade of blue, even in the thin light.

"Rex!" Charlotte whispered, grabbing his arm. "You were right, weren't you?"

"Good morning," the woman said in French, reaching into her pocket. When she pulled her hand out, a phone was in it. "Looking for this?"

Rex laughed, looking to an astonished Charlotte as he said in English, "Charlotte, this is my aunt, Viviane Mercier."

Chapter Nineteen

Femmes Fatale

CHARLOTTE LOOKED FROM Rex to his aunt to the phone in her hand, at a loss for what was most incredible. "Viviane Mercier is your *aunt*?"

"Only by blood, Charlotte, and most definitely not by affection. *Bonjour*, Viviane. *Comment allez-vous?*" Then he was on her, holding his hand out as he continued *en français*. "Now give me my fucking phone."

"Oh do cut to the chase," Viviane said in their own language, throwing it at him. "I wouldn't want you to mince words, you ungrateful ass."

"And I wouldn't want to wring your neck," he said, catching it. "At least not for all the neighbors to see." He went straight to the voice recorder, tapping it. "It's there," he said, letting out a visible sigh of relief. "How the hell did you get my phone?"

"It wasn't that difficult. Policemen still take bribes, you know." She rubbed her arms, shivering a bit. "I've been sitting out here for over an hour. You could at least offer me a coffee."

"Did I hear right?" Charlotte felt like screaming. "We've just been running all over the East Coast because of her, and she wants you to make her *coffee*?"

"Your woman there," Viviane said, *en français*, eyeing her blandly, "she's rather excitable, isn't she?"

"Actually," Rex said in their own language, "she's my attorney."

"Oh really?" His aunt gave her a quick once-over. "Well, with that hair she looks more like a tart. Are you sleeping with her?"

"What the hell!" Charlotte cried. She glared at the older woman. "And you look like something out of a Mickey Spillane novel," she said in French. "Why don't you go stand under a streetlight."

The woman turned red with rage. "Why didn't you tell me she speaks the language!" she said in English.

"Because it's more interesting this way, don't you think?" Rex said. "But let's keep to English so we're all on the same page." He grabbed her arm. "I'm going to give you ten seconds to tell me what part you're playing in this drama, or I swear to God I'm calling the police and having you—"

"*Arrêtez—arrêtez!*" she cried, shrugging him loose. "Believe it or not, if you give me a chance to explain you'll find out I'm very much on your side."

His brow arched. "Excuse me if I find that extremely difficult to fathom."

The elder woman straightened, righting the scarf over her midnight-black hair. "I'm not asking you to believe me. All I'm asking is for you to listen." She shivered again. "And maybe take an old and very tired woman out of the cold."

"Old—*you*?" Rex scoffed. "Why Viviane, you're ageless." Then he took her arm, a bit more gently, yet no less firmly. "You have ten minutes. Let's go."

THERE WAS NO milk and very little sugar, so Charlotte bypassed what Rex and his aunt would call *café américain* for a French espresso her grandmother had been fond of. Which either impressed or irritated the older woman immensely. Charlotte found it hard to tell the difference and couldn't care less about either.

How she was feeling toward Rex right now was quite another story.

"You could have told me," she whispered as they stood by the stove, his aunt settling herself at the kitchen table. She turned up the fire under the kettle. "You're Marcel's first cousin, for Christ's sake."

"I've hardly seen her more than ten days my whole life. The fact she's my *tante* is purely an accident of birth. Marcel doesn't even know about me."

She stared at him in disbelief? "What?"

"It's rather awkward sitting in someone's house you don't even know the name of," Viviane said, slipping her scarf around her shoulders. "Don't you think it's time you introduce us, Rex?"

He turned from the stove. "As if you don't already know, but I'll say it anyway." He flung his hand from one woman to the other. "Charlotte Andreko—Viviane Mercier."

"*Enchantée*," Viviane said, nodding her head to Charlotte. "I've noticed your accent is too good for an American," she added with a regal lift of her nose. "Are you French?"

"Her *grand-mère* was a *Parisienne*," Rex said, appearing to enjoy how that stiffened her shoulders. "Her mother was born there and lives there now. Charlotte is half French."

"Ah." Viviane lifted her chin. "That explains the attitude."

Charlotte ignored that, bringing down the coffee press. "That was you in the Rolls-Royce the other night, wasn't it?"

"It was," Viviane said.

"But how did you find us?" Charlotte said. "No one knew we were here except the police . . ."

"Seems my aunt gets her money's worth out of a bribe," Rex said. "You must have dumped quite a load of cash for the privilege of screwing with my life."

"You really shouldn't talk like that, nephew," she said. "Because in just a few minutes you'll be thanking me."

"Can we save the cryptic dialogue for later, please?" Charlotte said. "I'd like to know why you were here Tuesday night, then in Washington yesterday, and why you grabbed Rex's phone." She stifled a yawn. "I'm working on very little sleep, and I'd really like to get this over with so I can go to bed."

"No doubt you do." Viviane said, fuming. She glanced to her nephew. "You *are* sleeping with her, aren't you?"

"Do you think I'd share that information with you or anyone else? Now," Rex said, "get to the point already. I've been accused of a felony, and—"

Her voice stopped him with the barest sound of derision. "As if you would have to force yourself on anyone. How ridiculous—"

"Viviane!" He charged at her, looming over her at the table. "Why have the directors been talking about going public again? The last time that happened you came to me at Richette, ready to sell out the family. It's the same now, isn't it?"

"You've got it all wrong," she said, mirroring his glare perfectly. "I didn't come looking for them. This time Richette came looking for me."

"Now why would they do that," Rex said, standing back, "if they didn't figure you'd be open to it?"

Her mouth crooked with a such a potent mix of cunning and seduction, it was a wonder the world wasn't laid at her feet. "Because I led them to believe I was."

Apparently, Rex wasn't buying it. "How?" Then he smiled as well. "Not that I'm questioning your skills." Or, Charlotte figured, perhaps he was simply immune.

"I was in Paris over the summer where I went to a cocktail party. At Jean-Paul Levere's."

"Who?" Charlotte said.

"Richette's CEO," Rex said, his eyes never leaving his aunt's.

"He said he invited me specially to introduce me to an

American businessman," she went on. "By the name of Brendan Hitchell."

"Representative Hitchell," Charlotte clarified, glancing to Rex, scooping coffee into the press. "Did he tell you that?"

"Not right then," she said, crossing a pair of very shapely legs. "Jean-Paul only said Monsieur Hitchell was looking into expanding his oil and gas business to Europe, and perhaps there was something our companies could do for him."

"How interesting he approached you instead of Marcel," Rex said, joining her at the table. "I'm assuming this was when both your son and I were in America?"

Her gaze shot to his. "I was perfectly aware of what he was doing."

"Then why did you play along?"

"You've heard the rumblings in the board about taking the company public," she said. "How their shares weren't paying as well as they could. The things they were saying about Marcel and André taking the company down."

"Fueled by your cogent criticism of each, no doubt," said Rex.

Those stunning eyes turned downward. "I'll admit my reputation as a mother isn't the best." Then she looked up, burying her gaze into Rex's. "But wait until you become a parent and you bear the betrayal of your oldest to a family that's taken someone so dear to me, and your youngest, hating you for trying to get justice. Then tell me how you'd feel."

"How horrible it's been for you." Rex's hands clenched.

"You sit there with that Hermès scarf around your shoulders, your Rolls-Royce on the street—covered in diamonds and euros falling out of your pockets—and yet you're trying to tell me the Merciers have ruined your life?" He clasped his chest. "Have they ruined *my* life, too?"

"You're the worst! You're like a knife right through my heart," she said, grasping the edge of the table, her eyes narrowing. "You ruined *everything*."

Rex shot to his feet, enraged. "Because I had the *audacity* to be grateful?"

"Wait a minute—wait a minute," Charlotte said, coming between them. She needed to defuse this situation before they killed each other. "I'm thinking it's time you clue me in on a few things. If Mercier's a family business and both of you are part of the family, then why aren't you playing on the same team?"

"Because of her grand plan to destroy Mercier," Rex said sardonically. "And she tried to use me to do it."

"The Merciers killed your parents—killed *my* only sister, and you'd do well to remember that," she snapped, her jaw twitching. "And they would've left you to rot back in that stinking little village if I hadn't fought for you."

Viviane turned away from her nephew, looking to Charlotte instead. "This is my life, *avocate*. They say I'm selfish, but all I've ever done was fight for people who don't give a damn about me and even less for themselves. I grew up in Le Havre, around ships, too. All day I used to watch them coming and going, wishing I could get on one and get the hell out of there. My sister did, though not in the way I wanted to. She met a farmer at *carna-*

val with more filth under his nails than a dockworker, and married him two weeks later. I was so brokenhearted when she said she was moving away I thought I would die." She lifted a delicate finger, flicking the corner of her eye. "We were inseparable up until that point. She was my twin sister, and we were barely eighteen." She glanced away, the years clouding her eyes. "I never saw her until years later when I brought her home in a box."

Her face filled with anger. "But after she left all I wanted to do was get even with her, though my escape wasn't much better. Not long after my sister left home I met an American sailor. He promised me the moon, and I believed him. I left with him for America, but what did I get? A broken-down farm, a drunk for a husband, and a baby son at nineteen. And what's even worse, when I went home to visit a couple years later, all I heard was how happy my sister was, especially now that she had a baby boy."

She made a distinct sound of derision. "She's picking grapes and living in a hovel, and she's happy? I never heard of such a thing. I knew I was meant for better than that. On one of my visits home from America to Le Havre I met a man in a nightclub named Victor Mercier. When he offered to buy me a drink, I knew my life would change."

"Which was how her grand little foot got in the Mercier business," Rex said.

"Wait a minute," Charlotte said, pouring coffee from the kettle into the French press. "You got a share of the company just by marrying into it?"

"Previously, only blood relatives would be given shares," she said, "but Victor's fifteen years older than me and was an only child and without an heir when I married him. So when Marcel was born, he was so happy he not only gave me a family share, but my son André as well."

"How generous," Charlotte opined.

"Victor was considered a very good catch. A sound investment, you could call it," Viviane said, looking quite satisfied with herself. "This may sound odd, but two of the best financial decisions I've ever made in my life was to make sure this man here"—she nodded to Rex—"got a good education, and the other, giving birth to my son, André. Both of them are excellent managers." All at once her expression soured. "But both of them went ahead and destroyed everything that I wanted to accomplish."

"Which brings us back to Richette," Charlotte said. "You used your family shares as leverage?"

"Although the Merciers own most of the shares, it's possible to turn over ownership of the company if the board of directors decide to sell their shares along with just one family member," Rex said. He looked to his aunt. "Which is what Viviane tried to do seven years ago."

Charlotte brought two cups of espresso to the table. "Enlighten me," she said.

"Seven years ago when the financial markets nearly collapsed in the U.S.," Rex said, "everything convulsed in Europe as well, including shipping. The board went into a panic as our net worth was tanking. Victor tried to tell them it was just temporary, that everything would even out if they just remained patient. But the board wouldn't listen." He glanced to his aunt. "And neither would Viviane."

"And why should I have?" Viviane said, on the defensive. "Victor was starting to care more about keeping his mistresses in penthouses than taking care of business. And Marcel was no different." She huffed in disgust. "He was running around with his pants around his ankles just like his *papa*."

"You hardly gave a damn about that," Rex said. "You figured your time had come as Mercier was just ripe for a takeover."

"But why?" Charlotte said, not following. "Weren't you thinking of Marcel?'

She shrugged, lifting her espresso. "Why should I? He certainly wasn't thinking about running a company. And André wanted nothing to do with the corporate culture, even though he knew more about the practical end of the business than anyone. He was happy just sailing around as an engineer. So I turned to my nephew."

"You were at Richette then," Charlotte said.

"As their *directeur général délégué*," Rex said. "She said the board was behind her, and her share of the company would tip the scales to allow it." His expression darkened as he looked to his aunt. "When Victor found out he had a massive stroke."

"Between the legs of his mistress, the old *queutard*," Viviane added.

Charlotte looked to Viviane. "So you decided selling out the family was the best for business?"

Viviane looked shocked at the boldness of the statement. "This one speaks her mind, doesn't she?"

"She came to me with the idea of a takeover," Rex said. "What the hell did I care about Mercier? They had outlived their usefulness as far as I was concerned. I put it before Richette's board of directors and they were all for it. Since the market was down, we'd be able to get them at a great price. Someone then leaked we were interested in Mercier, and Richette stock soared, while their value kept sinking even lower."

Viviane laughed, deeply and throatily. "It finally got André to dry land."

"That's true," Rex said. "I had never met him before, though I had heard about him. He came to my office fresh off the ship, still dressed in cargo pants. Even so, he was one of the most imposing men I had ever met. And, I could tell from the start, one of the most intelligent. He told me he was taking over for his stepfather temporarily, and he was offering me a deal. He said he was using his own money to buy out one of the investors, the one who had originally wanted to sell out. He was now offering that seat to me on the board, as well the same position I had then as DGD at Mercier. I'd become a shareholder of the company, and not just a *mere*"—he spun the word—"employee, making me richer than I could ever imagine—*if* the market rebounded."

"Which it did," Charlotte said.

"But back then, I was taking a chance," Rex continued. "Still, there was something convincing about André that made me trust him. He said if I'd do that, then Mercier would retain enough control to repel the takeover. But all I could see was a deal too good to refuse."

Charlotte looked to Viviane. "You must have gone through the roof."

She laughed lightly. "*Avocate*, there are some who haven't let me hit the ground yet."

"Marcel," Charlotte said.

"When he found out, he swore he'd never forgive me for what I did," Viviane said.

"And now she's trying to do it again," Rex said, his eyes turning very dark.

"No," Viviane said sharply. "I know you won't believe me, but I can't play those games anymore. The fight's not worth it." She lifted her cup, setting it down before she could even take a sip, all at once growing very quiet.

There in that kitchen, amid the silence that yawned between the three of them, Charlotte saw a woman aging before her eyes. For all her seeming advantage, for all her natural beauty, Viviane Mercier was worn to the core, the fine lines around her eyes and mouth settling even deeper as she bent into her coffee. And then, in an instant, she knew why.

Vendettas, in the end, are pretty cold comfort.

So are ideals, a little voice told her.

"I can either grow old or be alone, but I can't do both things at once," Viviane said wearily. "It's too hard. I found that out when André came to visit me a few months ago. Before he came I would have gladly sold myself to the other side. But as soon as I saw those two little boys of his, well . . . it made me realize how time is marching on without me."

Rex stared at her for a few long moments, sipping his coffee. "I've never known you to be quite so sentimental, Viviane."

"Call it sentimental—call it whatever you want, but you'll see what I mean"—her gaze flashed dismissively to Charlotte—"when it happens to you." Then she flung her hand to Rex's phone. "Isn't my getting that back for you proof enough?"

"Only after whatever goons you hired hacked it."

"Goons, huh?" She eyed him wryly. "Think what you want but I swear, nothing was stolen or erased."

"And don't think I won't check it out," Rex said.

"If you need any more proof I'm on your side, how about this bit of information." Viviane leaned in. "Congressman Hitchell has been buying stock in Richette."

Rex's eyes widened almost imperceptibly, but Charlotte noticed. "How do you know?" he said.

She seemed to take exception. "I have my spies as well, you know. He's buying so much stock he's now one of their principal stockholders."

"Why, that's an ethics violation," Charlotte said. "You can't sponsor a bill that'll benefit a company you're going to make millions off of."

"But he's buying Richette stock through a blind trust, so it looks like he doesn't know what's going on," Viviane said. "From what my spies are saying, once Hitchell's bill passes, the price of Richette stock will go through the roof."

Rex sat back, crossing his arms. "So if Richette gets control of Mercier, they'd control enough to practically corner the LNG market in Europe."

"And they're using your little congresswoman friend as the pipeline to you," Viviane said. "She never had any intention of trying to get that dredging bill passed, and that little escapade with the lobbyist was all part of it."

"Are you saying Lilith knew?" Charlotte said. "That she was complicit in setting Rex up?"

"I wouldn't go that far," Viviane said. "But discrediting Rex in order to devalue Mercier's worth was definitely part of Richette's plan. At least that's what Jean-Paul intimated to me." Her mouth curved seductively. "You see, I still know my way around a man, a martini, and a moonlit terrace."

He looked to his aunt. "But what proof do you have the congresswoman is implicated?"

"How about lots of Richette stock in *her* blind trust?" Viviane said. "Deposited in her account in the last two months. That's what they say, at least."

"Deposited during my sabbatical away." This time Rex was openly smiling. "How convenient." He looked to his aunt. "Marcel knows about this, surely."

Viviane flicked her hand dismissively. "Oh surely. That's one man who knows *everything*. So what are you going to do with this little bit of information now?"

"There's only one thing we can do," said Charlotte. "Confront Lilith with the recording of the lobbyist and if she doesn't play along, we'll take all this info to the assistant DA. Codicil that with the fact that my phone was stolen from the property room."

"*Quoi?*" Viviane said. "Then what will happen to me?"

"Nothing," Charlotte said. "No one will ever own up to it. But my righteous indignation will speak volumes for sure."

"Lilith will be ruined," Rex said. "Absolutely and—"

"Completely," Charlotte said. "And it couldn't happen to a nicer girl."

Viviane peered at them. "You two. You finish each other's sentences. Interesting." She looked to Charlotte. "*Où est le toilette, s'il vous plaît?*"

"Just up these steps," Charlotte said, pointing toward the stairs.

"*Pardon.*" She left for the bathroom.

When she was gone, Charlotte slumped against the sink with a sigh. "Jesus Christ, Rex. Do you believe her?"

He rose, going to her. "I don't know. But it won't take me long to find out. I'm throwing this ball right into Marcel's court just as soon as she leaves." He reached up, his hands on either side of her face. "You're exhausted, *chérie.*"

"Which I'm sure is just a polite euphemism for how shitty I look."

He brushed a strand of hair behind her ears. "Would you like to go to bed?"

"Please? Or do I have to beg?"

He slid his finger along her bottom lip, making her shiver. "I think I'd love to see you beg."

"Me too. I'd be a first."

"You know, we got cheated out of the éclairs again. I'm still waiting to lick the custard off your—"

"*Excusez-moi*," Viviane said, "but I must be going."

Rex turned, all playfulness vanishing from his face. "I'm going to check out everything you said."

"I wouldn't expect anything less," she said, reaching in her pockets for her gloves. "You know Julie's pregnant again."

"I know," he said. "We saw her just a couple of days ago."

"With twins," she said wistfully, looking away. "Just like me and your *maman*." She looked back to Rex. "Knowing that, how can you think I'm not telling the truth?"

"Maybe if you go see Marcel while you're here I would," Rex said. "Maybe it would help if he could hear what you told me from your own mouth."

She huffed with distinct Gallic dismissal. "He should come and see me. He knows where I live." She pushed down the leather gloves between her fingers. "Beside, he's on his honeymoon. Maybe this time it'll even stick." Her gaze shot to Rex. "Maybe you should tell him about yourself, you know."

"That should've been your job, *tante*, not mine."

"Well, nonetheless, someone should." She offered her hand to her nephew. "*Au revoir, neveu.*"

He stared at her hand a moment, looking unsure what to do, then suddenly took it. "*Au revoir, tante.* No one hopes more than me that what you're saying is true."

"You'll find out before too long." She turned to Charlotte. "*Au revoir,*" she said. "You can do far worse, you know." Then she nodded her head and walked out.

As they watched her walk across the street to her car, Rex said, "If what she says is true, what's the legal implications? At least as far as my charges are concerned?"

"Well, let's see . . ." Charlotte thought a moment. "False arrest and conspiracy, for starters."

"Against who?"

"Now, that's a bit trickier," Charlotte said. "It would all depend who's specifically behind this whole thing. I would expect that anyone connected with Richette would deny involvement. Hitchell would claim no knowledge of anything because the blind trust handles his investments. As far as the lobbyist is concerned, that's a classic case of he said/she said."

"Hm." Rex tapped his finger against his cheek. "Then it would all come down to Lilith?"

"I'd imagine they'd be looking for a scapegoat, and she's the most likely candidate if she knew what was going on while she was"—she eyed him up and down—"*with* you."

He cast her a wicked smile. "Couldn't happen to a nicer lady."

"In the end, they all could be complicit. But what do I know." Charlotte shrugged. "Like I told you, I'm not a criminal attorney."

"That's right. You're a goddess. Now come here." He pulled her to him. "Let me thank you."

"For what?" she said, slipping her arms around his neck.

"For the coffee. What do you think?"

She yawned, the best she could do at the moment.

"My sentiments exactly," he said, nipping the corner of her mouth. "Let me just give Marcel a quick call, and then . . ."

"And then we'll be just fine," she said, finishing the rest of his kiss.

THIS TIME IT took Marcel a little longer to pick up. "Talk to me," he said.

"Your mother just paid me a visit," Rex said.

"I was waiting for that," he said.

Not the reaction Rex had expected. "And why is that?"

"Because I figured she was behind this whole thing when I found out she had your phone."

Now Rex was really stymied. "And how did you figure that—oh, wait a minute. *You* were the one who hacked the phone. Or, Lee rather. Why didn't you tell me?"

"You never asked. Lee turned it on remotely, and then we did a location search. When it came up with a hotel in Philadelphia, we called and asked for Viviane Mercier. When they put us through to her room, we knew we had her."

"You slick son of a bitch. But you've got it all wrong this time. She came to see me and told me everything. How Brendan Hitchell is pushing though his own bill to fill his bank account, how Lilith was in on it, too."

"Yeah, well." Marcel hardly sounded convinced.

"We'll have to check on everything she said. I don't trust her, Rex. And you shouldn't either."

"I don't have to. She's *your* mother."

"And she's something infinitely worse to you," Marcel said. "She knows where all your bodies are buried. Watch it. *Ciao.*"

Chapter Twenty

Filles et Femmes

CHARLOTTE PULLED HER legs up against her on the bed, wrapping her arms around them. She could hear Rex in the bathroom, doing those little things that people usually did when they got ready for sex, like brushing their teeth, taking a quick look in the mirror. With women, that quick look was more like an assessment, checking to see if the curves were still curvaceous, if that bit of pooch here and there would just be another thing to obsess about. Which was ridiculous, really, as Rex had probably explored every inch of her body in the last three days. Even so, while she waited for Rex she dragged the teddy from her bag and slipped into it, not so much to add to the mystery, but to make sure the mystery stayed right where it was.

The sun had fully risen now, but the day was dawning

cloudy and cool, just the type of fall day to stay snuggled under the blankets. Not that they could, as they needed to get back to Philadelphia. But for now she needed to sleep. *Sleep*, she thought, yawning expansively, oh for just a few hours of sleep, glorious sleep. But first there was that other imperative, that one thing that they both couldn't seem to do without. They seemed to crave each other every few hours like the smoker did his smokes, the drinker, his drinks. And she craved him, more than she ever had anyone. In a perfect world she could see herself curled around him, head against his chest, riding its rise and fall, so happy.

A moment later she heard him turn out the light then pad into the hall, entering the bedroom in the dull light a cloudy day brings. But she seemed to sense him more than she could see, almost able to pick him out in total darkness, his naked body shining like a beacon. Was it through instinct that she knew him, their mutual attraction nearly primal? Whatever it was, it was as pervasive as it was persistent, a constant need, an unrelenting desire. She wasn't used to feeling like this, certainly not so quickly, and it scared her a bit to think about what she'd feel like when he was gone. Because no matter what he had said to her in the moment, he *would* go, and maybe that's just how it should be.

She needed to remember why she was in Margate to begin with. She'd left a lot of angry women behind. And although her initial impression about him had been wrong, and Rex hadn't made her compromise her principles in any way, there were still too many men out there who would never give women a fair shake, and abandoning them for Rex would mean abandoning all that she believed in, and all the woman who believed in her. It was a dilemma she could angst long and hard over. Until she realized one thing.

He had never asked her to make that choice.

"Charlotte," he whispered, crawling in beside her. "Charlotte, are you awake, *ma petit*?"

She turned, and there he was, eyes so black some would think them sinister. "I'm awake," she said. Not so much sinister as boundless depth. Into which she could fall and fall.

"Charlotte," he said, then he kissed her, his hand sliding down her back. He lifted up in surprise. "What's this?" he said, his finger looped under the thin strap of her teddy.

"It's called lingerie." She affected a seductive pose. "I think you guys invented it. Don't you like it?"

He bent over her as she lay against the pillow. "Of course you look lovely in it, *chérie*, but may I take it off?"

"You don't like it," she said.

"It's not that." He pulled the lacy string that held together the bodice. "You're just a bit overdressed for this party, *mon amour*. Now come here."

He rolled to his back, taking her with him, Charlotte settling atop him to straddle his hips. As she braced her hands against his chest his fingers fell to her crotch, unsnapping tiny snaps. Once opened, Charlotte raised her arms and he lifted the teddy over her head, tossing it to the floor.

"Ahh," he murmured, resting his hand lightly on her hips. "That's better. Now, let me take a look at you."

"What?" she said, suddenly embarrassed. "You want to take a look at me?"

He reached up and opened the curtain behind the bed. "*Oui*," he said, gazing at her.

She laughed, a nervous titter. "But it's not like you haven't seen me naked before. Why do you have to—"

"You talk too much," he said, swirling his hand lightly over her belly, his eyes never leaving her. "Can't I take a look at *ma femme*?"

"*Femme*?" she whispered. "That means 'wife,' doesn't it?"

"Or woman," he said, "*my* woman. That's who my *tante* thought you were."

"Am I?" she said, barely breathing it. "Am I your woman?"

"*Oui*," he said, his thumb sliding against her belly. "You are my woman."

"Oh . . ." she murmured, still not sure what he meant. Because the modern woman inside her, the one who battled the routine injustices women endured every day, rebelled at such a notion. But the elemental woman, the one sitting naked atop him, was secretly thrilled at his claiming her. *His* woman. And yet . . .

He tilted his head to the side, his gaze still grazing over her. He slowly slid one hand up her side until it curved under her breast, her skin pebbling as he let it rest in his palm. He slid his other hand up and let it circle her round and round. "So lovely," he murmured, "so soft. How did I go so long not knowing you?"

"I don't know," she said, and she honestly didn't, having wondered the same thing herself. As he slid his hands over her shoulders and down her arms she felt herself loosen, not realizing she'd been so tightly wound. With each sweep of his hand, with each press of his fingers, with each languid gaze he uncoiled her, breaking off all her fastenings, letting her glide smoothly down to earth. He brought his legs up and she leaned back, stretching herself as she relaxed against him. Now he could see her better, but she didn't feel any more exposed. He had her in his grasp now, inside and out, and she went willingly, emboldened by his touch and in awe of it.

She could feel his cock under her, hard and slippery at its head, ready to enter her. "How do you feel now that you know me?" she asked, hoping it was more than just this.

"Amazed," he said, sliding his hands all the way down to grasp her hips, his fingers hot against her skin. "I feel amazed to know you."

He was being quite effusive in his praise, and she wondered where it came from. Then all at once she figured it out.

He had nothing to lose.

It would have been one thing to have him kiss her good night after a party, hoping he'd call the number she left in his contacts. It was quite another to have him fly off in his jet to another world. Either way he'd be gone. So what did it matter what he said now? Or how she felt when he said it? It didn't necessarily mean they'd never see each other again. Perhaps they'd run into each other now and then. Maybe at a party or on a social network. Maybe even on the Rive Gauche.

"Knowing you was amazing, too," she said. "And I'll miss you."

"Don't miss me," he said, his brow knitting as he palmed her belly. "I'm right here."

"You are," she said, her hand over his. "For now."

"And you really have no idea what the future will bring." His hands grasped her hips and he lifted her up over his cock. When he set her down, he thrusted.

She jolted, huffing, thoroughly impaled, as he flexed his hips, filling her, again and again and again. She braced her palms against his chest, falling forward, her mouth over his. He lifted his head, kissing her.

She closed her eyes, savoring his taste, the sweep of his tongue, the urgent press of his lips, the slightly manic way he wanted her, the way he always wanted her. Like she might suddenly poof away. He pulled back, his hand on her cheek.

"*Êtes-tu ma femme?*" he whispered, sweeping his hand up and over her hair. "*Êtes-tu?*" He stilled inside her, waiting for an answer.

She pushed up, her palms again at his chest. "Don't ask me that," she said. "I can't give you an answer."

"Why?" he said, slowly swiveling his hips. "Tell me what you feel. Or don't you feel anything for me?"

"I feel . . ." Could she tell him? Then suddenly he thrust hard and deep. She smiled. "Well, I certainly felt *that*."

"*Très bien . . .*" he growled, thrusting again and again until Charlotte fell back against his upraised legs with a groan. "Because that's me making love to you, and tell me, Charlotte—doesn't it feel good?"

She groaned again, sparks shooting behind her eyes. "Oh yes, *si bon* . . ."

He slid his hand over to her pussy, thumbing her clit. "You're so wet, *ma belle*, I can slide around inside you." He stroked her a few times, Charlotte's hips swiveling languorously. "Does that feel good, *belle*? Do you like that? Maybe because it's me, Charlotte. It's me inside you." He kept on stroking her, thrusting at the same time. "That's because I love to fuck you."

"Oh *God*." When she lifted up, he thrust into her hard, and kept thrusting until she was coming, clamping herself around him. Her orgasm rocketed through her in a violent, jolting crest, and so thoroughly she virtually shook around him. Then just before the last waves left her he lifted up then fell back, his hands grasping her hips so tightly she could feel his nails digging into her skin, his head arcing back into the pillows. She could feel him pulsing inside her with such a convulsing force it once again sent her over the edge.

"*Mer-de* . . ." he choked out, collapsing against the pillows, his chest heaving as she fell back against his legs. After a moment he looked up, his mouth curving. "Was it good for you, too?"

"Damn . . ." she said, swiping the hair from her face as she bent into him, meeting his kiss. "Rex, oh God, it always is."

He shifted, pushing himself up against the headboard, still buried inside her as he pulled her into his arms. "*Ma *femme,*" he whispered, kissing her lightly. "You're like a marvel to me."

She looked away. "You need to stop saying these—" She flipped her hand in front of her, embarrassed now that they were through. "Stop making this more than what it is. We both know the truth of it."

"And what's that?" he said, his arms still firmly around her. "Why don't you tell me?"

"I've told you already. We're just two people filling the time in a mutually interesting way." She looked at him. "We're fucking. That's it."

"Jesus," he said. "You make it sound so filthy."

"And you're wasting your shtick on me. Believe me, I'm sold. All you have to do is look at me and I'm already coming."

He laughed, a barely audible burst of incredulity. "Those three sentences were the oddest combination of insult and praise I've ever heard strung together." He shook his head. "No—I've never heard them strung together. Charlotte, no doubt, you're the strangest *fille* I've ever known."

"Is that so." She slipped from his arms and lifted off him, climbing from the bed. "Excuse me," she said, leaving for the bathroom. As she did, she could feel those dark eyes burning into her back all the way out.

REX CLIMBED INTO his trousers, and throwing on his shirt, left through the French doors for the small porch off the room. There was a striped canvas awning covering it and a small table and chairs, and he thought it would be a lovely romantic spot to have breakfast in the summer with its easy view of the beach. And with Charlotte on the other side of the table.

That stopped him cold.

"*Enculé de ta mère*," he cursed. He gripped the railing, looking down into the street. "Why now?" This wasn't the right time. This was so inconvenient. Didn't he have enough going on in his life?

Why did he have to pick now to fall in love?

Because he was, as surely as those waves crashed against the shore, she had crashed into him. And like those goddamned waves he couldn't stop it. It just kept coming and coming, relentless. What was it about her that drove this overwhelming need to keep her close? To drown in her if he had to. *Mon Dieu*, he thought, how did it happen? But it did, and in spite of everything, it made him happy. Indescribably so.

He loved the way her curly hair met the curve of her neck, how her lips parted just before he kissed her. How her nails looked a bit chewed, how her breasts tasted of salt and cream and how he could die, just lying atop them. He loved how he felt when he was inside her, like she could drive him out of his mind, yet how she also made him realize he was exactly where he was supposed to be.

She was so much more than any woman he ever imagined.

He loved her calculating mind, he loved how she held on like a dog with a bone. He loved her ambition, that when she believed in something there was no stopping her. He loved how she stood up to people and always questioned authority. He loved how much order she could find in chaos, and how that chaos defined her. He loved her fearlessness, and how she bowled over those seemingly tougher than she. But most of all, he loved how she could lay bare his many flaws, and still leave him a stronger man for it.

There was no denying it, he loved her.

But the bitch of it lay in what to do about it. The door opened behind him. He turned.

She was wearing a sweater, probably an ancient one, and most likely one that only saw daylight from this vantage point. It nearly reached to her knees, a collection of mottled colors, pills, and frayed yarn, with a shawl collar and ribbed, folded-over cuffs. He could tell she wore nothing beneath it, as it molded each luscious curve it flowed over. It probably should've been thrown out a long time ago, but it was the comfort food equivalent of all her clothing, like a pastry or a warm mug of cocoa. She came up beside him, her fingers wrapping around the railing.

"I'm sorry. I think I was mean to you back then," she said. She looked up. "Are you angry with me?"

He didn't answer right away. He wanted her to stew in that awhile. He wanted her to feel a bit of his confusion and anger and hurt, even if he wasn't confused or angry or hurt at all. He couldn't be, not with her. Because when you felt like he did, you could forgive everything.

"I'm not angry with you," he said, looking down on her. "I'm in love with you."

Her eyes widened and she gasped, moving almost imperceptibly away. "You can't be."

"Are you telling me how I feel?" He wanted to laugh. "You can't, Charlotte, because I am. This is one ruling you can't challenge. The proof is irrefutable."

"But . . ." She scratched her head, looking confused, like it was the last thing in the world she wanted to hear. "But I'm your attorney."

That time he did laugh. Loud and rib-crackingly hard. "You must be joking, *ma belle*. As if that makes a difference. Honestly, is that the best you can do?"

"But Rex . . . I . . ." She had no answer, and that was hardly what he wanted to hear. He wanted her to say out loud she loved him, too. He wanted her to throw herself in his arms, kiss him all over his face. He wanted to feel the warm press of her body against his. He wanted to make love to her until neither of them could breathe. He wanted to . . .

"You love me now. In this warm little cocoon," she said, as reasonably as she did most things, in lawyerly tones meant to convince. "But what happens when it's time to go home? How will you feel about me then?" She came closer, her hand on his arm. "How will you feel when it's time to step on the plane?"

He looked at her. She had a point. But he hadn't thought it out that far. All he knew was what he felt now, looking at her through the lens of his heart. "I'll know I'll feel wretched."

"You might," she said, "but you'll go."

"Come here," he said, throwing his arm over her shoulder.

She snuggled into him as they looked to the sea, its gray waves crested and angry. He could feel its spray or was it just the rain, intermittently pattering on the lightly flapping awning. She had called where they were a cocoon and maybe it was, but it didn't feel like it. Not with the fresh air and the ocean off in the distance, a long expanse of open sky and sea and beach yawning before them. He couldn't help seeing the analogy of its endless possibilities, hardly something as insular as she imagined. He could dream of something more expansive, couldn't he? Because what was a cocoon besides an incubator?

"To tell you the truth, I don't know what will happen," he finally said. "It's all come to me so quickly. All I know is when they arrested me you're the first person I thought of." He looked down at her. "Now why do you think that was?"

"Because you were in Philly and I'm a lawyer," she said. "It was a natural segue."

"True," he said. "But that all changed when you walked in that room."

"How?"

"Because then you became much more than just my lawyer. You became *Charlotte*."

She smiled, looking embarrassed. "You make me sound like such a formidable thing. I'm no one really."

He kissed her temple. "You were formidable today with my *tante*. Especially since she intimidates everybody." He smiled. "Except me, of course. But then I never really got to know her. She was just some abstract legal guardian, a gatekeeper, a name scrawled on my permission slips. Her own children avoid her, though André seems to be seeing more of her lately."

"How is it your cousins don't know about you?" she asked. "What's the big secret?"

"André does, but then he's twelve, thirteen years older than Marcel, and by the time Marcel was old enough to be told, I was already making my way in the world."

He shrugged. "Who knows, maybe it just comes down to the simple fact Viviane is incapable of loving anyone because she needs to own them, and who can stand for that? And Viviane's jealousy couldn't allow for her sister to love someone more than her, and then go off and leave her alone. So she married the first person who came along—André's father—thinking she could punish her sister by moving far away. It didn't work. Then when my father died and my mother committed suicide, she realized how precious the years are that you lose. But where most people would see the lesson in that and try to mend things, it only made her angrier and wanting to seek revenge. Because really, that's all Marcel is—a revenge tactic for all the hate she felt toward the Merciers. She tried to play him against his own father, much like André's father had come between his own son and Viviane, demanding André tell him which parent he loved more. Maybe she learned it from André's dad, who knows. But it didn't work with Marcel. Maybe it's why he keeps his own daughter from her. It just keeps going on and on."

"Maybe he'll see the futility in that now that he's married Dani," Charlotte said. "But what's that got to do with you? What would be the harm in his knowing who you are now?"

"I've wanted to tell him, really I have. But Marcel needs to find his footing or he'll never live up to what he could be. If he knew I'm his mother's nephew, he just might hate me for it, especially since André hired me. It would almost be like a vote of no-confidence."

"Isn't that what the board of directors have essentially given him?" Charlotte said.

"Exactly. Which is how his knowing who I am could only make it worse. The Merciers pay me well to help him find his way, and I've never minded doing it. They've been very good to me, and I can't ever forget that."

"But his apprenticeship has to end sooner or later, and you have to think about yourself." She stood back, her gaze very stern. "Rex, you're a natural leader and the strongest man I know. You shouldn't let yourself be second to anyone."

He laughed softly. "Maybe I'm not as strong as you think I am." He wanted to pull her into his arms her, but he resisted the urge. "Not when you can bring me to my knees."

"Oh Rex." She sighed, going to him. He curled his arms around her, loving the way she fit against him. "Don't think of me that way. Know for now you have my heart."

"Then that's enough." He kissed the top of her head. "For now."

"Let's go back to bed," she said, yawning expansively. "If I don't get a few hours of sleep before we go to Philly, I think I'll just end up babbling."

He turned them toward the door. "That's an invitation I can't refuse."

They crawled into bed, Rex spooning behind her, her body a warm press against his. Almost immediately he fell asleep, warm and comforted, for now.

A FEW HOURS later, Rex's phone rang. Still half asleep, he reached for it. "*Allo?*"

"Oh, you're so going down," Lilith said.

Chapter Twenty-One

Sounds Like . . .

REX SAT UP, Charlotte snuffling awake beside him. "I'm sorry, but did you have something to say to me, Lilith?"

"You may have thought you had me," the congress-woman said, "but here's the thing. You can't go around being a bastard your whole life, then suddenly turn the white knight."

Charlotte sat up, leaning into Rex. *Lilith?* she mouthed. He nodded, switching to speakerphone as he pulled her closer, his arm over her shoulder. "I think you have me confused with someone else, Lilith. I'm never tried to be a good example for anyone. All I've ever wanted to be was a credible threat."

"Well, here's one for you, except it stopped being a threat when you taped me talking. You're being deported. I'm getting your L-1 visa canceled."

"Seriously, Lilith? Is that the best you can do?"

"You won't take it so lightly when you're not allowed in the country anymore."

"Now isn't that a tad ungrateful? Especially when I had every intention of going to you and working things out."

"As if I'd believe you, you son of a bitch. Gone are the days when you could hand me the tape and we could play like *Mission: Impossible* and it'd self-destruct in sixty seconds. For all I know whoever stole it sold it ten times over to someone before you got it back."

"Lilith, why are you arguing over a recording when at the present, that seems to be the least of your problems?" Rex said.

Silence, then, "What the hell do you mean?"

"I know how Richette's been buying your loyalty. And they've been rewarding you by filling your blind trust with their stock. How this thing with the lobbyist has been a setup by Richette to make me look bad. How you've been bought."

"What are you talking about?" she said, with a distinct catch in her voice. "No one buys me."

"The hope was to build a scandal around me, to make Mercier look bad, so our value would tank and the investors would flee, and make it so much easier for Richette to swallow us up. Which would make you and Hitchell rich in the process, now wouldn't it?"

"Where are you getting this from?" she said, sounding a little desperate.

"From the source," he said. "But blood will always be

thicker than your bank account, *chérie*. It's not going to work."

Rex could hear her sputtering, cursing under her breath. "You son of a bitch—you took me for granted. You never cared about me. You just used me."

"Arguably, but at least I've always been up front about it," Rex said. "And I always paid for the privilege. You, on the other hand wanted things I could never give you."

"All I really wanted was your heart," she said, tears in her voice now.

"That never was for sale," he said, holding Charlotte closer. "I would have given it away for free, had I wanted to."

"You bastard, you'll ruin me." She was crying now. "My life is over."

"It doesn't have to be," Charlotte said, breaking in. "Use whatever influence you have with Hitchell or Richette to see that the girl recants. If you do that, Rex will make the tape go away."

"For good," he added.

"And how can I be sure of that," Lilith said.

"Because you have my word as an honorable man," Rex said. "Believe it or not, I am one. But if you don't . . ." His voice turned hard and steely. "Don't think I have anything against spilling my guts with what I know to the DA."

"And go now," Charlotte said. "We're due in court to-morrow, and if those charges aren't thrown out—"

"I still have a witness tucked away that'll attest to your

collaborating with Hitchell to buy up Richette stock," Rex said.

"And it won't even matter whether or not it's legal," Charlotte said.

"Because it'll make you look like you're in Richette's pocket, and that's never good."

"What—are you two finishing each other's sentences now?" Lilith grunted derisively. "What a pair of sharks."

"Thank you," they said simultaneously.

"You go to hell," Lilith said. "Both of you."

"Fine," Charlotte said. "As long as you get that girl to the DA first."

Rex hung up. "So what happens now?"

"If the girl goes to the DA—which I'm sure she will once Lilith gets ahold of her—they'll have to throw out the charges against you due to lack of evidence."

"Which only solves one of my problems." He sighed, sliding his phone to the nightstand. "This whole mess is making the board of directors lose confidence, and that doesn't look good for Marcel. Did you know the way our company is set up he can be replaced if he doesn't perform?"

"And what does that mean?"

"They can ask André to step back in."

"Do you honestly think he would?"

Rex tossed his hand. "I don't know. But what I do know is I'm getting awfully tired of all this corporate intrigue. It all seems a bit pointless."

"Why Mr. Renaud, you shock me." Charlotte slid down into the sheets, turning toward him. "I thought you loved this business. Loved the competition and the spreadsheets and"—she glided her hand down his leg, grinning wickedly—"that sharp, clean scent of money."

"Which only goes toward making more."

She made a face at him. "Some capitalist you are."

He lifted his chin. "I have nothing against making money. I think I'm pretty good at it. All I'm saying is there has to be more to life than that." His hand fell to her back and he rubbed it. Charlotte groaned with contentment, laying her head on his thigh.

"It's you who's made me see that," he said. "You and your causes and those crazy women who think you walk on water."

"Who throw bricks through my window and threaten me with bombings?"

He laughed slightly. "*Oui.* They're passionate about you, Charlotte. They'd put themselves out on the line not only for what you stand for, but for *you*. Now who would get that passionate over a corporate executive made ridiculous by a twenty-two-year-old lobbyist? Who would get that excited over me?"

"What are you saying?" Charlotte said, eyeing him wryly. "You want me to toss a bomb at your house?"

"You already have," he said, slinking down to her. "Or you've at least done the damage. Charlotte," he said, kissing her lightly. "Do you have any idea how you wreck me?"

"Oh, Rex," she said, "I don't know how to . . ."

She didn't continue, and perhaps she couldn't. She simply slid down further and took him down her throat.

"Mon Dieu—oh Charlotte," he choked out, sprawling back against the pillows as Charlotte worked her way up and down him. She took it slow, torturously so, alternately licking and sucking, almost lovingly, he liked to think. As she did, her hands roamed across his belly, slid around his thigh and hip, stroking, exploring in tender caresses, teasing every pore to life where her hands passed. This time it was altogether different than the time she'd had him in the shower. This wasn't any Cosmo girl version of fellatio. This was a long way from mechanical. He could be wrong, and chances were damned good that he was, but he couldn't help thinking this was her way of telling him how she felt about him. This was her way of saying that she loved him. At least he could imagine it was. At least that's the way it felt.

"Charlotte," he murmured, his fingers threading through her hair as she weighed his *couilles* in her hand, her fingers wavering under them. Her tongue trailed down and down, her lips parting to take them into her mouth, her hand wrapped around his shaft, gently sliding up and down. What he felt was beyond description though he tried—pleasure, comfort, intimacy. He wanted her to go on and on, but he also wanted more. He wanted to give her some of what he felt. He wanted her to feel as he did, only more so.

He wanted to give her everything.

"Come here," he said, his hands at her shoulders. "I want to be inside you."

Her mouth trailed back to his shaft and she swallowed him again, her tongue teasing the tip of his cock until a groan escaped from deep within him. Then she let go and pulled herself up, sliding her leg over him. He groaned again, sinking himself deep inside her, his hands over her breasts, holding her up.

"Charlotte," he whispered, "*qu'est-ce que je ferais sans toi? J'ai envie de toi, si mal . . .*"

"I'm right here," she said, falling forward, her lips over his. "I'm right here . . ." she murmured, kissing him.

Rex's arms flew around her, holding her so close his heart beat next to hers. He kissed her deeply like he'd drown in her, the taste of her so exquisite it made him dizzy. He pushed himself up, turning her until he was on top of her, lowering himself.

She looked up at him, her blue eyes as clear as day, his own, black as night. The irony wasn't lost on him, and never had he felt more undeserving. His life had been open-ended until he met her, and now that he had, for the first time he could imagine it complete, if only she were beside him.

"*Je t'aime*," he whispered, kissing her. "With all my heart. Please believe me and know that I mean it."

She sighed, laying her head in the crook of his as he drove himself deeper inside her. "I know, Rex, you've told me and I do believe you. But it's been so fast, I can't . . ."

"I know," he said, kissing her again, stilling as he caressed her cheek. "I know what I am. Believe me, I understand. If I were you, I would feel the same way. But just know that I do love you and you're everything to me. *Tu es l'amour de ma vie*."

"Oh Rex . . ." she said, arching against him, her hands

at his hips as he began to move again, pulling him closer until there was no space between them at all. "I wish I could say what you want to hear, as there's no one else I've ever really wanted to say it to. But I just can't, Rex. I can't. I'm so sorry, but I just can't."

"*Je t'aime,*" he said, over and over and over, until he couldn't breathe and all words were gone, Rex taking them over the edge, his heart breaking as they fell.

A FEW HOURS later Charlotte awoke to find herself alone. A state, it surprised her to discover, she was beginning to find a bit foreign. "Rex?"

He didn't answer, and suddenly she panicked, scrambling out of bed and into her robe. Then she spied him on the little porch outside the room, sitting in one of the chairs at the table, his phone atop it. She went to him.

"Rex?" she said.

He looked up and smiled, holding his hand out to her. She took it, curling into his lap and his bare chest. For such a cool and cloudy day he was surprisingly warm.

"I'm sorry," she said, the tears falling.

"*C'est bon, calmez-tu,*" he said, holding her close. "The last thing I want to do is push myself on you. I understand. My reputation leaves a lot to be desired and you are perfectly right to feel wary."

"No," she said, pulling back. "It's not you, really it isn't." He stroked his cheek. "You're wonderful. I've never met anyone like you. And to tell the truth, no one is more surprised than me that you can love me. The fact is . . ."

She swiped her eyes, snuffling. "I'd come to believe I was unlovable and suddenly there's you, telling me I'm not."

"Unlovable? You?" He laughed. "See? That's why we're perfect for each other. You thought you were unlovable, and I thought I couldn't ever love anyone. Then I met you and I suddenly knew why." He kissed her. "I was just waiting for you to show up."

"Oh, Rex." She started crying again, snuffling against her hand.

"Jesus." He reached into his pocket. "Here," he said, producing a handkerchief. "Blow your nose before you drench us both."

She eyed the linen square, taking it. "There are men who still carry these?"

"Real men do," he said. "Tissues are for mama's boys."

"No," she said, blowing again. "I suppose I really don't know much about men after all."

He held her close. "The only man you need to know anything about is right here," he said. "And he loves you enough to wait for as long as it takes."

"That's good to know," she said, curling against him again. "What are you doing out here besides freezing to death?"

He looked at her. "Do I look like I'm freezing?"

"You *feel* like a furnace. But answer my question."

He glanced to his phone. "I got a phone call, so I didn't want to wake you up."

"Marcel, I'll bet."

"*Oui.* He said they're bringing the *Esther Reed* into Penn's Landing this afternoon, and he wants to talk to me." He thought a moment. "And Jesus, do we have a lot to talk about."

"I can drop you there. What time?"

"You're not dropping me anywhere," he said. "You're going with me."

She bolted upright. "Oh no. There's no way I'm doing that. Dani's okay, but Marcel hates me. He sees I'm with you and—"

"He already knows you're with me."

"You told him I'm you're lawyer?"

"*Oui.*" He grasped her by the shoulders, holding her out. "But I made it plain you're much more than that."

"Why'd you do that? Why should he know? What business is it of his?"

"Because I took a punch from him in Boston over a crack I made about Dani. And if he thinks I'm going to tolerate any remarks from him about you . . ." He flexed his fist. "Then he can expect the same thing out of me. And let me tell you, I pack a mean left hook."

She smiled. "Talk about a real man."

"No shit." He stood her up, patting her behind. "Now let's get dressed, *belle*. We have business back to Philly."

Chapter Twenty-Two

Courting

By the time they were crossing the Ben Franklin into Philadelphia, the cloudiness hugging the coast was behind them and the sky was bright and clear. From the bridge they could see Penn's Landing Wharf and the double masts of the schooner, the *Esther Reed*, her sails now tightly furled as she idled in port.

Charlotte remembered the time she had spent on the ship with Dani Lloyd down there at Penn's Landing. She and Occupy Vagina had been protesting the misogynistic practices of Liberty Sail and Mercier, the then-parent company who owned the *Esther*. Dani had chained herself to one of the masts, prompting Marcel Mercier to fly over from Cannes to attempt to toss her off. Who knew they'd fall in love, and he'd end up buying the schooner for his new bride as a wedding gift? And now here they all were again, in port under such different circumstances. It just showed how much things stayed the same.

Until they changed. Irrevocably.

Because Charlotte had fallen in love with Rex just as deeply and just as fast as Dani and Marcel had. The difference was Charlotte couldn't bring herself to tell him, and for a very good reason. For as much as he'd been saying how much he loved her, not at any point did he tell her what he was going to do about it. And until he did, she wasn't about to give him her heart. Not so he could just fly away to Marseille with it.

This time, she promised herself, unlike all her other relationships, it was going to be different.

This time, she needed to know he loved her for sure.

"There she is," Rex said, looking down from the bridge into Penn's Landing. "That's what all that fuss had been over? That boat?"

"Not just any boat," Charlotte said. "That's the *Esther Reed*. I still find it hard to believe Dani could love anything more than that ship, let alone Marcel."

"And now she has both," he said, steering Charlotte's car down the off ramp.

"Only because she couldn't take one without the other," Charlotte said. "Though if Marcel had been honest with her from the start, maybe they wouldn't have had to go through what they did." She looked at him. "Honesty goes a long way."

Rex looked askance. "Is that some kind of hint? Because if it is, I've learned my lesson."

"Of course you have—turn here." He did, and soon they were in the parking lot walking toward the ship.

For the first time since they'd been together, Charlotte got to see Rex out of his work clothes and in something a bit more casual. He had put on khakis, a polo, and boat shoes, things he had purchased when they'd gone shopping in Margate, and he looked so unlike himself she hardly recognized him. Even so, although his clothing was relaxed, she could see no reflection of it in his demeanor, his whole body seeming to tense the closer they got to the ship.

"Are you okay?" she said, rubbing his shoulder.

"I'm all right," he said, quickly flexing his fingers.

"You're about as *all right* as I am," she said, taking his hand. "For one reason or another I feel like we're both walking up the gallows."

He brought her hand to his lips, kissing it. "Well, don't. You have nothing to worry about. And for what it's worth, you make me feel better just by being here."

"Hey," Charlotte suddenly said, looking toward the ship. "That's not Marcel. Who is it?"

Rex craned his neck, squinting, as they trotted down the steps to the pier. On deck was a large man coiling a rope around his massive arm, resembling a larger and more intense version of Marcel. He looked up and spying them, waved.

"That's André," Rex said. "Or as he likes to be called, Andy."

"Andy Devine?" Charlotte said. "Julie Knott's husband?

"That's him," he said as they approached the ship.

"Should I be afraid?" she whispered, taking the hand Rex offered as they climbed aboard. "He looks kind of scary."

"Nicest man in the world," Rex said, helping her down. "Unless you cross him. Do that and you might as well slit your wrists."

"*Bonjour!*" Andy said, meeting them at the gangplank. He shook Rex's outstretched hand. "*Alors, qu'est-ce que tu deviens?*"

"*Comme ci, comme ça,*" Rex answered. "How about you?"

"Not bad, not bad," he said, looking to Charlotte.

"Andy, this is my attorney, Charlotte Andreko," Rex said. "And, I'm happy to admit, a bit more."

"*Enchanté,*" he said, shaking her hand. Charlotte noticed he spoke French with much the same American lilt that she did, and then it struck her. Andy had an American father, although all three men—Andy, Marcel, and Rex—were linked through the contentious Viviane, all possessing her smoky allure. "Dani told me you crewed on the *Esther* for their sail to Boston."

"That's right," she said. "Though I didn't make it all the way. Marcel kicked me off the ship on Martha's Vineyard."

Andy laughed. "That sounds like my hothead brother. Never lets his emotions get in the way. Sheesh."

"Is your wife here as well?" said Charlotte. "We just saw her a couple of days ago."

"She's at the TV station," Andy said. "She'll be here

shortly. She can barely fit behind the wheel, so Denny's dropping her off." He laughed. "I think she's had it after this. Even *I* can feel her pain."

"Where's Marcel?" said Rex, and Charlotte could tell, a bit impatiently. "I feel like I've been summoned."

"And don't think you haven't," said Andy, going to the other side of the ship to a table covered in linen, fine china, and a centerpiece of white roses. Aside it was small liquor cart. "Can I offer you both a cocktail?"

"I think I'll need one," Rex said and Andy smiled, holding up a bottle of forty-year-old scotch. "Jesus, you're certainly softening the blow, aren't you?"

"After this, you'll never know what hit you," said Andy, pouring two fingers. "What'll you have, Charlotte?"

She looked to Rex, and he smiled. "Whatever he's having. Though pour mine around some ice."

"You got it," Andy said, pouring the same for himself. "Marcel and Dani should be up any minute. They're below decks getting ready for a sail to Bermuda in the morning. Dani is still in the habit of filing a float plan. Which, of course, is a good thing."

"Sounds like a nice, long honeymoon," Charlotte said.

"Not that he hasn't been working all along," Andy said, glancing to Rex. "Proof of that will be apparent soon enough."

"Like now," Marcel said, climbing out the companionway with Dani behind him, both carrying steaming trays of hors d'oeuvres. There was enough food to feed an army with, but Charlotte didn't think she could swallow a thing. As calm and collected as Rex appeared on the outside, Charlotte could tell he was wired beneath. Something was coming and it was always worse waiting for the other shoe to fall.

"How are you, you fucking bastard," Marcel said, shaking his DGD's hand. "You've been giving me heart attacks lately."

Andy slanted Charlotte a glance. "My brother, the master of subtlety."

"Charlotte," Marcel said, eyeing her warily. "Still hate me for leaving you at the Vineyard?"

"For the record," Dani said, reaching to clasp Charlotte's hands, "I was hardly all in with that idea. But who listens to me anyway?"

"I do," Marcel said to his wife, the two exchanging a smoldering glance. "Now go get yourself a drink, and me too, if you'd be so kind."

Charlotte felt a small pain deep within her. *What must it be like to be that secure in your relationship? It must be wonderful.*

"Outside of the obvious, you're probably wondering why I asked you here," said Marcel, taking a beer from his wife. He took a slug and set it down. "Am I right?"

Rex shrugged. "Of course."

"Then I won't keep you in suspense any longer." He whipped out his index fingers like the barrels of two six-shooters. "You're fired."

"*Excusez-moi?*" Rex said, nearly dropping his drink. Charlotte grabbed Rex's arm as he charged at Marcel. "Why you mother—"

"*Calme-toi, calme-toi!*" Marcel cried, jumping back, a

look of elfish glee on his face. "Just hear me out before you freak out on me. I think you may even like what I have to say."

Rex glared at Marcel, his face a study in barely contained rage. "Go ahead," he said.

"Primarily, let me apologize," Marcel said. "Seems I've kind of taken you for a ride. That whole mess over at the Ritz with Lilith and the lobbyist?"

"*Oui . . .*" Rex said, hardly breathing it.

"We kind of knew about it," Andy said.

"*Quoi?*" said Rex, his fist clenching. "You knew about it and you didn't warn me?"

"Now hold on," Marcel said. "All we knew was something was going to happen to try to make you look bad."

"To ruin your credibility and Mercier's," Andy added. "So our value would sink so that Richette could make their move. And to do it, they had to get you and your dreams of harbor expansion out of the way." Andy's brow arched. "Seems you're a very persistent man."

"Did you get this from your mother?" Rex said to Marcel. "Did she tell you this?"

He thumbed his chest. "Me? Hell no. She could be dying on my doorstep and wouldn't even try to knock."

"My family and I visited her in Marseille a couple months ago," Andy said, his deep blue eyes smoldering with intrigue. "You have no idea the transformative power behind a couple days with the grandkids." He looked to Charlotte. "Though the real leverage kicks in when you try to bring them home." He shook his head, like still amazed. "Viviane was crying like a baby."

"And babbling like she was shot full of sodium pentothal," Marcel said. "After that, she started telling Andy everything."

"She told me about meeting up in Paris with Jean-Paul Levere, the Richette CEO," Andy said. "She told us about his wanting her cooperation in another takeover attempt of Mercier. I told her to play along with whatever they'd try to do."

"You see, we had no idea what kind of move they were going to make," Marcel said, "and then you were arrested."

"If you thought they were behind it, why didn't you tell me?" Rex said, still seething.

"We still weren't sure. But then you told Marcel about those recordings," Andy said. "We suspected Lilith may be working with Richette when she was dragging her feet with the dredging bill, but we had no proof. But when she tried to steal your phone, we knew."

"Knew what? That evidence of her infidelity could ruin her career in Congress?" Rex laughed. "What's that got to do with anything?"

"It doesn't," Marcel said. "It was because your recording tied Lilith to Brendan Hitchell, when she said she'd be meeting him for lunch. Which she never actually would, no matter what she told you. And no matter how much she was meeting him in private."

"I still don't get it," Rex said. "Why wouldn't she want to be seen with him in public?"

"Because she and Hitchell were both gobbling up Richette stock," Andy said. "And the last thing she wanted was to be seen within a mile of him."

"So they were both trying to use inside information to hopefully make themselves rich." Charlotte looked to Rex. "Seems their blind trust wasn't so blind after all. And that's the ethics violation I told you about."

"If not criminal," Andy said. "Lilith didn't give a damn about her reputation in Congress. All signs were pointing to her getting crushed in the election, and that's the way she wanted it. By the time Hitchell's bill passed, she'd be out of office. So she needed to steal your phone so any evidence of what was really going on would be gone."

"And then *maman* snatched that possibility away," Marcel said.

Rex looked away a moment, absorbing it all. "Goddamnit—you should have told me."

"I'm sorry, *mon ami*," Andy said. "Perhaps we should have. But once you decided you were going down to Washington, Marcel said it would send Hitchell and Lilith into panic mode."

"You're like a fucking car crusher when you get pissed," Marcel said. "I knew you'd scare the shit out of them and make them get sloppy. And that's when they went nuts and started buying Richette stock like there was no tomorrow."

"So where did all of this lead to?" Rex said.

"We called Richette's bluff on the takeover attempt," Andy said. "As of this afternoon, they're now on their way to becoming a wholly own subsidiary of Mercier."

"What?" Rex said, astonished.

"That's right," Marcel said. "We pulled all our resources together, and with a couple of low-interest loans from all that cheap American money floating around, we grabbed fifty-five percent of Richette stock and gained a controlling interest."

"And now they're all scampering like rats from a sinking ship," Andy said, pulling out his phone. He tapped it a couple of times, holding it up. "Look at this text I just got from Julie."

Hot off the police wire! Tell Rex that his little lobbyist friend just spilled her guts to the DA and she's been arrested on filing false charges.

"Damn," Charlotte said. "And I'll bet that's only the beginning of it. They're all going down." She looked to Marcel. "And I thought Rex was devious."

"They don't call Marcel the *enfant terrible* for nothing," Dani said.

"It was the recordings that really did it," Marcel said. "Now *that* was brilliant. That made her fuck up even more." He clapped his other hand over Rex's shoulder. "You're the best there is, Rex."

"So if I am," he said, taking a couple of steps back, "why are you firing me?"

Marcel glanced to his brother. "Well, now that we're so big, how can we leave you over in Marseille? Who's going to run our North American operations? Especially now," he said, glancing to Charlotte.

"You're joking," Rex said, almost as a whisper.

"I joke a lot," Marcel said, "but not about this. You'd control everything from the Hudson Bay to the Panama

Canal, and it'll be yours to run any way you want. You see"—he clasped him by the shoulders, his expression never more serious—"Mercier is and always has been a family business. We'd like to keep it that way. What do you say, cousin?"

Rex's gaze shot to Andy's. "You told him?"

Andy nodded. "After this, Marcel proved he was ready."

"I've been riding too long on your coattails," Marcel said. "But they're just too big and comfortable. If I don't get off now I never will. Like Andy said, it's time. And it's time for you, too. What do you say?"

Charlotte took a double sip of her scotch and set it down, as Rex's expression couldn't have been more impassive. No wonder he was such an excellent card player. A look like that could break the bank. But it did nothing to absorb the roiling in her own stomach. She couldn't help thinking her own future was being decided here as well. And for the first time in her life it hinged not on what she'd decide for herself, but hopefully, with someone else.

If only he'd ask. *Oh God*, she thought, *if only he'd ask*.

Then Rex looked to her, all his feelings toward her seeming to pool in his dark eyes. "I need to consult with my attorney first."

Charlotte let out a long breath. "Yes," she said, her arm in his. "If you'll excuse us we're—"

"Going to take a walk," Rex said, swallowing his scotch in a single gulp. A moment later he was leading her toward the gangplank.

They didn't speak until they were halfway down the wharf when he stopped, turning toward her. "So what do you think?"

She noticed he made no attempt to keep hold of her hand, slipping his own into his pockets. If anything, the expression on his face was much the same as it had been that night at the police precinct—cold, impartial, slightly sinister. But a lot of time had passed since then, even if it was only within the space of a few days. She now knew him well enough to read beneath that baleful mien and see a man weighing the rest of his life. But if he was asking her for advice, she couldn't give it. This wasn't a decision she could make for him. She could only offer him observations, what was balanced on either side of the scale. This was a decision he'd have to make it on his own.

Even if it broke her heart.

"Rex," she finally said, "It sounds wonderful, the opportunity of a lifetime. It sounds like you wouldn't have to answer to anyone but yourself. Just think of the things you could accomplish. But you're also a very rich man. You could fly back to France and live the life you always wanted to. Run for that office. Go sail a yacht. Finally do whatever makes you happy."

He didn't say anything for a few moments, his gaze washing over her. "You know what makes me happy?" He took her hand. "You do. For the first time in my life I finally met someone who does, and it's you, Charlotte. You."

Was it what she wanted to hear? *Of course it was.* But until he made a decision, she had to remain neutral. This was his life they were talking about, not hers.

She brought her hand to his cheek, her heart in her throat. She'd didn't want to ask him but she would anyway. "So what are you going to do about it, Rex?"

He brought her hand to his mouth, brushing his lips against it. "I'm going to ask you if you love me. Do you?"

It was as if her heart burst wide open. "Oh Rex, I do. After four days, and waiting a lifetime, I do."

His gaze was still on her. "And do you trust me, too?"

"You know I do," she said, slipping her arms around him. "In everything."

He kissed her quickly, reaching for her hand. "Then come on."

Charlotte had to trot to keep up with Rex as they hurried back to the *Esther Reed*. While they were gone Julie had arrived, the news van just pulling away as Andy helped her down onto the deck.

"I'm here for my scoop," Julie said, looking decidedly expectant. "What do you have for me?"

"Stick around," Charlotte said as they climbed aboard. "You'll hear it as soon as I do."

"Well?" Marcel said. "On advice of counsel, do you accept?"

Rex looked to Charlotte, saying, "Still trust me?"

She never trusted anyone more. "I do."

He turned back to Marcel. "I accept a variation of your first offer."

Marcel looked at him, mystified. "My first offer?"

"You know, where you fired me?" He looked to Charlotte. She beamed back at him. "I quit."

It was then Charlotte knew for sure.

Margate City
Christmas Eve

Charlotte's *grand-mere* had always spent the holidays in Margate, ever since she had bought the house. There had been just the two of them, but the house had never been empty. Every Christmas Eve they had filled it with each other, stringing greenery and singing *Noël* songs, and then on Christmas Day, they'd gather with the neighbors, a different house every year, for one big celebration.

This year she had much to celebrate, just two of them again, sitting before the tree. "Oh Rex . . ." she said as he slipped the diamond on her finger, "it's just beautiful."

"But you still didn't answer me," he said, one knee bent to the floor, firelight and illuminating his face. "Or it's just my diamonds you want?"

"Well, let's see." She set a forefinger to her cheek. "What do *you* have to offer? You're unemployed."

"Gainfully," he said. "It's just that I've decided not to work for wages anymore. I am now just a humble philanthropist, out to do your bidding. And look what I've accomplished already. Didn't I just buy that big building for your—what's it called, Operation—"

"That's *Occupy* Vagina. But we don't call it that anymore. It's the Women's Equal Employment Project."

"*Mon Dieu*. Do you realize its acronym is WEEP?"

"Because maybe that's what I'll be doing any minute. Do you realize an accused felon just asked me to marry him?"

"Hey, those charges were dropped," he said. "Or are you forgetting you defended me in court?"

"How could I? You still owe me the retainer."

"And you still owe me something else." Rex handed her another box from under the tree, this one white and tied with string.

Charlotte arched a brow. "And what could that possibly be?" She untied the string and lifted the flaps back, revealing two chocolate éclairs.

"Hey," she said, dipping into the chocolate glaze, "whose present is this anyway?"

Rex leaned in to kiss her. "I'll take it back unless you say yes, *chérie*."

"Yes," she said. "How couldn't I? You know it's my favorite dessert."

His mouth crooked wickedly. "And you're mine, *mon amor*." He kissed her. "*Joyeux Noël. Je t'aime.*"

"*Je t'aime*," she said as he lifted her into his arms, the best present yet to come.

About the Author

GWEN JONES IS an MFA, HEA addict, politics geek, and part-time native of the Jersey Shore. She lives with her husband, Frank, near Trenton, New Jersey.

Discover great authors, exclusive offers, and more at hc.com.

Give in to your impulses . . .
Read on for a sneak peek at five brand-new
e-book original tales of romance
from Avon Impulse.
Available now wherever e-books are sold.

An Excerpt from

VARIOUS STATES OF UNDRESS: VIRGINIA

by Laura Simcox

If she had it her way, Virginia Fulton—daughter of
the President of the United States—would spend
more time dancing in Manhattan's nightclubs than
working in its skyscrapers. But when she finds
herself in the arms of sexy, persuasive Dexter
Cameron, who presents her with the opportunity
of a lifetime, Virginia sees it as a sign . . . but
can she take it without losing her heart?

Virginia threw her hands in the air and walked over to face him. "Come on, Dex! Be realistic. You need a *team* to fix this store. An army."

"So hire one." He leaned toward her. "I need you. And you need me."

"I don't need you." She narrowed her eyes. There was no way she was going to tell him about dumping Owlton. Not right now, anyway.

Dex slid off the desk and covered the few feet between them, frowning. "Yes, you do," he said.

She stared at his mouth, her legs suddenly feeling wobbly. "No, I don't." She raised her hands to his shoulders to steady herself.

"You can choose to keep telling yourself that, or you can make a move."

"What do you mean by that?"

"Move forward."

She took a deep breath. "I don't know if I can." The words came out raspy, and the look of irritation in Dex's eyes changed into something much more focused. He hesitated for a moment and then leaned closer. "Make a leap of faith, trust your instincts, and take the job. You'll have my full support."

As she gazed up into his steady eyes, she was all too aware of her fear. Because of cowardice, she never acted as if she expected anyone to take her seriously—and so they didn't. It pissed her off. She didn't like being pissed, especially not at herself. Dex took her seriously, didn't he? She closed her eyes. "Okay. I'll do it."

When she opened them, he smiled. "Great. Now . . . about moving forward?"

"Yeah?"

"*Literally* moving forward would be fantastic. I never got to kiss you back, you know."

"I . . . didn't expect you to," she said.

"That might be, but the more I thought about your kiss last night, the more necessary kissing you back became to me. And now? I can't think about much else."

She gripped his shoulders and gazed into his eyes. "To be honest, neither can I."

"Please tell me we can try again. Kiss me and see what happens." His voice was low and thick.

Virginia's legs almost gave out from under her, and a shuddering breath left her body. She should be taking a step back, not contemplating kissing him again. Her body swayed forward, and she tightened her grip on his shoulders to steady herself. Just as she closed her eyes to think, his mouth descended, hot and sweet, angling over hers and stopping a hairsbreadth from her lips.

"Mmm," he uttered, the sound coming from deep in his throat, and it was all she needed.

She pushed up onto her toes, her fingers laced behind his neck, and she kissed him. He tasted earthy—wild, almost—

and that surprising discovery sent a shock wave through her brain. She kissed him again. "More," she murmured, even though she knew she shouldn't. His tongue invaded her mouth; he turned and, in one motion, lifted her onto the desk. Electricity sang through her body, and, as she twined her tongue with his, the idea of *shouldn't* started to become hazy. Her hands threaded through his cropped hair and she leaned back—arching her breasts toward him—wanting Dex to press her down with his body. *Please*, she whispered in her mind, *Please, Dex.*

His hands ran over her hips, but he didn't move closer, so she deepened the kiss, letting her hands trail over his smooth jaw, the taut sides of his neck; then she slid her fingers around the lapels of his suit and tugged. With a groan, Dex pulled her against his chest again, his hands skimming up her back to gently tug on the blunt ends of her hair. She complied, letting her head fall back, and his hot, open mouth slid down her throat and nestled in the crook of her neck. He kissed her there, lingering.

"More," she gasped out loud, clinging to his shoulders.

He kissed her throat again, his tongue branding a circle under her jaw. Then slowly, he pulled away. "We have to stop," he said, looking into her eyes. "If we don't . . ." He swallowed and she watched his throat work. She hadn't gotten to kiss him there, yet. Dipping her chin, she leaned forward, but he pulled away. He gave her a sheepish smile. "I think we sealed the deal, don't you?

An Excerpt from

THE GOVERNESS CLUB: LOUISA

by Ellie Macdonald

Louisa Brockhurst is on the run—from her
friends, from her family, even from her dream
of independence through the Governess Club.
Handsome but menacing John Taylor is a
prizefighter-turned-innkeeper who is trying to
make his way in society. When Louisa shows up
at his doorstep, he's quick to accept her offer to
help—at a price. Their attraction grows, but will
headstrong, fiery Louisa ever trust the surprisingly
kind John enough to tell him the dangerous
secrets from her past that keep her running?

Her eyes followed his movements as he straightened. Good Lord, but the moniker "Giant Johnny" was highly appropriate. The man was a mountain. A fleeting thought crossed her mind about what it would be like to have those large arms encompass her.

He spied her packed portmanteau and looked at her questioningly. "You are moving on? I thought your plans were unconfirmed."

Louisa lifted her chin. "They are. But that does not mean I must stay here in order to solidify them."

He put his thick hands on his hips, doubling his width. "But it also means that you do not have to leave in order to do so." She opened her mouth to speak, but he stayed her with his hand. "I understand what it is like to be adrift. If you wish, you can remain here. It is clear that I need help, a woman's help." He gestured to the room. "I have little notion and less inclination for cleaning. I need someone to take charge in this area. Will you do it?"

Louisa stared at him. *Help him by being a maid? In an inn?* Of all the things she had considered doing, working in such a place had never crossed her mind. She was not suited for such work. A governess, a companion, yes—but a maid?

What would her mother have said about this? Or any of her family?

She pressed her lips together. It had been six years since she'd allowed her family to influence her, and this job would at least keep her protected from the elements. She would be able to protect herself from the more unruly patrons, she was certain. It would be hard-earned coin, to be sure, but the current condition of her moneybag would not object to whichever manner she earned more. It would indeed present the biggest challenge she had yet faced, but how hard could it be?

"What say you, Mrs. Brock?"

His voice drew her out of her thoughts. Regarding him carefully, Louisa knew better than just to accept his offer. "What sorts of benefits could I expect?"

"Proper wage, meals, and a room." His answer was quick.

"How many meals?"

"How many does the average person eat?" he countered. "Three by my count."

Would her stomach survive three meals of such fare? She nodded. "This room? Or a smaller one in the attic?" She had slept in her fair share of small rooms as a governess; she would fight for the biggest one she could get.

"This one is fine. This is not a busy inn, so it can be spared." He rubbed his bald head. "My room is behind the office, so you will never be alone on the premises."

Hm. "I see. Free days?" Not that she expected to need them. She knew no one in the area and had no plans to inform her friends—her *former* friends—of where she was.

"Once a fortnight."

"And my duties?"

"Cleaning, of course. Helping out in the kitchen and pub when necessary."

"Was last night a typical crowd?" she asked.

"Yes. Local men come here regularly. There are not many places a man in this area can go."

"And the women? I am curious."

He shrugged his boulder shoulders. "None have yet come in here. I don't cater to their tastes."

Louisa sniffed and glanced around the room. The condition truly was atrocious. If the other rooms were like this, it would take days of hard work to get them up to scratch. It would be an accomplishment to be proud of, if she succeeded.

Ha—if I succeed? I always succeed.

She looked back at Giant Johnny, watching her with his hands on his hips, legs braced apart. She eyed him. He stood like a sportsman, sure of his ground and his strength. A sliver of awareness slipped through her at the confidence he exuded. This man was capable of many things; she was certain of it.

And if she were to agree to his offer, she would be with him every day. This mountain, this behemoth, would have authority over her as her employer. It was not the proximity to the giant that worried her; it was that last fact.

It rankled. For so long she had wished for independence, had almost achieved it with her friends and the formation of the Governess Club, only to have it collapse underneath her. And now she found herself once again having to submit to a man's authority.

It was a bitter pill to swallow. She would have to trust that she would eventually be able to turn the situation to her advantage. Nodding, she said, "I accept the position, Mr. Taylor."

An Excerpt from

GOOD GUYS WEAR BLACK

by Lizbeth Selvig

When single mom Rose Hanrahan arrives in
Kennison Falls, Minnesota, as the new head
librarian, she instantly clashes with hometown
hero Dewey Mitchell over just about everything.
But in a small town like Kennison Falls,
it's tough to ignore anybody, and the more
they're thrown together, the more it seems
like fate has something in store for them.

Waves of anger, like blasts of heat, rolled off the woman as she turned to the pumps. Rooted to the spot, Dewey watched the scene, studying the mystifying child. He was standing a little too close to the gas fumes, but irritation took a reluctant backseat to curiosity and captivation. What kind of kid couldn't follow a simple directive from people in uniform? What nine- or ten-year-old kid knew the year, make, and model of a fourteen-year-old fire truck, not to mention its specs—right down to the capacities of its foam firefighting equipment?

Asperger's syndrome. He knew the phrase but little about it. He certainly believed there were real syndromes out there, since he'd seen plenty of strange behavior in his life. But this reeked of a pissed-off mother simply warning him away from her weird kid. He knew in this day and age you weren't supposed to touch a child, but, damn it, the kid could have gotten seriously hurt. And she sure as hell hadn't been around.

Then there was the car. Over ten years old and spotless as new. The red GT did *not* fit the woman. Or the situation. You just didn't expect to see a mom and her son driving cross-country in a fireball-red sports car. She had some sort of mild, uppity accent and used words like "ire." In a way, she wasn't any more normal than her kid.

He tried to turn away. She wasn't from town, so he wouldn't have to think about her once the gas was pumped. But something compelled him to watch her finish—something that told him the world would go back to being a lot less interesting once she'd left it.

She let the boy hang the nozzle up, and then did something amazing. She opened her door, took out what appeared to be a chamois, and bent over the gas tank door to wipe and buff an area where gas must have dripped.

She doesn't deserve it if she doesn't know how to take care of it. That's what he'd said about her.

Dang. She sure knew how to keep it . . . red.

His observations were cut off by a sudden wail. The boy lunged like a spaniel after a squirrel. The woman grabbed him, squatted, and took his hands in hers, pressing his palms together like he was praying. Her mouth moved quickly, and she leaned in close, her forehead nearly but not quite touching her son's.

It should not have been a remotely sexy picture, but it was nearly as attractive as the sight of her polishing the Mustang. The over-reactive Mama Wolverine morphed into someone intense and sincere with desperation around the edges, and something he didn't understand at all tugged at him, deep in his gut.

The boy finally nodded and quit fussing. The woman dropped her hands and leaned forward to kiss him on the cheek. After straightening, she glanced over her shoulder, and the boy's wistful gaze followed. Dewey remembered that he'd begged only to look at the gauges on the truck. Should he just give in and let the kid have his look?

Then everything soft about the mother hardened as she met Dewey's eyes. Her delicately angled features tightened like sharp weapons, and the wisps of hair escaping from a long, thick brown ponytail seemed to freeze in place as if they didn't dare move for fear of pissing her off further. She stood, her shapely legs—their calves bare and browned beneath the hems of knee-length cargo shorts—spread like a superhero's in front of her son. She didn't say a word, so neither did Dewey. He didn't need to take her on again. Let the kid look up the gauges online.

With a parting shot from her angry eyes, she ushered the boy into the passenger seat, darted to her side, and climbed in. The engine came to life and purred like a jungle cat. She clearly cared for the car the way she did for her son. Or somebody did.

However angry she was, she didn't take it out on the car but pulled smoothly away from the pump. Dewey smiled. It was her car all right. Had it not been, she'd have peeled out just to punctuate her feelings for him.

Impressive woman. A little crazy. But impressive.

An Excerpt from

SINFUL REWARDS 1
A Billionaires and Bikers Novella
by Cynthia Sax

Belinda "Bee" Carter is a good girl; at least, that's
what she tells herself. And a good girl deserves
a nice guy—just like the gorgeous and moody
billionaire Nicolas Rainer. Or so she thinks,
until she takes a look through her telescope
and sees a naked, tattooed man on the balcony
across the courtyard. He has been watching
her, and that makes him all the more enticing.
But when a mysterious and anonymous text
message dares her to do something bad, she
must decide if she is really the good girl she has
always claimed to be, or if she's willing to risk
everything for her secret fantasy of being watched.

An Avon Red Novella

I'd told Cyndi I'd never use it, that it was an instrument purchased by perverts to spy on their neighbors. She'd laughed and called me a prude, not knowing that I was one of those perverts, that I secretly yearned to watch and be watched, to care and be cared for.

If I'm cautious, and I'm always cautious, she'll never realize I used her telescope this morning. I swing the tube toward the bench and adjust the knob, bringing the mysterious object into focus.

It's a phone. Nicolas's phone. I bounce on the balls of my feet. This is a sign, another declaration from fate that we belong together. I'll return Nicolas's much-needed device to him. As a thank you, he'll invite me to dinner. We'll talk. He'll realize how perfect I am for him, fall in love with me, marry me.

Cyndi will find a fiancé also—everyone loves her—and we'll have a double wedding, as sisters of the heart often do. It'll be the first wedding my family has had in generations.

Everyone will watch us as we walk down the aisle. I'll wear a strapless white Vera Wang mermaid gown with organza and lace details, crystal and pearl embroidery accents, the bodice fitted, and the skirt hemmed for my shorter height. My hair will be swept up. My shoes—

Voices murmur outside the condo's door, the sound piercing my delightful daydream. I swing the telescope upward, not wanting to be caught using it. The snippets of conversation drift away.

I don't relax. If the telescope isn't positioned in the same way as it was last night, Cyndi will realize I've been using it. She'll tease me about being a fellow pervert, sharing the story, embellished for dramatic effect, with her stern, serious dad—or, worse, with Angel, that snobby friend of hers.

I'll die. It'll be worse than being the butt of jokes in high school because that ridicule was about my clothes and this will center on the part of my soul I've always kept hidden. It'll also be the truth, and I won't be able to deny it. I am a pervert.

I have to return the telescope to its original position. This is the only acceptable solution. I tap the metal tube.

Last night, my man-crazy roommate was giggling over the new guy in three-eleven north. The previous occupant was a gray-haired, bowtie-wearing tax auditor, his luxurious accommodations supplied by Nicolas. The most exciting thing he ever did was drink his tea on the balcony.

According to Cyndi, the new occupant is a delicious piece of man candy—tattooed, buff, and head-to-toe lickable. He was completing armcurls outside, and she enthusiastically counted his reps, oohing and aahing over his bulging biceps, calling to me to take a look.

I resisted that temptation, focusing on making macaroni and cheese for the two of us, the recipe snagged from the diner my mom works in. After we scarfed down dinner, Cyndi licking her plate clean, she left for the club and hasn't returned.

Three-eleven north is the mirror condo to ours. I

straighten the telescope. That position looks about right, but then, the imitation UGGs I bought in my second year of college looked about right also. The first time I wore the boots in the rain, the sheepskin fell apart, leaving me barefoot in Economics 201.

Unwilling to risk Cyndi's friendship on "about right," I gaze through the eyepiece. The view consists of rippling golden planes, almost like . . .

Tanned skin pulled over defined abs.

I blink. It can't be. I take another look. A perfect pearl of perspiration clings to a puckered scar. The drop elongates more and more, stretching, snapping. It trickles downward, navigating the swells and valleys of a man's honed torso.

No. I straighten. This is wrong. I shouldn't watch our sexy neighbor as he stands on his balcony. If anyone catches me . . .

Parts 1, 2, 3, and 4 available now!

An Excerpt from

COVERING KENDALL
A Love and Football Novel
by Julie Brannagh

Kendall Tracy, General Manager of the San
Francisco Miners, is not one for rash decisions
or one-night stands. But when she finds herself
alone in a hotel room with a heart-stoppingly
gorgeous man—who looks oddly familiar—
Kendall throws her own rules out the window . . .

Drew McCoy *should* look familiar; he's a star player
for her team's archrival, the Seattle Sharks.
They agree to pretend their encounter never
happened. But staying away from each
other is harder than it seems, and they both
discover that some risks are worth taking.

"**Y**ou're Drew McCoy," she cried out.

She scooted to the edge of the bed, clutching the sheet around her torso as she went. It was a little late now for modesty. Retaining some shred of dignity might be a good thing.

She'd watched Drew's game film with the coaching staff. She'd seen his commercials for hair products and sports drinks and soup a hundred times before. His contract with the Sharks was done as of the end of football season, and the Miners wanted him to play for them. Drew was San Francisco's number-one target in next season's free agency. She'd planned on asking the team's owner to write a big check to Drew and his agent next March. And if all that wasn't enough, Drew was eight years younger than she was.

What the hell was wrong with her? It must have been the knit hat covering his famous hair, or finding him in a non-jock hangout like a bookstore. Maybe it was the temporary insanity brought on by an overwhelming surge of hormones.

"Is there a problem?" he said.

"I can't have anything to do with you. I have to go."

He shook his head in adorable confusion. She couldn't think of anything she wanted more right now than to run her fingers through his gorgeous hair.

"This is your hotel room. Where do you think you're going?"

She yanked as much of the sheet off the bed as possible, attempting to wrap it around herself and stand up at the same time. He was simultaneously grabbing at the comforter to shield himself. It didn't work.

She twisted her foot in the bedding while she hurled herself away from him and ended up on the carpet seconds later in a tangle of sheets and limbs, still naked. Her butt hit the floor so hard she almost expected to bounce.

The number-one reason Kendall didn't engage in one-night stands as a habit hauled himself up on all fours in the middle of the bed. Out of all the guys in the world available for a short-term fling, of course she'd pick the man who could get her fired or sued.

He grabbed the robe he'd slung over the foot of the bed, scrambled off the mattress, and jammed his arms into the sleeves as he advanced on her.

"Are you okay? You went down pretty hard." His eyes skimmed over her. "That's going to leave a mark."

He crouched next to her as he reached out to help her up. She resisted the impulse to stare at golden skin, an eight-pack, and a sizable erection. She'd heard Drew didn't lack for dates. He had things to offer besides the balance in his bank accounts.

"I'm okay," she told him.

She felt a little shaky. She'd probably have a nice bruise later. She was going down all right, and it had nothing to do with sex. It had everything to do with the fact that, if anyone from the Miners organization saw him emerging from her room in the next seventy-two hours, she was in the kind of trouble with her employer there was no recovering from. The interim general manager of an NFL team did not sleep with anyone from the opposing team, especially when the two teams were archrivals that hated each other with the heat of a thousand suns. Especially when the guy was a star player her own organization was more than a little interested in acquiring. *Especially* before a game that could mean the inside track to the playoffs for both teams.

Drew and Kendall would be the Romeo and Juliet of the NFL. Well, without all the dying. Death by 24/7 sports media embarrassment didn't count.

He reached out, grabbed her beneath the armpits, and hoisted her off the floor like she weighed nothing.

"I've got you. Let's see if you can stand up," he said. His warm, gentle hands moved over her, looking for injuries. "Why don't you lean on me for a second here?"

She tried rewrapping the sheet around her so she could walk away from him while preserving her dignity. It wasn't going to happen. She couldn't stop staring at him. If she let him take her in his arms, she'd be lost. She teetered as she leaned against the hotel room wall.

"I'm—I'm fine. I—"

"Hold still," he said. She heard his bare feet slap against the carpeting as he grabbed the second robe out of the coat closet and brought it back to her. "If you don't want to do this, that's your decision, but I don't understand what's wrong."

She struggled into the thick terry robe as she tried to think of a response. He was staring at her as she retrieved the belt and swathed herself in yards of fabric. Judging by his continuing erection, he liked what he saw, even if it was covered up from her neck to below her knees. He licked his bottom lip. Her mouth went dry. Damn it.

Of *course* the most attractive guy she'd been anywhere near a bed with in the past year was completely off-limits.

"You don't recognize me," she said.

"No, I don't," he said. "Is there a problem?"

"You might say that." She finally succeeded in knotting the belt of the robe around her waist, dropped the sheet at her feet, and stuck out one hand. "Hi. I'm Kendall Tracy. I'm the interim GM of the San Francisco Miners." His eyes widened in shock. "Nice to meet you."